BLURRED LINES

OLIVIA LUCAS

CHAPTER ONE

MIA

I'm in a coffee shop, stewing.

"Don't be late. We need to talk, she says. God, I'm such an idiot. Stood up twice in one week. You'd think I'd learn, but here I am, hoping for the best!" I'm all jazz hands, but when I glance up, I realize I must've spoken out loud because a wiry-haired woman is tutting and pushing past some spindly child in a green Hulk mask. "Keep moving, Sheldon. May've gentrified the area, but still far too many crazies around for my liking."

I glance left and right.

What? Me?

Look, I might be ranting, but I just got stood up for the umpteenth time. Yet again, my on-off girlfriend, Nadia, has failed to show for a catch-up she organized.

When the woman eventually turns to ogle a cinnamon bun on display, the child leans back with a wicked grin and flicks his wrist, firing a small yellow disc from a shooter. It hits me in the shoulder.

Is he serious right now?

Angrily swiping the disc from the floor, I make a point of chucking it in my bag. But this only emboldens him because the brat fires another two rounds into my torso, then puts his finger on his nose and wiggles his fingers.

That little...

I maturely do the same, and he finally runs away.

Shit. I've totally lost it.

I pick up another disc off the floor and drop it on the table. I have no idea where the other one is. Snatching my phone from the table, I angrily stab at the keys.

Where are you, Nadia? I've been waiting for thirty-five

No, wait. Delete, delete, delete.

THIRTY-FIVE minutes!!

I hit send and slump into my seat.

Thank God I have my best friend, Amy, and a barrage of *women suck* type messages keep me from hurling abuse Nadia's way. But when the flurry of messages ceases, I sigh and stare longingly at the fried chicken place across the road. Hardly noticing the buzz of the coffee shop or the lingering smell of freshly baked goods, my gaze soon drifts over the clock on the wall and then snaps back.

Oh my God, it's twenty to nine.

My interview!

I hastily throw my phone into my courier bag, slip the leather strap over my shoulder, and slide out of the booth with my Venti Americano in one hand and umbrella in the other.

Only now do I notice it's packed like sardines and have to push past a crowd of soggy patrons.

"Excuse me. Sorry," I mumble to a sweaty young woman wearing her tank top inside out and squeeze past a grumpy teenager with a solitary knitted eyebrow who is being summoned by the barista.

The linoleum floor is also a bit slippery from everyone tramping in and out of the rain, so I end up going for a bit of a slide on my right heel and latch onto a man wearing a tweed jacket and a monocle. "Whoops," I say quietly, then straighten the plastic carnation in his pocket.

No sooner am I congratulating myself for not snapping my ankle than I go skating with my left foot, arms windmilling in the air, and this time there's nothing to grab onto.

No blazers, no bodies.

Just glorious air and I realize I'm about to slam face-first into the glass door like an ill-fated bug. Only it miraculously swings open, and I instead collide at speed with a human-shaped blur, coffee cup launching from my grip, and tangle in a dark mane of hair that isn't mine.

We topple over, and I land with an unceremonious thud on my backside. "Why don't you watch -"

"Oh, for God's sake," a voice grumbles.

My head snapping up, but when our eyes meet, a jolt goes straight through me, and my heart starts beating fast. Piercing blue eyes. Scratch that. Silvery-blue, blistering cold, and looking straight through me.

Their owner, a corporate woman in a black pin-stripe power suit, is in her mid to late twenties. Her perfume smells of money, and she has a fancy air about her.

"Honestly, you should slow down and watch where you're going. Someone could get hurt," she says with a scowl.

"Wait, just a minute. The floor was wet, and I'm not the idiot who burst through the exit -"

"Which is also an entry, by the way," she challenges, and for a moment, I can't find my words. Her face stamping with a grimace. "Are you injured?"

"Nothing an icepack taped to my butt won't fix," I mutter, but the woman seems distracted. Her gaze drifting downward, pausing at my chest.

Hang on a second. Is she -

"Your shirt is wet," she says suddenly.

Huh?

I blink out of my stupor, looking down at my coffee-drenched shirt.

Oh, right. Not checking me out in the slightest.

"Great. Just great," I quietly scoff. "I've got a job interview. Don't even have time to get changed."

The stranger yanks at a cream cashmere sweater she has draped over her handbag. "Here."

I glance up, but she doesn't make eye contact. "Oh no, I can't."

She waves her hand dismissively. "Take it."

I'm a bit flummoxed by this kind gesture from the stranger and stare at her, not sure what to think or do. Taking a short, sharp breath, I remind myself how much I want this job. I mean, I certainly can't turn up like this, so I reach forward and take the sweater. When our fingers brush, the stranger simply stands and turns to leave.

"Um. Thanks," I say to the back of her navy Manolo Blah-nik's, but I don't think they hear me because they're already stabbing the pavement at high speed.

CHAPTER TWO
MIA

I whisk up to the giddy heights of a shiny metal tower in an elevator with a couple of posh women who are regaling their weekend at a yachting regatta off Catalina Island.

And boy, do I feel out of place.

I've worked from home for over a year, primarily in my pajamas. My new bra feels too tight, my pencil skirt like a straitjacket, and my feet are already pinching inside my kitten heels because, apparently, they've been molded into the shape of slippers.

I'm not used to 'fancy' anything anymore.

The doors eventually ping open on the twenty-second floor to an ivory-colored marble floor. Dark leather adorns the reception lounge, and the two gazelles next to me clip-clop out in a plume of brand-name perfume and then disappear behind a frosted door marked Dalton Media.

Wiping my clammy hands on my skirt, I walk up to a broad desk with floor-to-ceiling windows offering a view of San Diego Bay under a stormy sky.

A prim, older lady with a steel gray bob looks up from behind her computer and stops clacking away at the keyboard. Her eyes so green I wonder if she is wearing contacts. "Good morning. May I help you?"

"Yes, hi. I have an interview with Miss Natalie Dalton," I say with a squeak.

"Mia Andrews?"

"Yes."

"I'll let her know you are here. Please take a seat over there." She gestures to the corner of the room with a couple of intern-looking types shifting nervously in their seats and then whispers, "She's not even half as scary as she makes out."

Scary?

Oh, great.

"Do I have time to go to the bathroom?" I look down at my phone, then at her nametag. "Joan?"

Joan glances at her computer screen just as the phone rings and covers the mouthpiece of her headset. "Her meeting is running about ten minutes late, so yes." She smiles and winks, and I dash to the left, then realize I have no clue where I'm going. I look over my shoulder. Of course, Joan is pointing to the right.

"Thanks," I mumble and shuffle through the door.

I lock myself in a stall, phone in one hand, and pull out my compact mirror from the depths of my bag to gauge just how catastrophic I look.

Wow.

Actually, not that bad at all, considering I've been stood up, shot by a kid multiple times, and dunked in coffee. And all before nine am. If only I were this productive in all facets of my life.

Well, bad things come in threes, apparently, so I've had my quota for the day, right?

Either way, sweater looks great and hides the stain, and even though I ran most of the way, I'm only a little bit shiny and wind-swept. I fuss over my hair, smoothing down the wispy blonde bits determined to stick up on end.

Suddenly, an emerald-laden hand appears beneath me, and I startle, dropping my phone in the toilet.

Oh, for fuck's sake. That's number four!

How do I end this absolute -

"Any toilet paper?" shouts a voice.

I look at my phone, the roll, and finally, at the hand.

Such a difficult decision.

Ugh.

I shove my compact mirror in my bag and quickly snap off a few squares. "Here you go." Then roll up my right sleeve, lunging for my phone. I pull it out with my index finger and thumb.

God, gross. I'm gross.

"More. I need some more."

The demanding hand is back.

Okay, who is this annoying person?

There are also only two squares left, and I'm faced with a dilemma.

I huff and rip off one. She's not getting both. "Here. There's no more," I tell the hand with finality.

What kind of shit day is this?

Wiping my phone with one unsatisfactory square of paper. I wait for the woman next door to hurry up.

I hear a zipper. It must be her bag. Then she starts fossicking around for what feels like forever. Something hits the floor, and a ballpoint pen suddenly appears next to my foot, and then a tampon. I kick them both back and roll my eyes. Another zipper.

What the hell is she doing in there?

Come on! I mouth angrily through the partition.

Finally, there's a flush, and when I hear the bathroom door open and close, I slink out of my stall and aggressively wash my hands, then blast them and my phone under the dryer.

When I walk out to the reception area, Joan is waiting in her beige knitted dress by the entry door and waves me over. "Mia. Miss Dalton is ready to see you."

"Oh, okay." I smile, trotting past some golden planter boxes with ferns, and follow her down a pale carpeted corridor. The whole office buzzing with ringtones and chitchat.

Joan pauses outside a door, then gestures for me to step inside.

Straightening my shoulders, I thank Joan, take a deep, steadying breath, and shuffle forward into a mainly monochrome office with a designer light hanging from the ceiling and a large, commanding glass desk in the center. I immediately note an alarming number of awards on the wall and a tall display of products that Dalton Media must've marketed.

Suddenly, a head wheels around in the far corner near a sleek bar area, and my stomach drops the whole twenty-two floors.

Shit.

It's her.

The woman I rammed into at the coffee shop.

The woman I also called an idiot.

So, it's official. The universe hates me.

There's a flash of recognition across her face, and her lips part like she is going to say something, but then they close again. A quick glance at my sweater confirms that she knows who I am.

I feel my face burning.

This is... not good.

My heart pounding at the ridiculousness of it all. She was a stranger. Strangers are supposed to disappear into the ether, never ever to be seen again. Not turn up at your job interview. And certainly not be your potential mega-boss lady.

Well, that has taught me. My stepmom Mimi always said to be kind to everyone because you never know if you might cross paths again, and here we are.

There's an unbearable pause as she pours us both a glass of water.

"Miss Andrews. Please take a seat," she says coolly and walks to her desk, sinking into a large cappuccino-colored wingback chair that looks like it's worth more than all of my furniture combined. She slides the glass of water over to me.

"Oh, thanks. And it's Mia."

Unbelievably, my voice is only slightly squeaky.

"Natalie," she simply replies, and I take a sip from my glass.

Up close, she's even less of my type than I remember.

Stiff as a board, too polished. Eyes still the color of icy crystals. Those chestnut waves that were draped all over me half an hour ago now perfectly set in place. Not to mention her pin-stripe suit that looks like it has been sewn on. My God, the woman doesn't even have smile lines.

I sit in a squashy leather chair and wince internally, feeling every bit of my bruised tailbone, but I'm determined not to let it show. Instead, I opt to feign a smile and glue my knees together because it's been over a year since I donned a skirt.

Natalie looks across her desk, cool, calm, and even. The panoramic backdrop of the San Diego skyline spreading out behind her. "So, Anna, our recruitment manager from Hayes, tells me good things about your work... No college?" she asks, interlacing her fingers.

"No, self-taught," I reply. "I fell in love with graphic design in high school and have done plenty of courses. I believe my experience in the industry and my work speaks for itself."

Natalie nods. "Do you enjoy it?"

"Well, I wouldn't turn up to an interview with a coffee-soaked shirt if I didn't... " I pause, waiting for a response, but there is none. Christ. My ability to tell a joke has fallen flat. "Anyway. Yes, I'm very passionate about what I do."

It's true. To be honest, I can't believe I get paid for my imagination. Given my experience, these days, it's more about concepts than pixels. Still, there's nothing better than seeing my ideas come alive on the screen.

"So, why Dalton Media?"

"I've been freelancing for a while, but I miss human contact and would like to be part of a successful team again. With your clientele and reputation, I know that would be a given."

"Okay." Natalie taps her desk with her fingers. "Do you have some of your recent work to show me?"

I pull out my iPad and hand it to her.

Natalie swipes across the screen, making perfunctory noises. "Interesting. Impressive... " After a while, she pauses, looking up. "Look, at the end of the day, it doesn't really matter. I just wanted to see what the hype was about. The job is yours if you're happy to proceed? Here's our offer." She hands me my iPad and a contract.

What?

That was fast. Suddenly, my day from hell has a silver lining.

I skim-read the important details, and it's a very impressive package. I don't know what to say, but obviously, I can't wipe the smile from my face. "Yes. Of course. Thank you so much for the opportunity."

"Don't thank me. Your hire wasn't my call." Her cheek flinches, and suddenly, I'm not so sure about this conversation. "It was the board that wanted you. Today was really just a formality. A meet and greet. Frankly, I don't think we need to add to our headcount, and you're certainly an expensive overhead."

Wow, just what a new employee likes to hear.

I try to channel Buddha for my inner Zen as Natalie continues. "You'll be working closely with designers – Theo and Kayley. Kayley works from home most of the time, given that she has a baby. We offer flexibility but prefer employees come to the office on a regular basis. Theo and Kayley will be there to support you, and I, in turn, expect you to impart some of your knowledge to them."

I nod, trying to rise above her comments. "Of course. When would I start?"

"How about now?" Natalie raises a perfect eyebrow. "Unless you need to go home and get changed?"

"Practically dry," I lie.

"Good," she replies but doesn't look happy. Instead, she picks up her phone. "Margot, can you please come into my office?"

A minute later, an Amazonian woman with a swishy platinum blonde ponytail, hooded feline eyes, and the longest legs in human history strolls in. She's rocking a brilliant red sheath dress and looks so perfect I think she is airbrushed. I try to find one flaw, one imperfection, but there are none.

"Margot, this is Mia, our new senior graphic designer. Mia, Margot is the office manager."

"Hi." I can detect a fake smile a mile away. "Also part-time account manager and head of the social committee," she adds unnecessarily.

And bingo, there's the flaw.

Margot extends a perfectly manicured hand, and I realize that I need to shake it, not stare at it.

Wait.

I narrow my eyes with recognition. That's the mammoth emerald from the bathroom. The ring so large it could double as a weapon. It catches the overhead light, winking at me conspiratorially.

I proffer my hand that was down the toilet, and Margot and I shake.

Honestly, I don't feel bad about it one bit.

Margot wrinkles her small, upturned nose at my chest. "Don't you have the exact same sweater, Natalie? Same G logo on the right."

Natalie looks up, somewhat disinterested. "Hmm. Similar." She picks up a wad of files and glides toward the door.

"No. Exact. I have an eye for detail. Twenty-twenty vision at my last optical exam with Mr. Monroe. Could even be a pilot if I wanted -"

Thankfully, Natalie cuts her off. "Margot, please show Mia around. I have a meeting with production, then the board," she says with a grimace. "Mia, welcome to the team."

"Thanks again," I reply, wrestling my iPad into my bag. As I move to stand, a singular yellow disc plops to the floor from between my legs. What the –

I hate that freaking kid.

When I look up, they are both staring at it.

"Right. I shall see you later," says Natalie, thankfully not making eye contact. I'm not sure I could bear it.

She disappears out the door while Margot folds her perfectly toned arms across her dress and huffs, "Well, pick it up. . . Chop, chop. I don't have all day."

I angrily bend over, crushing the disc in my grip, and fight the overwhelming urge to chuck it at her head. With little choice, I shuffle after her onto the office floor.

Margot flicks her expensive ponytail like a prized mare but never stops walking. "So, have you *actually* worked for a media company before?"

Is she seriously questioning me?

"I have ten years of design experience. I've mainly free-lanced but have provided graphics for Ashley Peters, Hewitt and Robson, Genesis Media -"

"Good for you," she interrupts with all the subtlety of a chainsaw. "Kitchen here. Lunchroom at the end and bathroom over in the far corner." She uses hand signals, and for a brief moment, I feel like I'm about to take off on a flight. "And

Mia, the coffee machine. This is an official warning. Break it, and you're dead." She throws me a look, and oh my God, she means it.

"Fresh fruit is delivered every Monday. Two pieces only, or you'll be reported to HR like Sally Morton. We found a whole fruit shop in her top drawer. Don't be like Sally." Margot claps back to the present like some drill sergeant. "Now, let's meet the team."

She spends ten minutes, and that's being generous, in a whirlwind trip around the office, doing the introductions so fast that I think she is deliberately trying to fuck me up.

I can't remember one name by the end of it, and why are there so many Amandas?

Before I know it, we are standing beside a shiny white desk overlooking the bustling Gaslamp Quarter. "So, that's it. This is your workstation. Ben from IT will be with you shortly to give you your security pass, network access, and login details. If you have any questions, ask. . . " Margot pauses, tapping her finger on her lip. If she says Amanda, I swear to God. "Joan."

"The receptionist? Um, she looks very busy."
"Mmhm. We're all very busy in this industry." Margot glares at me. "And Mia. . . "
"Yes?"
"Don't get in my way."

A few Amandas snap up from workstations sensing danger.

"See you're still trying to make new friends, Margot?" A short, stocky woman clutching an extra-large iced coffee shuffles past with glossy hair the color of wheatfields. She dumps an armful of printouts on her desk and gives me a wink.

"Watch it, Kayley," Margot hisses, then mutters, "And your fat ass." And with that sublime gesture, she simply swivels on a single Miu Miu heel and saunters off.

I just stand there blinking while Kayley gives her a deathly glare and takes a comically loud slurp of her coffee.

"Oh, don't worry about her. She's just the office bitch."

I swing around, and there's a tiny woman with eyebrows capable of launching a thousand ships smiling at me in an adorable polka-dot silk blouse. She has big blue eyes, straight mousy brown hair that is cut to her chin, and a cute gap between her teeth.

"We can't get rid of her because her daddy Jeff Gold owns half the city and sits on the board. But we certainly all fantasize about hurling her out the window."

I nod in agreeance.

"Anyway, I'm Nancy. Natalie's PA," she says with an infectious smile and comes at me with a bowl. "Want some Maltesers?"

I smile back. "Nancy, we're going to be *excellent* friends."

* * * * *

So, the Maltesers cost me twenty minutes and a couple of ounces.

I learn all about Nancy's fireman fiancé, Roy, his unsuccessful DIY projects, and their planned wedding next month in Long Island. She even shows me a photo of her massive meringue of a wedding dress.

Interestingly, she tells me Margot wanted an assistant, but they hired me instead. She is also desperate to get into account management, so they gave her some piddly account in the back of the beyond just to appease her.

Every now and then, I catch Margot giving me dirty looks. At least I know why. I just pop a few extra Maltesers. Keep this up, and I'll be scheduling a visit to the dentist next week.

The rest of the morning is a little awkward because Natalie barely acknowledges me, so I drop off my signed contract to HR and wait for Ben to set me up online.

I don't have any office knickknacks to move in because who knew I would start today, but I do unload twenty-five stabby pens from my bag and raid the stationery cupboard.

Natalie seems to spend most of her time in the glass-walled meeting room with Nancy, who is diligently scribbling note after note while she's hunched over a long, bronze table, so I have a perfect view of her ignoring me. Oh, and her backside.

A tall, ruddy-cheeked man wearing a double-breasted suit and shiny Rolex I can spot from my seat spends quite a bit of time in there, too, bouncing around on the tops of his toes. His chest is puffing with rage, and he's getting redder and redder.

"Hi, I'm Theo. UX designer. Nice to meet you," says a voice, and I turn to a man, waving, with squirrelly eyes and cropped curly hair. He rushes toward me in a navy vest and brown tasseled shoes, whispering, "That's Natalie's idiot father, Ron Dalton. They're always at it. I would've decked him by now. Straight between the eyes with a sucker punch."

There seems to be an unnerving undercurrent of violence here, but I just smile because what else do I do?

Theo rubs his chin. "Rumor has it that when he bought his stripper girlfriend a condo, Mama Dalton ran him over. That's how he got his limp."

"What?"

"She ran over his toe," he says with a lopsided grin.

"Well, good on her," I mutter under my breath.

Kayley's whiskey-colored eyes come alive, and she scurries over in her shapeless muumuu, itching to contribute. "His prized Bentley ended up inside the foyer of the house, but he made the story go away with his influence. The man is a grade A -"

The door slams, and we almost jump into the roof.

Ron Dalton is angrily limping across the office floor with a white shock of hair falling over his brow. "No need to leer, you lot. Back to work," he grunts.

It's like drama central here.

In any case, I decide to briefly run my eye over company policy before getting started on my online induction training. Five minutes in, I'm bored to tears, and I have to remind myself why I'm giving up freelancing from home.

Am I insane?

It's even more difficult to reconcile when Margot continues to lurk around in the background being a straight-up dick. Every time I go to the bathroom, she intercepts me. I've already made her a double-shot latte (so I know how to use the coffee machine) and photocopied an entire catalog of headshots. Same reasoning.

When I get a crick in my neck, ironically while completing a multiple-choice quiz about ergonomics, I decide to have a breather and text my best friend, Amy. I scan the ceiling for any cameras. It is my first day, after all. Then slip my phone under my desk and summons her to an after-work meeting.

Just after five, I hobble out of the office, completely wrecked. Heels no longer my friends, it seems.

Joan is on the phone in hushed tones. "Well, now Irene needs a colostomy, so... " She startles when she sees me, and I wave. "One second, Deidre." She fumbles with her headset. "Congratulations, Mia! I knew you'd be perfect the moment I saw you."

"Oh, thank you." I smile back because she is genuinely lovely.

"What did you think of Natalie?" Joan asks, green eyes glinting. "Nice, right?"

Actually, I was thinking more of a demon, but she seems oddly protective of her, so I just nod. "Mmhm. Certainly made an impression. See you tomorrow, Joan."

CHAPTER THREE

MIA

"Wow. Lots to dissect, but calling your new boss an idiot on your first day is my personal favorite." Amy starts snickering on the sun-speckled street in her bouclé midi dress.

While it's nice to see the sun out because it has been unseasonably wet and cold, I'm still grimacing when Amy cheekily asks, "Why does this make my day?"

"Because you're a sadist, and I hate you." I hook her arm into mine, and she grins. "I just can't believe you did that. So gutsy. Next time Errol is hovering over my shoulder, I'm going to let him have it."

I roll my eyes. "You're all talk, Amy Buchanan. Oh, and please remind me to sit on a colossal ice pack when we get home," I say, not enjoying the shooting pain in my rear.

Of course, she gives me a solid whack right there.

"Amy!" I jump in the air.

Her whole face breaks out into a grin, and I just shake my head, smiling, because it's impossible not to.

My literal pain-in-the-ass friend works across the street as a cool copywriter at the coolest ad agency in San Diego, Satchi &

Co. Although she always complains about her job, I know deep down that she loves it.

She is also my roommate, and we've been sharing a quaint two-bedroom apartment in Mission Valley for four years. Prior to our upgrade, we lived in a grubby doll-sized place in El Cajon with paper-thin walls and a resident weirdo, Mr. Hoffmeister, who used to sit on a stool outside his front door with a stopwatch and notebook and record all our comings and goings.

Amy and I first met after I answered her flatmate ad on Craigslist. While I was only her second choice (Amy likes to regularly remind me. First choice was a mega-hot ex-real housewife with a turtle called Rafi. I don't ask questions), I still believe it was a kismet moment because her friendship is a gift, and I can't imagine life without her.

Like all great love affairs, however, it was a slow burn. I was slightly terrified by her purple pixie hair and vegan leather pants, and she was unsure of my rotating plaid shirt collection and perennial bum-part hairstyle.

Needless to say, our friendship was helped along by a bit of tequila, and our reluctance to get to know one another was soon forgotten.

Our fashion choices and style have also progressed over the years. Mine, albeit at a slower and less voguish pace.

Amy's hair now a more mature chocolate brown and almost the same shade as her eyes, and although she is averse to any exercise unless it's shopping, she is blessed with a lean runner's body. She is also honest and funny and never ever laughs at my misfortune.

Naturally, she is still sniggering beside me, so I punch her in the arm. "Ames! Not helping! Anyway, there's also the office manager, Margot -"

"The one that wears red and has legs up to her neck?"

My head whips around. "Wait. You know her?"

"No." She sidesteps a puddle. "I can see everything from my office window."

"What like on your freaking telescope?" I reply.

"I'm a very perceptive person, Mia." Amy grins. "Think you need to reel in your pen count, by the way. Borderline obsessive."

Okay, no one knows about that.

I shake my head. "Oh my God. You're not joking." On the curb, I watch yellow traffic lights turning red with jaywalkers gliding past in thick streams.

Amy turns to me. "Perfect line of vision. Wave back next time. This isn't a one-way relationship, you know."

"You're an idiot," I snuffle as we scurry across the street.

"Definitely," she grins, and so do I.

Predictably, Amy asks, "So, Margot?"

Amy Buchanan is a serial dater and never misses an opportunity because she *always* has her feelers out. No woman is outside her scope.

"Ugh. Apparently, she's the office bitch. Also, thankfully straight." I pin her with a glare. "Trust me. You don't want to go there. I can't help but feel that she'll go out of her way to make my life difficult. Which reminds me, walk faster because I need to pee. Every time I passed her desk to go to the bathroom, she had me doing jobs for her. Third time, I decided to hold it in."

We maneuver past some slow-walking map-wielding tourists and start to walk-run.

"Don't worry," Amy says between breaths. "You know I always have your back. I'll keep an eye on her."

I start to laugh. "Do you do any work at all?"

"Occasionally. When Errol isn't at his summer house in Malibu screwing around."

I giggle and then give an exasperated sigh. "Honestly, maybe I should just go back to freelancing. I forgot about office dynamics. It's difficult being the new girl. My boss, for one, is frosty as. No clue how we will ever have friendly relations."

"Maybe she just takes a bit of getting used to."

"Hmm. I think I'll need to get my job satisfaction from elsewhere, or I'll just end up eating Nancy's endless candy."

Amy laughs. "Well, it's not all bad. You love what you do, so that's a start. And apparently, Natalie is gay, so you know that adds a bit of spice to the job."

I do a double-take and accidentally shoulder-charge a petite woman carrying five shopping bags. "Sorry," I say as she bounces off me and throws me a murderous glare. "Hang on. Natalie Dalton is gay?"

"Uh-huh. She always has a beautiful woman on her arm. Dates CEOs, fashion designers, models. And at work, she's like this amazing powerhouse. Not known to be friendly but is well-respected among her peers. She's been there for two years. The board wanted to go in a new direction, and her father was shafted from the top job. They co-own the business, but there appears to be a lot of bad blood between them."

"How do you know all this by staring out a window?" I ask, panting slightly as we reach the stairs to the subway.

"I don't. I vetted her once you told me you were applying. *Media Guru* called her 'one of the brightest sparks in the industry.' No way I'm letting you work for someone evil."

"You're an excellent friend."

"So, I keep telling you."

We grin at each other and disappear down the tunnel.

* * * * *

Christ on a bike.

"Who the heck owns cashmere?" I yell from our kitchen.

"Fancy people!" Amy hollers back.

I stare at the washing machine and grimace at the melodic thud of her sweater hitting the drum. Why does gentle cycle suddenly not look that gentle?

"What if it gets deformed? You know, like most of my clothes." I look down at my cropped t-shirt.

Amy walks up behind me in an off-the-shoulder top and denim shorts, peering over my shoulder. "Just give it a bit of a stretch."

The machine comes to a singing stop, and I anxiously open the door to pull out the sweater.

I hold it up.

"Wait. Is that the same sweater?"

"Shit," I mumble.

It looks half the size and wider. I lay it flat on the counter and pull the hem down a bit.

"Hmm. Looks a bit different than when you had it on."

"No kidding, Sherlock."

Amy covers her laugh with her hand. "Does she have any toddler siblings?"

I groan and hang the sweater on our drying rack. "Oh my God. She is going to hate me even more."

"Donate to kid's charity." Amy bumps my shoulder. "And buy a new one to replace it."

"It's four hundred dollars! And that's on sale."

"Might whip out my telescope for that conversation." Amy laughs and narrows her eyes. "Speaking of conversations, have you heard from Nadia since her latest stunt?"

I really don't want to have this conversation, but there's no point lying to Amy because she has the instincts of an FBI agent and always, *always* knows when I'm fibbing.

"No," I sigh.

Amy snorts and toes off her heels onto the kitchen tiles.

Sure, Nadia had been cute and fun when we started out. Leaving me love notes in my desk drawer and handbag. There were spontaneous Vespa drives down the Baja coast. An endless supply of free toothpaste and floss (she's a dentist, after all).

In fact, Nadia was always there for me when I needed her. Until she wasn't.

"Surprise, surprise." Amy wraps her arms around me. "I'm sorry, but if she shows up on our doorstep again with a stupid bunch of weeds in her hands, I'm going to commit an act of violence."

Amy might be small in stature, but she's extremely protective of me, and I believe her.

When we played a 'friendly' tennis match against one of my more forgettable exes, Billie, and her new partner, Gilda, Billie deliberately smacked a ball right at my head. Amy leaped over the net like some superhero and gave chase to Billie around the court. She never gave up, and on the ninth lap, she decked Billie with her racket.

Funnily enough, I haven't heard from her since.

"They were posies," I say to Amy. "Granted, a little dehydrated. And thank you for your unwavering loyalty, but..."

"But what? I will not let you be treated like that. Also, I need to let you know that your sister called."

"What?" My voice immediately goes up an octave at the mention of Janet. "Why is she calling you?"

Amy shrugs. "Wanted to know if you were anorexic. You weren't answering her calls."

I wander out to the living room, slump on our navy corduroy couch, and zero in on our palm tree wallpaper for some serenity.

Light and airy with gorgeous, reclaimed hardwood floors, this is my favorite space in our apartment. Scattered on the walls are bright pop art paintings that we bought dirt cheap in Downtown L.A., while a large faux fur rug in the center of the room injects that little bit of luxury.

"Yeah, because she is completely annoying. Last month, she told me I was breathing too loud and needed to go to the gym."

Janet is my sister and only older by a year, but she likes to boss me around. She also speaks to me in this condescending way that really irks me. Like she has the perfect life.

Sure, she's a chartered accountant with twins, Leo and Marley, but her husband, Harry, a heart surgeon, is a total shithead. He's arrogant, far too blunt, and has a know-it-all attitude. Last time he came to a family event was four years ago when Mimi and my dad (Robert) hosted Thanksgiving dinner, and he managed to offend everyone. Even their six-year-old Boston terrier, Alfie.

'Mimi, I don't think you rested the turkey. I almost broke my molar.' 'Rob, why don't I hook you up with my personal trainer friend, Patty Mills, so you can get rid of that beer belly?' 'Ha! That's not a dog. Aren't you embarrassed walking it?' 'But what exactly *is* the purpose of your life, Mia? You're going nowhere. Soon, you'll be sent out to pasture, and then what? Die alone?'

Like I said, total shithead. Suffice to say, we don't get along.

Still, this likable couple appears to live a glamorous lifestyle. Constantly jet-setting around the globe to fabulous locations while owning a McMansion in the glitzy Carmel Valley, which is only fifteen minutes from where I live.

One of the "benefits" of living so close to one another is that Janet likes to impart regular feedback on every aspect of my life, whether I want it or not. (I do not).

Our mom passed from a brain aneurysm when we were nine, and obviously, dad, Janet, and I were all devastated. But Janet, Janet became an angry human overnight. Perhaps because she found mom slumped on the kitchen floor, not me, I regularly drew her ire.

One of the first things she did was deface my favorite Backstreet Boys poster, and I could never prove it, but I think she peed on my ant farm too.

She also bleached her hair and went on a shoplifting spree, primarily Seventeen magazines and Gobstopper candy, which she liked to hide in my bag. At school, she became violent and doled out Chinese burns to anyone that looked at her the wrong way. Kimberley Kitchener copped a whole armful.

Eighteen years later, Janet is still unpleasant. I mean, I think she cares about me deep down, but she just goes about it the wrong way. She can't seem to wrap her head around the way I live. No steady partner, freelancing, sharing a rental with my 'uncouth' best friend (Amy likes to rile her up). Heaven forbid – a social life.

Horrible existence, I know.

There's also been a frightening escalation in contact. She used to casually check in, but that soon progressed to weekly probes. Now, if I don't answer her texts, she calls. If I don't answer calls, she contacts people I know. If that doesn't evoke a response, she rocks up unannounced on our doorstep, which always requires a recovery period.

Amy pops her head out of the kitchen. "Want some food?"

"No."

"Want some wine?"

"Yes."

Amy fixes her eyes on me.

"Are you testing me? This has nothing to do with what Janet said. Also, this is not to be communicated to her." I cross my arms. "Anyway, it's a perfectly normal response after the day I've had."

"Ha!" Amy grins. "I know." She pops open the microwave and reheats some pizza. Thirty seconds later, the slice is sizzling on the plate, and she's shoving it in my face. "Here. Eat."

"Thanks," I say and blow on it several times, knowing her habit of serving molten lava.

Amy whips out her phone when I have the piece attractively jammed in my mouth. "Say cheese!" The camera clicks. I shoot her a glare and then hear the whoosh of a message being sent.

"What? I have to get back to your sister, or she will turn up again!" she says, horrified, and collapses beside me. "Shit! Far too hot."

I giggle as Amy drops her slice. I could've told her that.

A bit of cheese oozes onto Lorenzo's head, and I peel it off with my finger. I don't know what my sister is on about when she says we are a mess.

Lorenzo is our landlord Mario's incontinent Burmese cat. Mario is a cranky old Italian man with a barrel-shaped body and greasy hair who communicates through grunts. One grunt means yes. Two grunts, no. He also lives on the top floor of our building.

Every February, he jets off to Calabrese in Southern Italy to spread his cheer with his family. We couldn't believe it when he asked us to look after Lorenzo last year. We're hardly responsible pet owners or responsible anything. But being our landlord, we couldn't say no.

We also love our apartment and can't imagine living anywhere else, even though it is hardly big enough to swing a cat (or Lorenzo). It borders arty Hillcrest, but it's way cheaper on this side, and there are heaps of cool restaurants and bars close by. It's also only a short subway ride into town.

Anyway, we must've done a stellar job with Lorenzo because Mario was back on our doorstep early February with the furry man bundled in his arms and a gigantic box of diapers.

If he could only see him now. The sheen of mozzarella on his head glistening in the fading golden light.

"Thanks for this, by the way." I point to the pizza hanging out my mouth and mumble, "Maybe I was hungry after all."

After I scoff down my slice, my phone pings with a message from Nadia. It's full of emoji love and not much else.

"Another senseless text, I see," Amy huffs. "Emergency rosé?" I giggle. It's always an emergency around here. "In fact, let's do one better with a sparkling rosé from Sonoma!"

"Go on, then," I reply.

Amy grins, skipping gleefully into the kitchen.

Emergency rosé has been a thing for as long as I've shared an apartment with Amy.

When the dryer blew up into a small fireball, and Mario replaced it even though we forgot to remove the lint; when our Cypriot neighbors, who had a ginormous sound system next to our couch, finally moved out; when Janet found her multiple gray hairs in her eyebrow and nether region. Out came the emergency rosé. Sometimes the bottle would stay unopened for a month, and then bam, we'd down three in a week.

I have a hunch that this may be one of those weeks.

There's a loud bang and then some cursing. I grin to myself. Amy's popped the cork into the kitchen ceiling again.

I swoop down to cuddle Lorenzo on the couch, and he returns my affection with a little growl. Well, they do say pets mirror their owners.

Amy suddenly appears with two glasses filled to the rim. She's looking a bit frazzled. "Remind me to touch up the cork mark with some paint. We still have that tin from last time." She hands me a glass, and I start to laugh. "Okay, well, Mario's back in two days, so consider this your official reminder."

Amy freezes. "Shit. I better do it now." She places her glass down on the coffee table and bolts into the kitchen, and I giggle into my sleeve.

Amy is one of the most fearless people I know, yet something about the imposing four-foot-four Mario completely freaks her out.

I think she may still be traumatized from when he showed up with two policemen at our housewarming party. His double chin wobbled with rage, and he turned a worrying shade of purple before fainting on our living room floor.

Half an hour later, Amy flops down beside me. Her face shimmering with sweat and smeared with half a tin of paint. "Now, where were we?"

We have a drink, then another. Even though we live together, we never run out of things to say, and two hours later, we're still talking nonsense.

We've discussed everything from Amy's abnormally large big toe, rockets launching across Japanese airspace, to the possibility of joining OnlyFans so we can become instant zillionaires. Of course, there won't be any mention of it in the morning.

Conversation eventually gravitates back to our poor choice in women, and I look out the window to a jet-black sky. The only light from a shimmery lonely crescent overhead.

"Maybe it's just me," I wearily conclude.

"No way! Come here. You're a verifiable goddess! Gorgeous, inside and out." Amy is being extremely charitable, but right now, I let it slide. "And you know you deserve better, right?" She gives me a warm – albeit a tad violent – hug like she is trying to shake some sense into me. "Have you ever really asked yourself what Mia wants? What Mia needs?"

It's true I've been killing myself over Nadia trying to keep her because I'm afraid to lose her, but I never really asked myself if that's what I even want anymore.

Perhaps it has to do with losing my mom so young. I grip a little tighter onto things knowing how fragile life can be.

If I'm honest, however, spending time with Nadia is no longer fulfilling. Something dying each time she let me down. Our conversations, if you can call them that, are now stilted, and physical attraction has all but cooled to an indifference.

I inhale sharply through a cloud of alcohol. "Mia wants to... Firstly, she needs to stop addressing herself in the third person."

"Okay, then... But I hate to see you like this. You really need to rip the band-aid off with Nadia. You're twenty-seven, not eighty-seven. It's holding you back, you know. Then you can fully crush on someone new and get back into the dating game."

"I can't. It's too late," I say, having no idea what the time is.

Amy raises an eyebrow. "It's eight o'clock."

"What?" I squawk, feeling rather smashed. Only eight? And on a school night? "I'm a disgrace."

Up goes her other eyebrow.

"No, Amy. She will think I have problems. Like more than normal!"

"Honestly, why do you care?"

I frown. "I'll speak to her when I'm sober."

Maybe.

My phone starts buzzing against my butt, and I pull it out, blinking at the screen. "Oh my God. It's her!"

"It's a freaking sign! Answer it!"

I fumble with my phone, swiping my finger over the screen. "Hello? Nadia?"

Amy drops to her knees and whisper-hisses, "Speakerphone!" so I press the button.

"The one and only! Mia, love. Just about to take off to Seattle. Have that national sales conference for dental hygiene. Going to be so exhausting." She gives an appropriately timed yawn, and I imagine her perfect shiny teeth. "I'm back Thursday, so let's catch up."

Amy rolls her eyes. Naturally, there's no apology for standing me up.

"You could swing by my practice, and we could do the freaky sixty-nine in the dentist chair again -" My hand flies over the speaker, and I feel my skin flare with embarrassment.

Stupid, idiotic speakerphone.

When is it ever a good idea when you have company?

Abby is erupting with laughter, so I push her over with my foot. I remove my hand from the speaker. "Look, Nadia -"

"How about six pm at Totti's by the wharf? We'll get a special window table with the best ocean view and watch the sunset. Have a bottle or two of Tattinger."

"Nadia."

She doesn't hear me. I feel as unheard now as I do when we spend time together. Empty companionship somehow lonelier than being alone.

"We can indulge in a seafood platter with grilled scampi fresh off the boat. You know, seafood is an aphrodisiac. Oysters, for one -"

Amy is pretending to puke in the background.

"Nadia! Listen! Please!" This time, the line goes quiet. "I need to say something to you."

"Look at me," Amy whispers, and she leaps onto the couch. She starts to sing, "We can't go on together."

"We can't go on together," I say into the phone.

I look at Amy, who has started dancing and snapping her fingers. Disturbingly, she's also swiveling her hips. "With suspicious minds."

"With suspicious minds?" I repeat.

"Hang on a second," Nadia says, sounding a little annoyed. "Are you wasted?"

"No."

"You're reciting Elvis lyrics."

I feel my ears pinking. "Okay, one *small* glass of wine. Point is... um... " Amy hands me a banana, and I actually think it's a microphone. Thank God I saw the new Elvis movie last Thursday because I remember the next line, so this time, I really go for it. I sing my heart out. "And we can't build our dreams on suspicious minds -"

"Honestly, Mia. I'm loving the mid-week serenade. It's cute and all, but can we do this another time?" Nadia lowers her voice. "I'm on a packed United flight, and the hostess is giving me a filthy look."

Serenade? Only her inflated ego would think this was a serenade.

A doorbell rings, and I hear a female voice. "Nadia?"

"On a plane with a doorbell, huh? That's a first!" My hand balls into a fist, and I watch my knuckles turn white. I seem to grow a pair. "That's it, Nadia. I've had it with you. Do not ever call me -"

"You sent a message asking me to ring?"

Yes, *twelve* hours ago.

"You know, whatever. It's over. Whatever this thing is between you and me. I'm sick of your lies. Your Houdini acts. I deserve better, and I... I don't ever want to see you again, Nadia Magdelena-Merlina Newman. I really mean it this time!"

There's a massive cheer from Amy as I end the call, then unceremoniously topple backward off the couch, right on top of our fluffy faux fur rug and my banana microphone.

Amy and her paint-stained nose peer over the top. "Feel better, right?"

"Totally," I nod, slightly winded with a banana smooshed all over my back.

"So, that means your free tomorrow nig -" Amy loses her footing and crashes on top of me, both of us groaning but far less than if we were sober.

"Oh, shit." I laugh-cry. "You're crushing my boob."

"Wait." Amy lifts her head from inside my armpit a moment later. "Is that really her middle name?"

"Uh-huh."

She squeals into my hair, and both of us dissolve into gales of laughter.

CHAPTER FOUR

MIA

"Amy, are you alive?" I whisper through the crack in her door.

"No. Fuck off."

I grin, unable to contain myself.

She's completely fine.

I pad over quietly to her fully-clothed body starfished across her bedspread. Her face is squashed against the pillow, makeup still unremoved. I leave a glass of water and two aspirin on her bedside table and then close the door as I leave.

After shoveling some protein bars and a hair tie or two into my handbag, I snatch the plastic bag with Natalie's newly washed sweater slash bib from the kitchen counter and head to the front door, only to have Jules from apartment number twelve greet me on the other side. She's all big gray eyes and shiny black suit.

I smile. "Hey, Jules."

"Mia! Perfect timing. Walk with me." She glances left and right. "Damn it. Mr. Marxson stole my paper again."

"Why don't you report him?"

"He's ninety-six. Seems a bit cruel to hand a senior citizen over to the authorities. What if he gets incarcerated?" We shuffle down the stairs. "Where's the evil one today?"

"She'll be working from home."

Jules clicks her tongue. "I see. Another rowdy night in the Buchanan and Andrews household."

"Just your average Thursday night, really."

Jules is a long-legged redhead beauty with a wide mouth and an oversized laugh to match. She's also a successful real estate agent with a gift of the gab and an uncanny ability to rock killer stilettos day or night.

We've lived in the same building for three years. Unfortunately, or fortunately, depending on how you look at it, she chose to knock on our door after locking herself out. She dazzled us with her charm, and we dazzled her with, I'm not sure. Our liquor collection?

Regardless, we bonded, and from that moment on, we *never* let her leave our tight circle of friends.

Personally, I feel blessed that two of my besties live within ten steps of one another. I don't even need to commute to catch up.

We push through the heavy glass door, and I wince into the garish glow. A beacon of searing light blinding me before my pupils adjust. "Oh, shit!"

"What's wrong?"

"My head feels like a block of concrete. I can't believe the sun has the gall to come out this early." We step out onto the sidewalk. "On the plus side, I finally ended things with Nadia."

"Oh, thank fuck!"

My head snaps around as fast as it can with a hangover.

"Sorry. But wow, you can do so much better!"

"So, everyone keeps saying." We stride up to a busy four-way intersection and cross.

"Well, that means you can come to my soiree tonight after work. I'm heading straight there after my showing of that spectacular seaside estate in La Jolla. It's two streets down from Walker Avenue at that little boutique gallery, U-ho. Max has set me up on a blind date with Bec from the Property Management team -"

I stop still on the street. "Oh. I'm busy."

"No. You're not. Amy sent me your schedule last week. There is far too much 'rest' blocked out in there and not enough play."

The one slightly irritating thing about living with your friends – they're always ferreting around in your business.

I roll my eyes. "Honestly, Jules. I don't need help. I'm fine."

"Of course you are." She places a smacking kiss on my cheek and doesn't hear a word I say. "So, I'll text you the address after work. Come straight after speed dating."

My face falls.

Speed dating?

Amy.

"Don't forget!" Jules beams and disappears down the subway exit in her killer heels while I'm left to wonder what the hell they have roped me into now.

As soon as I get to work, I'm going to text the living daylights out of Amy Buchanan. Always signing me up for the most ridiculous things.

Last month it was gay swing dancing, and I have two left feet and the coordination of roadkill. Obviously, it was a total disaster, and all my blundering on the dance floor meant I never got a date out of it. And now, she signs me up to freaking speed dating.

I'm still shaking my head when the subway car shrieks to a stop at my station, and I make my way up the twenty-two floors to our office.

I eventually settle at my desk and stare out to San Diego Bay in all its perfect crystalline glory, and then glance down to street level, where people are moving like ants on the congested sidewalk.

Lights are being switched on in the shops, and cars toot their way through traffic.

I scramble for my phone in my bag.

ME: Amy, you're dead.

AMY: Ha-ha. What's new?

Great. She doesn't even take me seriously.

ME: Speed dating?!?!

AMY: I know. Exciting, right? Priya, the psychic, says we're going to meet our soul mates!! You can thank me later xoxo

Ugh.

Well, if Priya, the psychic, said so...

Rubbing my forehead, I drop my phone on my desk and laugh-groan because even though it always seems to end in disaster, I know Amy is coming from a good place.

The bag with Natalie's elfin sweater catches my eye. "God. We better get this over with," I mutter, but when I swivel around, I notice my boss isn't in her office.

Brilliant. Even better.

Leaping up, I snatch the bag, and sprint over. I almost mow down Amanda from Legal on the way through. "Sorry," I say, flashing an apologetic smile. She just glares at me from behind her thick black glasses, then stalks off in her strictly black ensemble.

I nervously shuffle inside Natalie's office. I'll just bury it under some crap on her desk and -

"My sweater?" asks a voice, and I startle with the bag hovering over a bundle of draft designs.

Shit.

I turn around slowly. "Mmm, yep. Thanks again."

Natalie walks up beside me in a sleeveless arctic white blouse, tailored navy pants, and a pair of red Jimmy Choo's, and I start to feel very queasy all over again. "Good. I could use it now," she sighs. "They've cranked up the air conditioning to obscene levels. No doubt men are in charge of the thermostat."

Okay. Not what I want to hear.

Natalie peers inside the bag and pulls out the sweater. It immediately unfurls in her hands. "What -"

"Oh, um."

Natalie pauses. "And what am I supposed to do with this? Gift it to my next-born?"

Call me crazy, but I think I detect a slight bit of anger in her voice.

I laugh awkwardly, and she drops into her chair.

"I might've had a few issues with washing it. It's not my strong suit. So many buttons, different materials to consider, temperatures. There are a lot of variables."

Oh, God. Just shut up, I tell myself.

"Mmhm. Washing machines. Impossible to master. Need a college degree. Got it." Natalie glances at her computer. "If that's all, Mia."

Christ. I spin on my heel and rush out of her office as fast as my wooden legs take me.

Joan is wrong. She *is* scary.

Honestly, it brings me back to the day I stood in principal Howden's office in my freshman year of high school after hurling a cupcake at my archnemesis, Heidi Clinger, because she stole my prized SuperGirl pen.

My heart is still beating a hundred miles an hour as I barrel around the corner -

I instantly freeze. Margot is sitting in my chair with her dirty paws milling around in my pot of pens.

Why does history have a way of repeating itself?

Margot gives me a saccharine smile, and it's pure evil. "I quite like the view from this desk." I want to say that I imagine it beats the view of the wall, but I don't. She soon loses interest in my pens because her eyes viciously settle on my shirt. "And nice top. My mom has the same one in bottle-green."

It's not a compliment.

I grit my teeth, and I wonder if it's too early in my tenure to commit violence. "Anything I can help you with, Margot?"

"Hardly," she scoffs and then springs up, looking like she has been poured into her animal-print leather pants. "Guest speaker in the McMillian room in five minutes. Alan Moffatt from Expedia is giving a chat on direct marketing trends in the travel industry. You snooze, you lose."

I blink. "McMillian room?"

Did she even show me where that was?

I try to recall my manic office tour but come up blank. When I look around, I realize the floor is completely empty. And forget asking Margot, she's teleported her way down to the other end of the office.

"Come with me," says an angelic voice.

I whip around, and great, I'm starting to hallucinate because there's not a soul in sight. "I'm going mental," I mutter to myself.

"No. You're not," snaps a reply, and I jump a foot off the carpet.

A head popping up from under a desk that is covered in a kaleidoscope of sticky notes organized in neat rows.

Nancy.

"Lost my damn earring, but it'll have to wait." She springs to her feet, wearing one massive hoop in her left ear, heavy eyeliner, and a stripey top. A knotted leather headband sweeping her hair back into a ponytail. She looks like a pirate. "Yikes. We better go," she says, glancing at her watch, and I automatically reply, "Aye, aye."

Nancy eyes me cautiously. "Okay. . . "

I cough. "I mean, yes. Let's go."

She picks up a pen and paper, her posture relaxing. "You know, Margot did the same thing to me when I started. Except I ended up in Tijuana and then got detained by Border Protection. There may have also been an unflattering mug shot."

"What the hell?"

"Long story. Don't ask. But every morning, I practice deep breathing."

"Margot's a monster."

Nancy is nodding so hard I think her head may snap off. She plunges her spare hand into her bottomless candy jar and hands me a Twix. "Uh-huh, but chocolate always helps. Even at nine in the morning."

I give her a look. "Honestly, I'm starting to think you're my fairy godmother."

Nancy giggles. "Funny. Natalie says that to me all the time."

CHAPTER FIVE
NATALIE

I dread Fridays.

Usually, the favorite day of the week for most, but for me, it means enforced lunches with my father, Ronald, and my step-mom, Ronnie, under the guise of a company meeting.

As much as I love my job, working with these two bozos is one of the annoying caveats.

I only agreed to these lunches because I didn't want my father constantly getting into my business. Still, I rue this arrangement because this blip in my day sets me back precious hours. Beginning in the early hours of the morning, my work is never-ending.

Ronnie has been married to my father for eight years. She tolerates me, and I despise her. We are both brunettes. Both tall. And disturbingly, the same age. But that's where the similarities end.

She is a vapid, luxury shoe aficionado with a proclivity for soaking up the sun on their mega-yacht, Ambrosia. According to master sleuth Joan, she even has designs on my position. Ha. As if that would ever happen.

Ronnie is a complete contrast to my late mom, Jean. My mom was not born into wealth, but instead, a middle-class mid-west family, so when she married my father as a doe-eyed twenty-two-year-old, he had her fix her teeth and ditch her accent.

Wealth never really sat well with my mom. Far from being the arm candy my father envisaged, she was awkward at events and preferred to stay at home and care for me, where we indulged in Taco Tuesdays and, my favorite, our Sunday Scrabble challenge.

Being a bookish homebody didn't bode well for my mom either, and when I was nineteen, my father started an affair with Ronnie, who was an exotic dancer. Stage name Trixxy Tease. Barf. My mom was diagnosed with stage four ovarian cancer two years later, and the bastard moved his girlfriend into our family home while mom was in hospice. He married her six months later.

I've never forgiven him, and for this reason alone, I despise him even more than Ronnie.

Thankfully, my mom was able to transfer her share of the business to me before she passed, which outraged my father. He assumed he would take full ownership.

We were never close. Always a thorn in his side, when I was seven, he tried to have me carted off to a boarding school in Switzerland, but mom wouldn't hear of it.

My loyalty to my mom never wavered. I'm certain that's why I look more like her. Blue eyes, dark hair. The only thing I inherited from my father was his height and ability to get under people's skin.

Imagine his disgust at having to ask my permission on company decisions. Not surprisingly, I secretly relish his discontent, but there are times I wonder if all the angst is worth it.

My issues with my father so big sometimes I can't see the sky.

I spot the two Ronnies seated in silence at our usual corner table of the sky-high terrace restaurant. There's only one plus, the gorgeous view looking out over the Pacific. I always make sure I'm facing that way.

Dressed in all black save for the small white daisy pinned to her hair, the maître d looks up and gives me a bright smile. "Good afternoon, Miss Dalton. They're waiting for you."

"Just the usual Almond Chicken. Thanks, Cassie."

To speed up the meetings, I place my lunch order at the front desk. It easily shaves off fifteen minutes.

"Of course. Right this way," she replies, leading me through an arch-capped French door.

Silverware tapping porcelain and ice clinking in highball glasses amongst the quiet hum of conversation.

"Father. Ronnie."

I call him father because he's never been a dad to me. A father only on paper, and a father who wouldn't blink at the chance to turn the board against me and kick me out as CEO. In fact, if you came to my apartment, you'd think I was fatherless because there are only photos of mom and me.

As far as I'm concerned, she raised me all by herself. I can still feel her arms around me, smell her rose scent, hear her voice – *You deserve the world, my darling girl.*

She was everything to me.

Neither of them makes an effort to look up or return my greeting. Ronnie is too busy pushing a piece of charred kale around on her plate while my father is peeling king prawns with his stubby fingers.

I'm barely in my seat when he starts his dribble. "So, we need to have a united front for the IPO. There are millions of dollars to be made if we play our cards right."

I immediately stiffen.

We are offering fifty million shares to the public in November, and my father is right. It's all about perception. We need to market the crap out of our business for the take-up to be successful.

Still, I can't stand the man, so when he tells me what to do, I want to do the opposite.

He glances at me from beneath his bushy, gray brows. "No maverick moves or anything underhanded, Natalie," he says, tone dry.

"Sounds like a warning?"

"Now, now." He runs his hand over his slicked-back hair. "You have just as much to lose as me, so sensible heads must prevail."

My father wounded by my success in the two years I've been CEO. I was the one that turned this company into a multi-million-dollar business, not him.

According to Instagram, my father and Ronnie spend a lot of their time in bathrobes on luxury European holidays while I'm in the office slaving away.

Not that I mind, the more distance, the better, but I do take issue when he tells me what to do with the business.

My father checks his phone as he speaks. "I played squash with Rolf from Babcock yesterday, and he said we should contact Henry Adams at Channel Five to see if we can get on his morning show. Would be incredible exposure. Their viewer numbers hit a million -"

I tear a bread roll in half and butter it. "No. It's tacky and doesn't align with our branding," I counter flatly. "Just like your vision to promote cigarettes and environmentally unfriendly products. Not happening."

My father snarls at me. "We need to stay profitable, Natalie."

"And we are. We've always been in green since I've been at the helm," I reply, unable to resist a dig.

He drops a prawn shell onto his plate and wipes his perspiring face with a cloth napkin. "I'm not sure I like your tone with me."

"Why? It hasn't changed in twenty years."

So, I could be rude to him.

Just because we share DNA doesn't mean I like the guy. I've only ever known a selfish skirt-chasing man, even when my world was imploding into minuscule pieces, and he hasn't changed. Cheating on Ronnie whenever he can.

Apparently, he still hasn't received the memo that he's well into his seventies. Because why not be a douchebag when you can afford to be? Women would've slapped him into unconsciousness by now, bare for the fact that he was thoroughly moneyed.

An awkward lull is interrupted by a waiter bringing out the mains.

Ronnie finally looks up from her marinated duck breast, spaced out as usual. "Oh, hello, Natalie." She probably guzzled a packet of Xanax before she came here. I would if I were her. Her poker-straight dark hair appears to be set like jelly, and she's packed on so much powder she looks like a cake.

Something winks at me from her chest, and she catches me staring.

"The pendant or my boob job?" She gives a slippery smile.

I roll my eyes.

Definitely not the latter, though I do note an eyewatering enhancement which is hardly contained by her baby-blue size zero Marc Jacobs dress.

"Ron bought me both, but the diamond pendant is for our anniversary. We've been together for eight years. Can you believe it? Isn't he a peach? We're sailing down the Intercoastal Waterway to St. Bart's next week to celebrate."

I grit my teeth and stab at my chicken breast. Eight years since his betrayal.

"Going for long?" I ask hopefully, then stuff my mouth to stop me from saying more.

My father looks up from his bowl of steaming lobster bisque. "Don't get too excited, Natalie. It's for ten days. Honestly, you could be a bit more discreet," he snaps. "How's the new girl going? Myra? Mina?"

"Mia. She's fine. Even though we don't need her. We're trying to minimize our costs after opening an office in Paris last year. You really shouldn't be pushing through decisions when you don't even work here on a day-to-day basis."

He crosses his arms defiantly. "Looks good for the IPO. We need someone high-profile to create additional interest. I want her to attend all the media events, not that plain Jane. What's her name? Stephanie something. Oh, who cares." He scrunches up his face, and I want to punch him. "Use Myra. We'll cut her as soon as she's served her purpose."

I bristle at the comment and wish I'd at least ordered one vodka soda to get through this. So like my father. Use and discard. Much like he did to my mom. We are both business people, but he's brutal.

His pale-blue eyes are cold and empty, and I can't ever remember them being anything else. "Oh, and stop firing Margot." His thin lips turning into a snarl. "Jeff keeps threatening to quit and pull the plug on his twenty-million-dollar investment."

"She's as competent as a pet rock. A total liability. I will not have her bullying my staff, so I'll fire her every time I see fit." I put down my napkin.

"Goddammit, Natalie!" My father knocks back his wine. "You've fired her three times in the last three months! Jeff has me by the balls. For once in your life, do as you are told."

"You shouldn't have made a deal with the devil then. I'm sure I would've fired her a dozen more times, but I've hardly been in the office."

"Natalie," he growls, and I return his stare. "Ronald."

Not much he can say, really.

Gripping the table, he hisses, "Well, it should also give you great joy knowing that we'll be staying in your guest wing for a few days."

I pinch the bridge of my nose. "Can't you stay somewhere else?"

"It was my home before yours, and I still have a set of keys. Besides, it's closer to the marina. I'll expect you to move that wretched furball of yours too. You know how allergic Ronnie is." But she's just staring vacantly into the restaurant. She's off her face. "Christ," he angrily mutters under his breath. "How many did you take today?" The waiter reappears to refill my father's wine. He goes to top up Ronnie's. "No, not hers. She'll be on the floor."

And I make a break for it, glancing at my blank smartwatch. "Oh, would you look at that? Emergency at the office," I lie and spring to my feet as the waiter hands me my to-go bag.

My father is nonplussed. "Well, at least you stayed past the entrées this time."

CHAPTER SIX

MIA

"Honestly, I don't know how you talked me into this garbage," I say, shuffling across the street, my hands pinning down the sides of my dress.

In a brave attempt to revive my love life, I'm wearing a nude color dress that apparently screams sex (I have my doubts), but I trust my friends. While Amy is wearing a tight black corset top and even tighter black pants, plus a pair of pointy heels that I know give her blisters. No pain, no gain, she likes to say. Her hair as glossy as Belgian chocolate, flowing so seamlessly down her back it looks like it melted there.

We turn a corner and then another until we're standing in a small alley.

"Stop whining. You might meet the woman of your dreams tonight," Amy says.

Actually, I think it'd make more sense to hope I bear witness to the second coming of Jesus, but still, I try to remain optimistic.

"Hurry up. Are you deliberately going slow?" Amy glances over her shoulder, her brown eyes glittering in the passing headlights. "It's just up here." She eventually stops, and I see the dingy sign of Milligan's Bar poking out behind a dumpster.

"I never walk in heels this high. I should know my limitations," I mutter, trying to go as fast as I can, looking like some concussed giraffe. Amy starts to laugh. "Oh, you think that is going to make me feel better? And why is there a dumpster out front? Is that where I'm going to find the woman of my dreams?"

"Shut up, or I'll chuck you in there." Amy giggles and then almost yanks my arm out of its socket as she pulls us through the back door.

Honestly, everything is so dramatic with Amy. We couldn't go through the main entry?

We soon come across a lady standing behind what looks like a lectern, and she has spiky burgundy-colored hair, high-waisted combat pants, and about ten coats of mascara. She looks us up and down with something that is close to contempt. "Speed dating?"

"Yes," we reply nervously.

After we pay, she roughly slaps a mandatory nametag to our chests.

It's okay. I don't want to be here either, I tell her telepathically.

Pushing through a heavy velvet curtain, Amy immediately snatches two drinks off the oaky, red bar. "Here. Drink," she orders, and suddenly, I'm thirsty like a camel. I don't care what's in it. I just drink, shifting from one blistered foot to another.

"Oh, look. Two girls dressed as the red and green Power Rangers," I muse and stir the straw in my drink. "Remind me why I let you talk me into this again?" I ask my alleged best drink.

"Because you love me," she replies, scanning the room.

"Questionable." I barely put my glass down when some burly woman with strong arms maneuvers me into a chair. "Sit."

"Oh, um -"

"Sit!" she repeats, and I gulp down.

When I spot Amy, she is being whipped over to the other side and looks as panicked as me.

Isn't this supposed to be fun?

There's a loud ding, and I startle. A woman appears out of nowhere and drops into the seat opposite me. Massive glasses, crazy makeup, and I immediately know this isn't going to go anywhere.

I cross my arms in defiance. Oddly, she refuses to make eye contact. "Hi," I say reluctantly.

"Hi." She's looking at my chest, trying to see my name. "Can you move your arm?"

"What? Can't you just ask me?"

Silence.

She's still peering at my chest. Honestly? I drop my arms to the side.

"Hi, Mia," she says, still not meeting my eyes.

Am I completely hideous?

"Kasey."

Instead, she picks up a pen and starts firing questions at me. "What's your profession?"

"Graphic Designer."

"College?"

"No."

"Where do you live?"

"In an apartment in Mission Valley."

"Siblings?"

"One older sister."

"Health insurance?"

"Yes."

Oh my God. What is this? Twenty questions? Obviously, my brain snaps.

"Do you own a car?"

"No. A horse and cart."

Finally, Kasey looks up.

She narrows her eyes. "Any pets?"

"I have ten cats, five dogs, and a miniature pony."

"In an apartment?"

I cough. "Uh-huh. Ground floor. With a yard."

Kasey throws her pen down and refuses to look at me anymore, and I'm passed the point of caring. "You know, you could take this seriously. Some of us are on a quest for love."

I glare at Amy. "Twenty bucks!" I mouth, and she deliberately leans forward, squeezing the hand of a very attractive blonde.

The bell sounds, and I frantically look to the next woman in line.

Woman is a stretch. She's wearing pigtails, a baggy unicorn t-shirt, and blowing a pink bubble with her gum which pops on her nose. She looks like she's twelve.

For fuck's sake. This is going to be a long night.

* * * * *

Thankfully, there's a break for drinks twenty minutes later, and I launch across the room at the speed of light. I grab the door handle pushing with all my might, but it's stuck.

"It says pull," snips the wise but still unfriendly entry lady.

"Indeed, it does." I scrunch my nose and stumble out onto the street.

Well, I can forget all about Amy because she's apparently having the time of her life blabbing to someone that looks like Gisele Bündchen's lovechild. The disparity in candidates is not lost on me.

I will kill her later.

"Wow. Is it just me, or do you look happy to be here? I was expecting a brooding toddler." Jules grins from across the foyer of the gallery, resplendent in her spiky heels and flowy metallic dress.

Her makeup so expertly applied she looks like a work of art while masses of red hair are levered away from her face by hundreds of bobby pins. Jules is originally from Dallas, and although there's not even a hint of an accent, her hair remains, well... massive.

I skitter across the marble floor and almost squeeze her to death. "Yes! God, yes! I snuck out halfway."

Jules giggles, kissing my cheek. "So, you didn't meet *one* interesting person?"

"No. Of course not! Something appeared to be amiss with my table," I report rather grimly, and her mouth twitches. "Maybe you'll have better luck here," she says.

"How was the blind date with Bec? Did she show?"

Jules pulls a face and gestures over to an irate copper-haired woman in a strappy beaded top. She's walking around in a tight circle, yelling at her phone. "Motherfucker! I will chop you up into a million pieces if you let me down!"

"She seems nice," I observe sarcastically.

"Mmhm." Jules smacks her lips together, then adds quietly, "If you want to date a serial killer. Appears something's also amiss with my date." She nudges me, and I giggle. "Quick. Let's make a getaway through this door." I latch onto her arm, and we weave around a throng of drunk women dancing the macarena.

"God. All the weirdos are out tonight. Must be a full moon," Jules says wide-eyed, and I attack my dinner, a handful of pancetta crisps. "Here. Drink." She hands me a glass of bubbly, and for the second time tonight, I drink on command. "Honestly, what the fuck, Mia? Aren't there any normal single women in San Diego anymore? Do we need to look interstate? I haven't had one acceptable date in over three months." Jules shakes her head and then runs her eye over me. "You look gorgeous, by the way."

"Thanks. You, too." I take a sip from my glass. "Only problem with this dress is it keeps riding up my a -" I startle, almost spilling my champagne on the floor. "You've got to be joking," I mutter and quickly step behind Jules and her heavenly hair.

She turns. "What the hell are you doing?"

"No!" I grip her body mid-swivel, locking her into position. "Don't freaking move. That's my boss."

"The one I'm waving to?" she asks out of the side of her mouth.

Oh, for fuck's sake.

This is the third time this week I'm going to run into Miss Dalton.

"Natalie! So glad you could make it," Jules squeals.

"Oh, don't -" I squeeze my eyes shut and then step out from behind her.

Jules pulls Natalie in for a bone-crushing hug. Being a highly affectionate person, she often catches people off-guard, and I almost laugh as Natalie's body visibly tenses.

"Happy to be here," she replies. Funny how she doesn't even try to sound convincing.

"Natalie," Jules says, her eyes as wide as saucers. "This is my gorgeous friend, Mia. Mia, Natalie."

Natalie clocks me, my chest. . .

My chest? Again?

This time I don't look down because I absolutely know that I'm still wearing my nametag. Gritting my teeth, I feign a smile and mentally plot my exit.

"You again," she says.

"Me again." I turn to Jules. "Natalie is my new boss."

"Oh, wow," Jules feigns surprise. "Well, she also happens to be in my spin class with Bruno and his unbelievably tight bike shorts. Honestly, if we weren't gay, it'd be off-putting."

"Hi, everyone. I'm Georgia." A woman pops up behind Natalie, grabbing hold of her hand.

Okay, Natalie has a date, and now I'm a bit curious.

She's pretty like a Hallmark card with deep dimples in each cheek. Mid-twenties, wholesome, eyes like toffee, and gorgeous blonde curls. She all flowery perfume, glowy skin. Surprisingly, she seems genuinely nice.

Not at all what I expected Natalie's type to be.

"I love your dress," Natalie says to her softly, and Georgia flashes a big smile while giving a twirl in her cerise satin slip dress that's so bright I almost have to shield my eyes.

Over her shoulder, I spot Kasey. The weirdo from speed dating.

Oh, God. When did the lesbian pool suddenly get so small?

She's sans nametag and has the same look of alarm on her face as me, but I'll give her credit, she still waves even though she doesn't want to. I follow her lead.

I have to get out of here.

The second the women launch into a discussion about politics, I excuse myself and tell them I'm going to get some food, but instead, make my way to a door by the foyer, which I spotted when I arrived.

It's important I always know the exits.

I walk out to the terrace dotted with sofas, breathing in the crisp, salty air. Resting against the marble balustrade, I watch people stroll along the path by the ocean and listen to a message from my stepmom, Mimi, congratulating me on my job.

She and dad have been golfing and traveling a lot lately, and why not? Life is short. Dad recently retired as a computer programmer, and Mimi is taking an extended break from teaching. They've just landed in Amman, Jordan, and are heading to the carved city of Petra.

I adore Mimi.

My dad remarried the grade school teacher three years after my mom's death. Somehow, Mimi was there to pick up the pieces, and I recall her being nothing but patient and kind. Anyone less kind would've throttled Janet with her countless tirades and outbursts, but Mimi took it all in her stride. Though

I did see her cry behind closed doors on occasion, and it made me cry too.

Although I carry a photo of my birth mom, Alison, in my purse, it is Mimi, whom I think of as my mom. She always listened, stroked our hair after a nightmare, and made sure we had a hot meal on the table when dad worked late. Honestly, I feel blessed to have her in my life.

Janet, my sister, not so much.

She was horrible behind Mimi's back, but I never told her what she said. Mimi was so soft-hearted, and it would've hurt her. My dad worshipped her too.

Robert Andrews was a good man who always wore his jeans a little too high and drank a beer every night in front of the sports channel but never played favorites. Janet and I received equal billing for all things. Her straight-A report cards right alongside my solid B's on the fridge door.

They relocated from San Diego to Scottsdale, Arizona, when we finished high school so Mimi could care for her mom, who has Alzheimer's.

In my mind, Mimi and dad were perfect for each other and shared a love that I could only hope for. Maybe the stars will align for me one day.

I glance skyward. Not one freaking star in sight. Figures.

"May I join you?" a familiar voice floats behind me, and instinctively, I whip off my nametag before wheeling around. "Are you like following me?"

Natalie tilts her head back. "Yes, I'm deliberately seeking you out for what is it. . . like the third time this week?"

I narrow my eyes and then relax. "Okay, I buy it. For now. But if it happens again. Where's your girlfriend?"

"It's only our second date, and I forgot all about this party. Georgia is stuck in an enthusiastic conversation about knitting, so you know, thought I'd grab some air."

"Oh. Understandable."

Natalie moves beside me, leaning forward on the balustrade. So close I can smell her scent. Spring blossoms, heady and sweet, mixing with the night. "Are you here for the art exhibit? You seemed to know a few people?"

"No, not here for the art. I couldn't tell a Renoir from a Monet, but Jules hardly takes no for an answer. Recently single, so my best friends, Amy and Jules, won't leave me alone. And the woman that waved at me like I was from outer space was from a speed dating night across at Milligan's bar. Most of my friends don't usually bolt out the door when they run into me."

"I should hope not." There's a sparkle in her eyes and almost a smile this time. "Well, it's good they're keeping you so socially active."

I nod even though I'm not sure I mean it. "How long have you known Jules?"

"Couple of months. I sit next to her in Thursday night spin class. I'm usually late, so she saves me a seat up the back to avoid being scolded by other cyclists. She also yells if I go too slow. Or if I sit down. It appears to motivate me as I keep going back regularly to be tortured. Previously my gym visits were sporadic at best."

I laugh. "Doesn't sound like her at all."

Natalie smiles.

I study her face and the softness that I didn't see before. Her smile also unearths a deep dimple in her right cheek.

Like I said, not my type at all.

"You know, you're different out of work."

"Not such an idiot?"

I wince. "Great first impression, huh? I was just having a bad day. Sorry."

"I've been called worse," Natalie replies politely.

"Mmm."

She laughs, and I do too.

The moon glimmers over the ocean, and we lapse into silence, and unfortunately, the first thing that comes out of my mouth is, "So, you date a lot?"

I want to slap myself.

Natalie turns to me. "What? Another office rumor?" Actually, Amy's research slash surveillance, but she doesn't need to know that. "I don't know. I work a hundred hours a week. Guess I see different people when I have time."

"Scared of commitment?"

"I was married in my early twenties. Now divorced. She left me two years ago and moved to London to pursue greener pastures. Last I heard, Lara was pregnant with her second child and engaged to the love of her life."

"Oh, sorry. I have a way of putting my foot in it."

Natalie shrugs. "Enough time has passed, and I'm just not in a rush to get into anything heavy." She pauses. Curiosity makes the blue of her eyes lighter. "Can I ask why you broke up with your partner?"

"Nadia just never showed up."

Natalie blinks. "Sorry?"

"I mean, we'd organize to meet, and she wouldn't show up. Then she'd pop back into my life, expecting to pick up where we left off. I suspect she was cheating too. Last phone call, she said she was on a plane, and then I heard a doorbell and a woman's voice." I shrug. "This pattern went on for close to five months."

Natalie frowns. "Was there something wrong with her?"

Something about the serious way she asks this makes me laugh. "Probably. Definitely *nothing* wrong with me."

Natalie smiles, the moonlight playing over her perfect face, and I can't stop staring at her. I decide to change the topic. "You seem very close to Joan."

"Yeah. Too close sometimes. I've worked with her for ten years and consider her family. She is stubborn as a mule and rather manipulative when she wants to extract information. Always threatening not to eat her vegetables or take her meds."

I chuckle. "And I thought Joan was a saint."

"She puts on a good show," Natalie says wide-eyed. "She also takes great pleasure in meddling in my personal life and likes to spring things on me. Last month, it was a blind date with a four-foot gymnast. I had dinner reservations with Joan at Tequila Daisy, so imagine my surprise when I met Claudia from Newfoundland. Nice girl, though. An exceptional tumbler, too. She even taught me how to do a cartwheel at twenty-eight years of age. Something I could only dare to dream."

I can't help but laugh. "The more I learn about Joan, the more I like her."

"You see my dilemma then."

I can't explain it, and I'm not sure I want to. A sudden flash of awareness makes me break eye contact. I chant inside my head, "She is not my type, she is not my type."

But for some reason, I'm quite enjoying our chat.

CHAPTER SEVEN

M I A

"Knock, knock," I say, standing outside Natalie's office Monday morning, suddenly strangely nervous to be within a five-foot radius of her.

Natalie hunched over a massive stack of papers, looks up with her blue blue eyes, and my stomach kind of lurches to the floor. "Mia. Come in."

I smile, melting just a fraction. "I just wanted to show you the mock-up designs for the Addison campaign."

"That was quick." Natalie stands and switches on the light-board, taking them from my hand. "I love what you've done here."

"I can make some changes with the placement of the furniture."

"No, I think it's perfect. Perhaps just ask Theo to increase the point size on the logo." Natalie hands me the designs. "Then send it straight through to Adam Huston for sign-off."

"Okay. Too easy." My eyes fix on the brochure in her other hand. "Oh, cats."

Natalie rubs her brow. "Yes. You wouldn't know any cat sitters, would you? My usual sitter, Maya, has just embarked on a three-month cross-country road trip of the US with her boyfriend. My father and his wife have sprung a visit on me. Apparently, their bedroom flooded because she failed to recall she had a bath running. They've insisted on staying for a few days, and Ronnie breaks out into a rash -"

"I'll do it."

Why is my mouth moving?

The sun is behind her, and when she looks at me, the light catches her eyelashes. "You?"

"Yes," I gulp. "I love cats. We look after Lorenzo, my landlord's cat, but Mario is back from Italy now. Anyway, I'm trustworthy. I gave back your sweater -" I stop.

"Debatable."

My cheeks go beetroot, and I laugh awkwardly. "Hardly going to throw a cat in the washing machine, am I?"

"I should hope not. PETA would be all over you." Natalie lets out a breath. "You know, that would be... " She gives me another look. "Wait. It's very last minute. Are you sure?"

"Uh-huh." I nod.

Natalie blinks a few times, almost in disbelief. "Okay, well... great. I'll pay you extra, of course, and get him dropped off to you after work with food, bed, toys, et cetera. Oh, plus some aromatherapy oils for when he goes a little berserk."

I scrunch up my forehead. "Aromatherapy oils? Has he got a problem?"

"Oh, no. But we all know how cats become possessed at three am. I mean, he certainly has a lot of energy. Last Christmas, he climbed the Christmas tree, flipping it onto the iron, and it might've started a small fire." Natalie meets my slightly panicked eyes. "Oh, he's doing *so* much better with the oils. Especially the lavender and cedarwood blend. You just have to spritz his bed."

I nod. "Right."

"Fabio has become -" She stops when my eyebrows practically disappear in my hairline.

"Fabio?"

"He was a gift from Joan post-breakup. I could hardly rename him, or I would have."

I try to hide my giggle, and she grins.

Well, this is annoying.

The playfulness in her expression, her unwavering affection for Joan and Fabio. Natalie is turning out to have layers, and not at all like I imagined.

I tap my designs against my hand. "Right, on that note. I better get back to work," I say, turning on my heel.

"Thank you, Mia."

My heart skips a beat when she says my name, and I'm grinning all the way to my desk.

* * * * *

Fabio winds his way around my ankles with swirls of orange fur so symmetrical they look like they've been painted on.

I empty his locally produced, organic cat food into a bowl. "Okay, calm down. You're not going to starve, mister."

He shoots me a look like he doesn't believe me.

"What? God, are you always this demanding?"

He shoots me another look.

MIA

Right. I got it.

I place his food on the floor, and Fabio pounces. "Slow down, or you're going to get indigestion," I tell him, but he snuffles it down at record speed and then licks his paws, ignoring me completely. "Aren't you going to ask me about my day?" His tail disappears out the door. Sarcasm seems entirely wasted on cats. "Thought as much."

The buzzer sounds, and I jump.

Not again.

I shuffle past a wall of cardboard and press the button. "Delivery!" the intercom squawks.

Four already today. All the boxes are starting to make it look like an Amazon warehouse in here. Bed, food, litter, aromatherapy oils, and an assortment of balls and cat-nip-scented toys. Oh, and a see-saw thing.

What now?

I open the front door, and there's a pair of lanky arms struggling to hold a massive castle. "What on earth... "

A young man's tanned head pops out the side with a floppy, shiny brown fringe covering half his face. "Looks like a cat castle, ma'am."

Cat freaking castle.

"Oh, right. Of course. Silly me." I take it off him, and my knees almost buckle under the weight.

"It's pretty heavy. I'll close the door," he offers.

Brilliant help.

"Thanks," I mutter under my breath and blindly stagger inside under the weight, then ram my shins into every single piece of furniture in the living room like a human pinball. "For fuck's -"

Suddenly, there's an ungodly scream, and I drop the castle. Thankfully, not on my big toe because I'm not sure it would survive.

I bolt down the hallway and fling open Amy's door, surveying the room. All looks in order. Makeup scattered on her chest of drawers, smell of her perfume, wardrobe exploding with hangers and cool clothes. Claude doing leisurely laps in the fishbowl.

"What the hell? Amy?" I hear a very faint whimper from behind the door, and I peer around. "Amy!"

Amy is white as a ghost, back pressed into the wall. She's wearing a 'Don't Fuck With Me' t-shirt and ladybug underpants. There's a towel wrapped around her head, and it starts to unravel as she points under the bed, shaking her finger. "There's a massive rat in our apartment. I've read in the news that they are getting bigger each year, but Mia, this is obscene."

I cover my laugh with my hand, rather enjoying seeing her scared shitless. I haven't yet forgotten our calamitous speed dating night. But to be fair, her reaction is kind of warranted. It's only been two weeks since our last mice incident. We're understandably still on edge.

"I'm telling you, it launched at the speed of light under my bed. And it's freaking neon orange -"

Okay, enough.

I start giggling.

Amy narrows her eyes in suspicion, hands pinned to her hips. "Mia. What aren't you telling me?"

"That's Fabio."

"Fabio?" Amy swats the towel away from her eyes. "You've befriended a rat?"

"No! He's a thirteen-pound cat. I'm cat-sitting for Natalie. Might even help us with our mice issue."

"Oh my God!" Amy huffs. "Can you tell me next time?" She unpeels herself from the wall and yanks the towel from her head.

"Sorry. Well, you should probably also know that he is moody and vocal."

Amy is crouched over, waving to Fabio. He's just staring at her like she is completely mental. "Great. Just like living with a woman then."

I giggle. "It's only for a few days, plus it might get me in the boss's good books." I cross my fingers in the air.

Fabio leaps onto her bedside table and pries the top drawer open with his paw.

"Good books or somewhere more comfortable? More horizontal?"

"Jesus. You have a one-track mind." I shake my head, and Fabio disappears inside her drawer. The table toppling over. "Fabio!"

Amy giggles when Fabio emerges with a g-string looped over his head. "Don't lie to me, Mia! I know what she looks like! I'd babysit anything of hers. Regardless, the stress of it all calls for an emergency rosé."

"Naturally," I reply, lifting her bedside table upright.

Amy reclaims her g-string from Fabio and disappears into the kitchen. "We're also welcoming a new roommate."

"Technically, he's just passing through." I walk into the living room, flick on the television with the sound down and throw myself onto the couch.

Not long after, Amy reappears with wine and a bag of peanut butter pretzels. She hands me a wine glass that could double as a bucket.

"Oh, God. Are these new? They're massive!"

Amy uses two hands to sip hers. "Uh-huh. Sick of refilling. Cheers!" We clink glasses and settle on the couch. I tip my mouth back like a tiny bird, and she feeds me a pretzel. It's a best friend's thing we do that we've never grown out of.

Fabio suddenly launches onto my lap with an almighty thud, and I startle, laughing. "Oh, shit. Hi, Fabio. You don't seem that moody to me." I stroke his soft fur, and he seems to agree, purring thunderously. He doesn't even flinch when Amy squishes her face next to his.

Predictably with her beloved fur child in my arms, my mind soon drifts to Natalie, and I wonder if I fabricated that spark between us.

I lean my head on Amy's shoulder, sighing like a deluded loon. "You know, I think I actually *am* crushing on Natalie."

Amy leaps up onto the floor, pretzels launching everywhere.

"Christ. Please contain your excitement." A massive blush working its way up from my head to my toes while Fabio springs off my lap to hoover up some pretzels.

"Best news I've heard all year!" Amy chortles.

I blink at an invisible spot on the wall. "Damn her for being hot and bringing my lady parts back to life."

"Don't you see? This is progress. Plenty more fish in the sea. Like I keep telling you!"

"But she's my boss. There would always be complications. Not that she's even remotely interested, mind you."

Amy points to Fabio. "Look, you could learn a lot from this guy."

"Dining 101? Eating off the floor?"

She rolls her eyes. "Jumping on an opportunity when you see it. You're single. She's single. And how do you know she doesn't like you? She likes you enough to let you cat-sit, and that was even after you destroyed her clothing."

I nod slowly, considering her sage advice. "True -"

The door whips open, and we both jump while Fabio drops his pretzel mid-bite, diving straight under the couch.

"Evening, cretins. It smells different in here."

It's my sister.

Janet.

She strides in with her swingy blonde hair and gorgeous clear pale skin, dressed in jeans, Italian leather loafers, and a crisp, striped shirt.

Glancing around, she assesses the space. Oh, God. I mentally prepare for a tirade, but surprisingly, she says, "It smells clean."

Amy and I look at each other and shrug.

"Well, just waltz right in why don't you, Janet," says Amy, crossing her arms.

"Thank you. I will. *So* good to see you again," Janet replies with whopping insincerity. "And I'm well. Thanks for asking, Mia."

Oh, great. She is in one of those moods.

"Hi," I say flatly.

Janet toes off her loafers and fishes for something in her gigantic handbag. She used to be all sharp planes and angles, but two kids later, her edges have softened a bit. Unlike her tongue.

She spritzes herself with Bvalgari perfume, flicks her hair, and smiles at the mirror hanging above the sideboard. "Honestly, I knew you moving in with *her* would be a problem."

I wrap my arm around Amy. "Leave her alone. She's amazing."

Amy gives me an extra big squeeze. "Watch out, Janet. You may have noticed I am almost naked from the waist down. With the way things are progressing, I could be your sister-in-law soon," says a classic Amy, and a tiny snort escapes me.

Uberserious Janet visibly shudders. "Put some clothes on!" she snaps, immediately shielding her eyes from Amy's ladybugs.

"My house. My rules," grins Amy. "Please also adhere to the message on my t-shirt."

As usual, things are off to a strange start.

Unfortunately, it doesn't do me any favors because now Janet sets her sights on me.

"Mia, are you eating properly?" She studies me closely. "You look particularly haggard. Or is it just because you don't have any bronzer on? A potato or two wouldn't kill you, you know."

"Why are you here?" I snap. "Don't you have anyone else to push in the pool?"

"That was months ago. Get over it. I am."

"I spent two hundred dollars on my hair!" I yell. "And shouldn't you be in your holiday home in Aspen socializing with D-grade celebrities?"

"Actually, Harry and I just came back from Fashion Week in Paris, so you know... choices."

I grit my teeth.

"Anyway, stripper Amy didn't answer her phone." Janet throws her a glare, and Amy eye rolls. "I also had to take Leo and Marley to violin lessons. Martha Collins, you know, the daughter of one of San Diego's most famous families, thinks they could be maestros one day with the right direction."

God, my sister embellishes to no end. The way she talks about her twins, you would think they were halfway to being Mozart when I know for a fact their violin playing sounds like a screeching cat.

"Anyway, their teacher lives on this side of town. Unfortunate, but... thought I'd drop in and see if you looked any better -" Janet stops when her eyes lock on our glasses and gasps. I guess the size could be a little alarming. "Ever heard of a standard drink? Do you two drink every night?"

"Of course not," Amy replies. "Every second."

Janet exhales loudly. "Whatever. Pointless engaging in conversation. I'm going to the bathroom. Then I'm preparing an eggplant lasagna since you only seem to be capable of eating," she pauses, looking down. "Pretzels."

She walks off huffing something about vacuuming regularly, pretzels crunching underfoot.

"Oh, shit," I gasp to Amy a moment later and squeeze my eyes shut. "I forgot to replace the kitty litter and the light bulb in my bathroom."

"Oh. Excellent." Amy snorts and holds three fingers in the air. "Three, two, one... " She curls them one by one. "Showtime."

We hear a blood-curdling shriek.

Amy and I start to laugh.

"I just trod in freaking cat shit!" Janet storms into the living room with her cheeks flushed, her eyes darkened. And I try not to laugh, but the tears on my cheeks may give it away. "Honestly, are you two ever going to grow up?"

Amy giggles, sloping her chin up. "Never."

Janet just stares at us in shock. "This is why communal living shouldn't be encouraged. You just egg each other on. Achieve God knows nothing with your lives -" She slides into her shoes and screams, and then sniffs her shoe, staggering backward. Her neck immediately breaking out into hives. "Cat piss! That's it! Cook the lasagna yourself!"

This time Amy and I burst out laughing.

Suddenly, Fabio rockets into the room like he's navigating a parkour course. Leaping onto the couch, the lampshade, and then springing off the palm tree coated wall and onto our small table before crashing less gracefully through a mountain of boxes and careening around the corner in a blur of orange.

"What -? Arghhhh!" Janet shrieks, shielding her body as a wall of cardboard crashes around her.

"Fabio!" yells Amy, and we laugh even harder.

He's become possessed!

"I never knew what hell looked like!" Janet fumes, angrily flinging boxes. "But now I do! PS I'm never ever fucking coming over again! Even if you actually invite me!" she says it with such ferocity I'm sure she means it as a threat, but it feels anything but that to me.

"Hooray!" gurgles Amy between breaths, and forget me, I can't speak because I'm quietly shaking with laughter.

Janet fumes some more and then stalks off, slamming the front door, while Fabio saunters back into the room, apparently far less mental now, and happily snaps his tail back and forth like he's the star of the show.

Well, today, he most definitely *is*.

CHAPTER EIGHT
NATALIE

I've spent the entire cab ride back to my place trawling through five million photos of Fabio on my phone. Guess that happens when you don't have a partner/friends/life.

I've become a freaking cat lady.

My time at home in my industrial-style condo with its sleek black granite and oak paneling in the Gaslamp Quarter is usually spent glaring at a computer screen with the furry dictator pottering around somewhere in the background.

So, when I walk into my apartment, I'm hit with an immediate ache in my chest. I think I miss my cat.

Thankfully, I spot a note on the kitchen counter and quietly cheer. My father and Ronnie have just left for the marina. I quickly snatch my phone from my bag and call Mia to see if I can pick up Fabio. It goes straight to voicemail, and I mull over what to do.

Glancing at the wall clock, I mutter, "Only a couple of hours earlier than we had arranged. Oh, whatever." Swiping my keys from a glass dish, I rush across the parquet floor and head out the door.

I do a quick grocery run at Trader Joe's for all things Joan hates – health foods, green vegetables, and pressed juices. I chuck in some mixed berry vitamin gummies, too. Once I've dropped the box off at her duplex in San Carlo, I make a beeline for Mia's.

"Hello?" The intercom squeals at me.

"Mia. Hi, it's Natalie. Sorry, I'm early. Was just, um, passing by and hoping to pick up Fabio?"

"Oh, sure." At least that's what I think she says, but there's terrible feedback from the intercom. "Shitshitshitshit."

I hear things being thrown around. She mustn't have hung up.

"Mia?"

It goes silent.

"Yes?"

"Can you please let me in?"

"Sorry. Of course!"

The buzzer sounds, and taking the stairs two at a time, I make my way up three flights. A short Italian man grunts hello in the hallway, and I almost grunt back, but settle for a smile instead.

A door suddenly swings open, and there she is.

Pink-faced with those dark whirlpool-like eyes blinking at me. Her naturally wavy blonde hair sticking out in every direction.

A weird feeling ignites in my chest.

She's wearing a faded t-shirt that has seen better days, and I think she's wearing shorts, but they're obscured by her top. Her feet are bare, and I seem to be fascinated with the curve of her neck. A little shorter than me, her face has a sprinkling

76

of freckles on an ivory canvas while her lashes reveal a depth to those soulful eyes that she seems completely oblivious to.

I could stare into those eyes forever. Stupid me.

"Hi," I say because my brain seems to have forgotten other words.

She smiles cutely. "Hi."

I'm not blind.

Of course, Mia's attractive. Willowy and toned, with long, playfully mussed blonde hair and a perfect mouth. She's not my usual type, which is probably more refined. Women that wore expensive suits and chatted fondly about vacations on the French Riviera. Joan has been in my ear about being more open-minded, hence my dates with the wholesome Georgia, but that doesn't seem to be going anywhere either.

Still, Mia is intriguing. I never quite know what to expect, and for some reason, I like it.

"Sorry. Have I come at a bad time?" I peer over her shoulder, hoping she doesn't have a visitor, and my nose catches just the hint of her perfume. She smells of fresh-cut peonies and afternoon sun, and annoyingly, like a woman I want to know.

"Um, no. Just wasn't expecting you so early." Mia kicks something to the side.

"I tried to call."

"Oh, I was on the phone with my sister, and I didn't want her to show up again, so I let her waffle on about eliminating urine odor. Fascinating topic. Who knew white vinegar was so versatile?"

I just blink. Like I said, she's different.

"And, yeah, well, the place is a bit of a mess." A loud squeak emanates from under her foot, and we both look down at a squishy mouse toy. "As I was saying."

"Oh, don't worry about -" My face must drop when I scan the room because Mia's face flames red. "Oh... right. Looks like Fabio has taken over your entire living room. I didn't realize he had so much stuff." I sidestep a pink ping-pong ball, then hop over a decapitated bunny.

"He's around here somewhere. Last time I saw him, he was climbing the curtain." She shuffles over to the window. "He's certainly active."

"Oh, God. I thought he grew out of that. Or maybe it only stopped because I traded in my curtains for automated blinds. I'm sorry," I wince and then gasp. "Are those claw marks on your wallpaper?"

Mia shrugs calmly. "Fairly standard reaction to my sister visiting. Could be human, not sure."

I whip out my phone and start tapping a message. "So, so sorry. I'll get someone here this week to fix his trail of destruction." That little shit. I can't leave him alone for one minute. "Fabio!" I yell.

Fabio strolls into the room, then freezes when he sees me. I walk forward, and he dashes under the couch. "That's weird." Bending down, I reach out my hand, but he just darts across the hardwood floor and down the hall.

"I'm not sure what has gotten into him."

"He appears to have forgotten his owner. After three days," I say, mildly pissed off. A motorized mouse rams into my foot, then the other. "Ow! I don't think he wants to go home with me."

"Mmm. We did bond. Look, he can stay here for a bit. You know, until... "

I'm not sure where she's going with this.

"Until? What Mia? He gives me a call on his phone to pick him up and take him home?"

She tries not to laugh, but her eyes crinkle. "Okay, don't be mad. I mean, I guess he can stay here for a bit longer. Think of it as a short vacation."

Two green eyes soon appear from under the couch, aware that we are talking about him.

I sigh. "Well, I am going to that conference in Florida for a few days. Are you sure you're okay with all of this?" I look around and inadvertently step into a water fountain. I glare at it and shake my wet ankle boot. "I can't help but think it's significantly impacting your home life."

"Oh, no. We love him. Amy gets up early to feed him. Normally you need a forklift to get her out of bed. We take turns singing him lullabies at night. He's also become my cuddle buddy -" Mia stops because I must be turning a shade of green. "Um. Do you want to stay for dinner? I've just ordered some Thai takeout."

"Yeah, dinner sounds good," I blurt out without thinking.

What's wrong with me? I have reports to run my eye over tonight.

We end up having dinner on the floor with some makeshift rug because, well, I don't know why. There is a small table in the corner that would make more sense, but Mia says she wants to sit cross-legged, so that's what we do. Regardless, I seem to be enjoying the newness of it. Even with a pretzel digging into my butt.

We have chicken stirfry with basil and chili that sets my mouth on fire and a slighter milder Panang curry.

Mia starts fanning her face. "Oh my God, it's so hot!" She latches onto a bottle of cabernet, and takes a swig, then offers it to me.

After pausing for a nanosecond because that's not something I normally do, I snatch it out of her hands and tip my head back, putting the flames out in my mouth. "I can't believe I'm crying."

"Wow, that was intense. Here, have some more rice." She shovels some onto my plate and then hers.

I pick out a piece of chicken and try to de-sauce it with my knife. "Thanks. You know, when Joan gave me Fabio, I was inwardly angry. What was I going to do with a cat? I wasn't a cat person. All that damn cat hair everywhere. On my suits. In my bed. Even finding their way into my turkey and rye sandwiches. Somehow though, that guy helped me through the darkness, and we became friends." I throw her a look. "Well, we used to be."

"God, so dramatic," she replies with a playful roll of her eyes. "You guys can bond again. You probably just need to work on your relationship. All that time in the office, long nights apart, no play time -"

"Thank you, Dr. Phil."

Mia giggles. "You know, I had a Maltese Shih Tzu called Lily and a ferret named Zac when I was younger."

My face pinches. "Not strange at all."

Her smile climbing her cheeks and into her eyes. "Honestly, ferrets get such a bad rap, but it's unwarranted. Growing up, my sister was the devil incarnate. Locking me in confined spaces, tying me to trees. I needed all the support I could get, so I trained them. Lily used to latch onto her ankles while Zac ran up the inside of her pants, biting as he saw fit. It was like a two-pronged counterattack."

My eyes dance with amusement. "Hence your love of animals."

"One of the many reasons I have a soft spot for them."

Fabio suddenly trots in, burying his furry head in my lap. "Oh, he does remember me."

"Um. You're sitting in his spot."

"Huh?"

"For some reason, he likes to sit exactly there by the coffee table. He's rather particular." Mia points and I shuffle to the right. Fabio barges past with not a worry in the world, spreading out like an eagle between us.

Still my dickhead cat, I see.

While Fabio snores like a Trojan, Mia and I fill a couple hours of the night, teasing and joking. Oddly, I don't check my watch once.

Eventually, I help her clear up and wash the dishes, and I feel this strange happiness wash over me. I'm not even sure I want to leave, but I do. Trust me, no one is more surprised than me. Because who knew a night of mouth-burning takeout on the messy floor drinking cheap wine with Mia Andrews could be so pleasant?

Such a surreal blend but surprisingly perfect.

CHAPTER NINE

MIA

Next morning, I'm still buzzing from Natalie's visit, but she is nowhere to be seen.

Joan tells me she has been called away for last-minute contract negotiations, and suddenly without her, my day turns drab. But loose-lipped Joan *does* let slip that it's Natalie's birthday tomorrow, so we hatch a plan, and as soon as the clock hits five, I rush home.

When I open the front door, I find Amy spinning around with a slightly freaked-out Fabio in her arms. "Who's the best-looking cat in San Diego?" she coos. "You are!"

Oh, God.

"Amy. He's going home tonight," I say, dropping my bag on the couch. "It's Natalie's birthday."

Amy just picks up his orange paw and waves at me. I already know what she is thinking. She did the same thing with our old roommate Stella's goldfish, Claude, when she skipped out on the lease to follow some crush to Belize.

"You cannot keep the cat, Amy!"

"Why not? Finders keepers."

"You didn't find him!"

"Correction. I actually *did* find him in my room! Plus, he slept on my bed all day. Exhibit A." She points to her bed through the gap in the door. "Very large patch of orange fur on my duvet."

"Amy. Fabio is Natalie's cat!"

"You let me keep Claude!"

"Stella absconded to another country. Slightly different scenario."

Amy scoffs. "Fabio doesn't like Natalie. He doesn't even want to go home!" she says, still arguing.

"Of course, he likes her!" I can't dispute her second point, so I march over. "Hand him over right now."

"No."

"Yes."

"No. Ugh. You're so bossy, Mia." She drops him in my arms and storms off. "And you owe me a cat!"

"Wh -... Amy!" I watch her walk away and glance down at Fabio, scratching his ear.

God, I'll need to buy her a few emergency rosés to calm her down. It might even be time to get that Dwarf Roborovski hamster she has always wanted. There's certainly no disputing that this little guy has brought a ray of sunshine (or orange) into our life.

I quickly place Fabio in his carrier before he can dart off to one of his thousand hiding places.

After I bathe and have a healthy, balanced dinner consisting of Doritos and some salsa of unknown origin hiding in the back of our fridge, my phone beeps. Just like my very own secret agent, Joan confirms that Natalie is now in the office, so I snatch the carrier off the countertop and head out the door.

Unfortunately, I don't get the memo about the weather, and I run into a storm of epic proportions halfway there.

Wincing into the cold wind, rain slashes my face, and a downpour drenches me entirely. I stagger through the revolving doors with my hair plastered to my face and my t-shirt and jeans molded to me like a wet t-shirt competition.

After copping a sideways glance from an older security guard with dyed black hair, I fling myself into the steel box and jab at the button for the twenty-second floor. Only to be smacked in the face with my reflection.

Brilliant.

I'm a freaking disaster.

As for Fabio, he's completely unfussed in his shelter and purring like a tractor. Well, at least that's something, I guess.

Once we arrive on our floor, I bolt through the front door and up the corridor. I stop dead. "What on -"

There's a super skinny woman sitting on the edge of Natalie's desk, legs crossed. A pair of beach balls sticking out from her chest. She leaps to her feet in a tight shimmery mini dress when she sees me, eyes ballooning. "Oh my God!" she shrieks. "Call security! There's a homeless person, and they've stolen your cat!"

"Huh?" Natalie spins around, and I feel a tide of pink start to creep up my collarbone, a pool of water settling at my feet.

Natalie gasps. "Mia? What are you doing here?"

"You know her?" the woman snorts, and I stand there, dripping quietly. "Honestly, can't we aim a little higher? Such an undignified display."

What part of me thought this was a good idea?

Natalie swivels on her heel and snaps, "What's undignified is the way you are talking to her. She's a valued employee." My heart soars a little, and Natalie snatches a gaudy bag and shoves it into her beach balls. "And how quickly you forget that you were a stripper who had an affair with a married man."

Ouch. Must be the infamous stepmom.

Her face twisting into an ugly mask. "God. You know how to hold a grudge, Natalie," she snips and immediately starts sneezing. "You. Stay away!" she yells at me, holding out her arms, and then almost trips as she rushes down the corridor in her skyscraper heels.

"Good riddance," Natalie mutters under her breath.

"Mmm. She's pleasant," I muse and hold up the carrier. "Thought you might want your best friend back for your birthday. We had a chat, and he wanted to go home."

Not entirely true.

Natalie chuckles, stepping toward me. She puts a finger inside the carrier, and Fabio butts his head against her. She smiles. "Hi, to both of you. Well, this is a nice surprise and the best gift ever. Thank you. Let me guess, Joan and her big mouth?"

"Who else?" I grin, blinking rainwater off my lashes. "Sorry. I didn't know you had company."

Natalie pulls a face. "Ronnie turned up unannounced. Although it proved to be a rather insightful chat. She's surprisingly open about my father's infidelities when she's wasted."

She holds open the door. "Please come in. Don't suppose you're hungry?"

I walk into her office and spot a few empty bottles of wine and a half-eaten pizza still in its box. A trail of water follows me, my shoes obnoxiously squeaking with every step.

I stop, frowning.

"What's wrong?"

I peer into the box. "Is that pineapple on your pizza?"

"Yes. Controversial, I know."

"Why?"

"Because I asked for it."

I narrow my eyes. "You're very strange."

"Says the woman soaked to the bone, bringing my cat to my office in the middle of the night." Natalie glances at the pizza. "Tell me, then. What should I have got?"

"Loaded or Pepperoni. There are only really two options. Certainly, none with fruit." I look down at my clothes. "You don't suppose -"

"Yes," Natalie replies as though she reads my mind. She whips open a drawer and pulls out a fresh shirt, pants, socks. Even shoes.

Thankfully, no underwear. I hardly know the woman.

"Quite the drawer."

"I spend most of my life here. Plus, there's a gym on the third floor that, for some reason, is empty around midnight."

I nod. "Sorry. This is becoming a habit."

Natalie hands me the bundle. "It's okay. You look good in my clothes."

My blush is back in full force because I don't know what to do with smiling, charming Natalie Dalton.

"The shoes might be a little big, though."

"Oh, it's okay. I have fat feet, even bigger on the plane. I always go up a size or two." I regret everything that's coming out of my mouth. I laugh awkwardly. "Birthday plans?"

"None. Will be here working all weekend, unfortunately," Natalie replies, her elegant shadow cast against the window.

Beyond her, the city night beckons. Buildings gleam in a golden light as the night sky burns with stars overhead. The backdrop, her power – something makes me shiver even more, the tiny hairs on my arms up on end. The shadows of the room contrasting with the city glow, illuminating Natalie and all her angles.

I shake my head. "No candle-lit dinner with Georgia?"

"No. I don't think I'm made for relationships." Natalie shrugs. "It kind of fizzled. Perfect on paper, but... "

"Something missing?" I offer.

"Yes. That special spark," she says, staring back at me.

There's a brief lull in conversation, and I'm not sure if it's the way she's looking at me or the way my stomach is lolling around on the floor, but the temperature in my body definitely rises a few degrees. So, *this* is what chemistry feels like. Well, something tells me that the lines might have just started blurring between boss and employee.

Perhaps I'll have that slice of pizza after all.

* * * * *

So, I end up having two slices.

Obviously, only to extend my time with Natalie. I must've been in some sort of trance around her because, shock horror, I kind of liked the pineapple topping.

It's hard to wipe the smile off my face, and I'm practically floating on my way home. I stop at the store to pick up some fancy French rosé and Kinder chocolate (Amy's favorite), and then scrabble for my phone in my bag to make a call.

"Hello?" snaps an unpleasant voice.

"Janet?" My arm shoots out, and I stare at the phone in front of me, pausing under a street light. I dialed Mimi and dad, not Janet.

Goddammit. I can't escape her ring of influence.

"Darling sister… " Janet says almost venomously, and it starts to bucket down with rain. "I was just thinking about you."

I wish she wouldn't.

God, I'm a moron! Why didn't I ask Natalie for an umbrella?

"Pleasant thoughts, no doubt," I reply grimly, and for the second time tonight, I get absolutely drenched by a rather monsoon-like downpour because, of course, I do.

"What are you doing?" asks Janet casually, and I hold my bag over my head as I skitter down the sidewalk.

What's with all this chit-chat?

"Oh, you know, meaningful stuff like stumbling around naked, shouting out cuss words, starting brawls."

"I would expect no less in that household -"

There's a muffled noise, then a man's voice. "Hi, Mia."

I almost lose my footing. "Harry?"

"Uh-huh. That's me!"

God, gross.

Just when I thought it couldn't get worse. What on earth is he doing there!

"How's my favorite sister-in-law? Heard you got dumped again."

"Heard you finally developed tact," I reply as I fly around the corner, almost knocking over a pizza's shop easel sign. "But you can't believe everything you hear."

He growls to someone that isn't me. "I'm done speaking to her."

I grin. That was easy.

"Mia?"

My relief is short-lived. "Oh, for fuck's sake," I mutter under my breath. Janet *again*. "I'm after Mimi."

"She's watching Who Wants To Be A Millionaire?" she snips. "She's about to win the jackpot and doesn't want to be disturbed."

Why must she always make everything hard?

"Can you call her?" I ask through gritted teeth.

"No. Call back later -"

"Who is it?" I hear Mimi yell.

"It's Mia!" Janet yells back, deafening me for the rest of the week.

There's some shuffling.

"Hi, Darling," Mimi huffs into the phone, and I feel a familiar pang of longing. "Sorry, I'm out of breath. You know how I get bouncing along to my Jane Fonda VHS tapes in the lounge room."

Janet is the devil.

"Hope I didn't interrupt," I say.

"Of course not. I was mid star jump. I love hearing from you. I'm in the full spandex outfit you bought me. Even wearing my pink headband."

I giggle into the phone. Mimi is firmly stuck in the eighties and quite happy to stay there. Her refusal to conform to the norm just makes me love her even more. "I'm sure you're totally rocking it."

"Trying. Trying," Mimi laughs, and her pocket-size dog, Alfie, starts barking hysterically in the background. "When will I see you next?" she shouts.

"Christmas in July? I've just started that new job, so it'd be cheeky of me to ask for leave so soon."

"Too far away, but of course," she replies, disheartened. "And job is going well?"

"Yes. So far. I also have a thing for my boss, which is unfortunate."

"A thing!" she shrieks, and for the second time this call, I lose my hearing.

So, I spill it. The Nadia no-show. Colliding with my boss. The sweater. Speed dating. Fabio v Janet. Fabio v Natalie. How Natalie's stepmom thought I was a homeless person.

By the end of the debrief, we are in fits of laughter.

I've missed her laugh, its frequency.

"God, I do love hearing from you. Your life is so eventful." Mimi chuckles and gives me her weekly update. Apparently, she's put on ten pounds, her desert agave is growing at a rate of knots, and a rogue coyote has been terrorizing the neighborhood.

I climb the stairs to my apartment and shuffle through the front door, toeing off Natalie's soaked shoes. Jesus. I hope they can be salvaged because I cannot ruin any more of her belongings.

Padding down the hallway into Amy's room, I place the wine and chocolate on her bedside table. On a pink post-it note, I write in chicken scratch: *I'm sorry, Ames. Let's go hamster shopping xo*

Dad calls out, "Hi, pumpkin!" and I sing back, "Hi, Dad!" even though I know he won't hear me because he is one hundred percent sprawled out on their maroon couch in his favorite Rolling Stones t-shirt watching his Indy Car Racing replays. What's so fascinating about a car that goes round and round in circles? I get dizzy thinking about it.

"Sorry, you there, darling?" asks Mimi. "Your dad is watching his cars again."

"I thought as much," I laugh and wander into my bedroom, dumping my bag on the floor. I spot a box of my favorite Ferrero Rocher chocolates on my duvet and a yellow post-it note: *Sorry for being a dick. Can we please go get that hamster? xo*

I can't help but grin. Amy and I are so in tune.

"Tell her I'll call her after nine!" yells dad.

"He says he'll call you later," Mimi relays.

"Tell her to visit before Christmas!" he yells again, and I move my phone away from my ear. Honestly, I'll be hard of hearing by the end of this call.

"He says -"

"Yes, I heard Mimi."

"Jesus. Alfie! Stop humping -"

Someone screams blue murder as I try to peel off the sticky note that has attached to three of my fingers. At first, I think it's a woman, but then I realize it's Harry in falsetto tones. I enthusiastically press my ear against the phone. "Off! Off! Get that rabid thing off me! I need a tetanus shot!"

I think I hear Mimi say sorry somewhere in the mix, but there are too many voices crossing over. I try really hard to listen. Just when it starts to be entertaining and someone asks Harry if he wants a cuddle, the line clicks dead.

Either way, after that call *and* Natalie, I definitely deserve a lie-down.

CHAPTER TEN
NATALIE

"Joan. Why aren't you eating?"

I grab lunch with Joan every Monday, and today because the sun is out, we've ventured down to the Liberty Public Market. After picking up some food from the old navy building, we find a free table outside.

"Deep in thought." She slurps on a ramen noodle just as some live acoustic music starts up behind us. "Going to see Georgia again?"

"No. Probably not," I reply, pushing the seaweed in my bowl from one corner to another.

Sure, Georgia Mason is beautiful, polite, and ticks all the right boxes. She also stirred absolutely nothing in me.

Joan pauses. "Mia is quite lovely, isn't she?"

"I suppose she's fairly competent." I slide some vegetables over the table. "Dr. Yip said you're low in iron. Your blood pressure is also too high. Have you been doing your two miles on the elliptical each morning?"

Joan screws up her face at the kale. "When I'm not busy."

"Honestly, you're worse than a child." I pick out broccoli and put it on her plate. "Eat."

I say this, but Joan is as smart in her sixties as women in their sassy twenties. She is a widow and has two sons, Samuel and Nicholas, and five grandchildren that visit each Sunday for lunch. Apparently, I'm the daughter she never had, and she's, without a doubt, the closest thing I have to a mother.

Joan was my executive assistant for six years when I worked at Hartman Myer as a marketing manager. However, she wanted to step back from her role when I became CEO at Dalton Media, given she was nearing retirement.

She also said I was a bit much as a manager. And to be honest, I didn't really care for her constant interference in my romantic life as much as I knew that her heart was in the right place.

I tried to replace her. Franny talked too much. Neil couldn't type. Thankfully, Joan and I found some middle ground because I love her to pieces and couldn't be here without her. She works part-time in reception now but still likes to 'keep an eye on me.' Whatever that means.

A seagull lands beside Joan, and I batt it away when Joan tries to feed it some kale. It's hard not to laugh.

She sighs loudly. "I mean, she's like a breath of fresh air, isn't she?"

"Who?"

"Mia. Attractive too."

I draw a circle with my chopsticks in the air. "Where are you going with all this?"

"It's been a while since your divorce," she chirps, and I level her a look. "Joan. Stop meddling."

She giggles.

"Anyway, hardly my type."

"So, you've thought about it?"

"No."

"Will you think about it?"

"No."

"Am I still employed?"

"Just."

She continues to snigger, and I catch myself starting to smile.

"Honestly, what is this quest to find me a woman?"

"Partners can be a very nice part of life, Natalie. I mean, when they don't grate on your nerves."

"Like Barney?"

She huffs and rolls her eyes. "Barney is my friend."

"Like a friend friend? You see him Thursday and Saturday."

"What's a friend friend? Don't fish, Natalie. Nothing going on there," splutters Joan.

I can't help laughing.

Joan pulls out an ice cream sandwich from her handbag, and I drop my chopsticks into the bowl. "When did you get that?" I hiss.

"When you went to the bathroom, Natalie," Joan grins, her cheeks a mischievous pink. "What? I have needs on the rare occasion!"

I shake my head. "Sneak. I need to keep my eyes on you twenty-four-seven."

Joan chuckles, licking her lips. "So, excited for your conference in Florida this weekend?"

I grimace. "Where I'll be entering the seventh circle of hell with my father? No."

"Actually, he's canceled," she mumbles with a mouthful of vanilla. "Something about an anniversary? Anyway, Mia is going with you."

"Joan. I'm ripping up your contract."

"Idle threats," she sniggers like a naughty grandma, and her eyes start to gleam. "She's quite a win for the company, so it's only fitting. Your father suggested Mia, given her profile, and plus, there'll be media coverage. Obviously, we need to maximize our exposure if the stock offering is to meet expectations."

"Uh-huh." I purse my lips. "Purely a business-driven decision."

She slides on her red reading glasses, glancing at something on her phone, and says with mock seriousness, "I'm the last person to meddle in your life, Natalie."

I try desperately not to laugh. "Joan!"

She holds up a hand. "But, say if I was... " I get a conspiratorial wink. "Well, I think Mia Andrews could be *just* what you need."

* * * * *

Mid-afternoon, I'm at a strategy meeting, and it's the last place I want to be.

Already in a bad mood after a disagreement with two of our more grumpier board members, I'm yawning as Jeff Gold moves like a turtle in front of a PowerPoint slide and delivers his multi-page agenda on how we can milk more money out of our clients.

He's in his mid-fifties with iron-gray wavy hair that's set like a helmet. He's an intelligent man in an expensive navy suit, but God, he's boring and horrible at reading social cues. Half the room at risk of lapsing into a coma. I don't think he likes me either, especially given my intense dislike of Margot.

My stomach growls in irritation.

He says something about the opportunity cost of *blah blah blah* and points to a line on the graph. "We are here, but we should be here... "

God, who cares?

I just want my afternoon soy latte and a couple of macadamia and coconut protein balls.

I'm not sure what has happened to my patience of late, but it's out the door. When Jeff starts boring the room to death with a lengthy speech on managing expectations, my phone buzzes.

MIA: How's Fabio?

I shuffle in my seat.

ME: Won't make eye contact and still in his carrier after three days. He's also on a hunger strike. Appears to be morbidly depressed after having to leave the funhouse.

She is one hundred percent rolling her eyes right now.

MIA: A drama queen like his owner.

ME: I can't help but feel that you contributed to this situation.

MIA: BY PROVIDING A FUN, LOVING HOME??

I cover my laugh. I really enjoy getting a rise out of her.

I'm soon bombarded by photos of Fabio wearing a pink shower cap and getting his nails filed. Fabio wearing war paint and wrestling a chubby cat in a diaper. Fabio sitting in a seat at the dining table, napkin tucked into his collar, and eating freshly-cooked salmon. Fabio with his paw in a fishbowl, terrorizing a goldfish.

Honestly, the snapshot of his time away is unreal.

ME: What did you do to my cat?! I can't ever beat that amount of fun.

She has raised the bar far too high – he will never love me again.

MIA: :) :)

ME: Also, when are you returning my clothes? I have nothing to wear.

MIA: Hmm, if I knew the answer to such a tricky question, I'd have ascended to a higher plane... meaning they're currently in the wash. I'm crossing my fingers that it works out this time ;)
MIA: And, liar. I saw your drawer!

I snort behind my hand.

And just like that, we're off. We text back and forth for the best part of an hour.

"Natalie?"

I haven't heard a word Jeff has said, so there's only one thing to do, really.

"Brilliant. Let's head back to work," I reply, then stand and walk out the door before anyone can ask me any stupid questions.

CHAPTER ELEVEN
NATALIE

I'm in trouble.

I *like* her.

Even when she showed up to my office looking feverish and soaked mercilessly like a rat, she found a way to move me, consume me.

I watched her quietly as she yammered on about how pineapple on pizza was criminal and, not long after, how people should give pineapple a chance. All the while, taking in every one of her features, every curve, every smile, and truth be told, I haven't been able to get Mia Andrews out of my head.

Now, I'm forced to spend three days at this conference. The only saving grace will be a busy schedule and separate bedrooms.

The flight is far too long for my liking. Squirrel-sized seats making it impossible not to touch her and set off electric currents across my skin. Every breath, every movement, every flicker of eyelids, and I'm aware of it.

I practically leap out of my seat when we land, only to be subjected to a cab ride together to our hotel. I immediately call shotgun and slip on a pair of oversized sunglasses. Sure, the view isn't as good, but it's less stressful.

We drive in silence, the only sound coming from the purr of the engine and gusty wind blowing the car around. It takes twenty minutes of blinking vacantly at blue skies and palm trees until we reach Laguna Marco hotel, rising three stories high and shining bright white in the gorgeous sunshine.

Our driver drops us at the front, and we climb out onto the hot asphalt, where the valet collects our bags. Mia lifts her face toward the sun, her long hair teased by the balmy sea breeze. "Picture perfect," she hums, and it is – straight out of a storybook.

We're right on the shores of the glittering Atlantic, sur-rounded by emerald green lawns and lush landscape. Terra-cotta pots are clustered around a stone fountain by the entry.

We walk through the open-air lobby to the front desk. It's packed with conference attendees, and I smile at some fa-miliar faces. We're greeted by a young but beautiful girl named Rosa, who has thick black hair and chocolate-drop eyes. "Miss Dalton. You're in luck," she beams. "We have you ladies over-looking the beach in our honeymoon suite. Best room in the hotel! It's on the top floor -"

I think I mishear. "Sorry, what?"

"Oh -" Mia flaps her hands around.

"You're booked into the honeymoon suite," confirms Rosa with a nod.

Shit.

I blink rapidly as her words sink in. This can't possibly help my anxiety. "How many beds?" I ask, gritting my teeth.

"One," Rosa replies, straightening a stack of papers. "It's a king plus."

Like the plus means anything to me right now.

"Oh, no. That won't work." Suddenly, the Florida humidity isn't the only thing that's making me sweat. "I'm going to fire Joan."

Mia rolls her eyes. "You're not going to fire her."

I tug at my collar, which feels like it's tightening. "Can you please see if we can switch rooms?"

"I'm sorry," Rosa shakes her head. "There's nothing else. There's a conference this weekend, so we are fully booked."

"Yes, we are attending it. For work! We're not on our honeymoon!" I say, slightly exasperated.

"I'm sorry. The room was specifically requested."

I grip my handbag. "We'll try elsewhere."

"You won't find anything." Rosa taps the keyboard. "Wait. I can move you into separate rooms tomorrow. And I can arrange... " She coughs. "A rollaway bed for tonight."

I pause and rub my temple. Better than nothing, I guess. "Yes. Okay," I huff. "Thank you."

Once Rosa finalizes our check-in, we shuffle past white décor and potted palms to the elevator, and I jab the button at least three times, muttering under my breath.

The elevator ride seems to take years. Neither of us speaks.

Obviously, the honeymoon suite is a gorgeous space. There's a separate living area that has a couch, love seat, and lowered glass coffee table with a bucket of Veuve Cliquot on ice and two champagne flutes. As we walk through, I spot a dining nook off to the side and a rolltop bath by the window that I definitely won't be using.

Mia seems quite enraptured by the suite, tripping over at least twice.

I don't misstep, but I do stop by the large glass bi-fold doors that lead out to an incredible balcony overlooking clear blue water. Waves so close that I could probably dive straight into them. I briefly entertain sleeping out here, and when I turn, Mia is watching me. With far less enthusiasm, I say, "Okay. Let's see where we're sleeping, then."

One foot in front of another, the walk down the hall feels like a death march, but even I'm blown away by the size of the bed.

"I've never seen something so big," gasps Mia.

"Yeah. Wow," is all I can add.

The biggest bed ever is sitting in the center, all crisp white linen and cloud-like pillows. I try to pretend I don't see the entire rose bush worth of petals strewn across the top.

I'll let Mia deal with that.

"Right." I clap my hands together. "Well, I have to give that introductory presentation in twenty minutes, so I better go freshen up and then head downstairs to prepare."

"Okay. Do you need my help with anything?"

Ah, stop being so nice.

"No. All good," I reply, but I'm suddenly distracted by a walk-in shower behind a frosted glass partition which looks very honeymoon-ish. Brilliant. No privacy at all. "I'll see you later, I guess," I say faux casually.

Mia is still staring strangely at the bed.

Me, on the other hand? I'm charging into the bathroom and locking the door. God, I'm totally losing my cool. I need to get out of here as soon as possible.

I get ready in record time and am grateful that Mia is nowhere to be seen when I reappear.

Unfortunately, the rose petals are still there.

CHAPTER TWELVE
MIA

I had to get the hell out of there.

Natalie was going to be naked, having a shower, and there wasn't even a door. I couldn't listen to hot water splashing against her skin, running down her curves –

Dammit. I shake my head. I'm going crazy.

Instead, I choose to go outside into the blistering heat, which is incredibly smart. My hair instantly doubling in size. I find pockets of people sipping champagne and eating ceviche in the late afternoon sun, and do a lap of the facilities. Tennis courts, indoor/outdoor pool, sauna, gym. All impressive, but soon morbid curiosity takes hold, and I'm on autopilot back to the conference room where Natalie is due to present.

Sweat drips from my brow, and I discreetly wipe it away. I pat down my wayward hair and, with a deep breath and tiny prayer, slip in through the back entrance to a blast of arctic air-conditioning.

I take a seat next to a very tall man in chinos in the second last row. Salsa music is blaring from the speaker directly above my head, so I glare at it. Eventually, the lights dim, and a slightly hysterical event coordinator with a mousy brown perm named Helen introduces Natalie on stage.

My eyes move from her hands skimming the sides of her charcoal skirt, up over the rise of her chest to the smooth curve of her neck and those perfect red lips. Her mesmerizing ocean eyes popping from here against the light blue of her shirt.

There's an immediate reaction from my traitorous body.

Clicking through the slides, Natalie gives statistics and discusses current trends in the media industry, but I'm not really listening to her words. Rather I'm focused on how charismatic and stupidly good-looking she is. And I'm not the only one. Men and women are leaning forward in their seats because there's a way she carries herself that demands attention. She is good at this, a natural speaker.

Sometimes the universe seems so unfair.

I huff internally, uncrossing and re-crossing my legs, and try to ignore whatever is happening between my thighs.

Natalie seems to sense my gaze because her eyes find mine in the crowd. The contact is brief – no more than a few seconds. But the cartwheels in my stomach last far longer.

She concludes her presentation to rapturous applause, and the press starts snapping away with their cameras. Just as I'm about to dive out of the nearest exit, Natalie finds me, and I almost smack into a waiter serving honey-glazed crab cakes. "Oh, there you are," she says.

I freeze and turn, but a young woman with short straw-blonde hair and massive hazel eyes intercepts me. "Miss Dalton," she says in a breathless whisper. "Just wanted to introduce myself. Britt Diaz from iMAD Graphics. Here's a leaflet on our company and my card if you have any questions."

"Thanks, Britt. I'll have a look at this, and we'll be in touch if we need your services. Appreciate you reaching out."

"Amazing. Thank you so much." Her face explodes into a smile, and she backs away with stars in her eyes.

No sooner has she gone than a leggy woman in an Alexander McQueen red satin playsuit places a lingering kiss on Natalie's cheek.

It appears I need to get in line.

Tall and slim, she has luminous dark eyes, sharp cheekbones, and long jet-black hair, so shiny it looks polished. I'm guessing she's in her late thirties, certainly still attractive. Her hands are also ringless.

"Hey, gorgeous. Nice talk. You walked straight past me," she pouts, but Natalie just stares at her like she is an alien, and I have to hold in a laugh.

What's going on there?

"Sorry. Didn't see you," replies Natalie stiffly, but something tells me she did. Turning to me, she says, "So, this is Mia. Our new senior designer."

"Lydia Longman. Longman Media." She shakes my hand with a blatantly curious once-over, and I immediately note her amazing eyebrows. She has that disturbing glint in her eye that sets off my gaydar.

Great. Lydia and Natalie have history.

And, of course, I know Longman Media. It's one of the top three media companies in the country.

"Hi. Nice to meet you," I reply, and she circles her manicured finger around my face. "So, you're the star recruit? You're a lot younger than I expected. And prettier."

I settle for a faint smile, but in the corner of my eye, I catch Natalie frowning. Something about her distance tells me she doesn't like her much.

A hairy, bearded man in stonewashed jeans moves toward us, clutching a camera. "Photo, please, ladies. Look this way. Now smile," he says, chewing gum with a mechanical rhythm.

We shuffle together, smiling big phony smiles, and then break apart.

Lydia anchors her attention on Natalie. "You, Miss. Fancy a drink at the bar? For old-time's sake. You know my proposal was serious. We would make such a great team. Professionally and..." she purrs. The intonation makes me bristle. It only gets worse when Lydia runs a possessive hand over Natalie's arm, and I head straight for the back door because there's no way I need to see anymore.

Unfortunately, no amount of swaying palms can distract me from thinking about Natalie. So, I sit poolside under an unreal royal blue sky dotted with cotton-wool clouds that rush past overhead and try to eat away my stress by devouring a forty-five-dollar burger. Okay, it's good, but it's no In N Out.

Naturally, I have a couple of caipirinhas as well to wash it down. But this just seems to stimulate my imagination even more, and I stupidly think about Natalie and Lydia, lying entwined on some Swedish designer rug half-naked, toasting each other for being super-hot and successful.

Ugh, my brain sucks.

In an attempt to distract myself from my self-destructive inner gremlin, I noodle around the equally expensive hotel shops and buy a shark shape bottle opener for Amy, a few souvenirs for my parents, and a mug for Janet that says, 'I want to be a nice person, but everyone is so stupid.' Even though she is a jerkface most of the time, she does look out for me. It's fifty-fifty on how she'll take the mug. She'll either use it every day or blow it up into smithereens.

Despite my determination to keep busy, the low hum of unwanted sexual attraction to Natalie remains, and there doesn't appear to be much I can do about it.

My brain hurts from too much thinking and not enough caipirinhas, and I know I can't sleep out here.

Giving a resigned sigh, I decide to walk back via the private beach, white sand seeping between my toes as the sun finally tips over the horizon. The sky is already streaked with red and pink, and I have only one wish this evening.

That Natalie Dalton is fast asleep.

* * * * *

So, turns out Natalie never did have that shower when we arrived.

How do I know?

Because she is having one now to torture me.

My boss is showering ten feet away, naked, behind a glass panel with no door. My legs feel like jelly under me. White noise from the water and steam billowing out from the side sending my mind racing with visualizations.

All of it – unfuckingbelievable.

I start rifling through my bag, looking for my phone, desperate for any distraction, and there's a text from Amy (Are you two naked yet?), which absolutely does *not* help my cause. I want to scream, but instead, fling my phone back into my bag, change into an oversized t-shirt ten sizes too large, and then make myself useful, removing approximately five million rose petals from the bed, repeatedly cursing the genius that came up with that idea.

The water turns off, and Natalie emerges a few minutes later in a dark skimpy singlet and matching shorts showing miles of leg. Her hair is towel-dried, water droplets still clinging to her forehead and neck.

Nope. None of it even registers.

Her mood brightens when she sees my petal-stained hands, and with a headache building, I disappear into the bathroom. "So, how did it go with you and Lydia?" I call out, scrubbing my hands, and then reach for the toothpaste.

"Fine. Lydia is just Lydia. I made another pitch for the Longman Fashion account. I've been trying for years. Obviously, it's a separate entity, and their focus is Longman Media, but it would look great to have them on our books. Unfortunately, I don't think Lydia's ego could handle it."

"I sensed some… history between you two," I say with a mouthful of toothpaste.

"I interned at Longman Media many moons ago as a booking assistant after I finished my business degree at Berkeley."

Not what I meant.

I rinse my mouth and walk out. "She was a bit handsy." I'm not going to ask. I'm not going to ask. "Did you guys ever have a thing?"

Natalie angles me a look, and I shrug. "We never dated," she replies.

"Wait. You slept with her?" my voice kind of squeaks.

She sighs. "Lydia can be very forward and charming when she wants to be. I won't say I was naive because I knew what

I was doing. Young and stupid? Maybe. There were a couple of incidents when I was working at her business. She is known in the industry to be quite... friendly to females, particularly younger ones."

Oh, why did I even ask?

"What did she mean when she said she wanted a partnership?"

"Get married."

My browns snap up to meet her blues. "What?"

"Business decision. She controls thirty percent of media advertising in the country, but we're obviously more niche, focusing on digital strategy. We hold key accounts. Accounts she will never get. If we merged, we'd be a powerhouse and pretty much control the entire west coast. But you always need to read between the lines with Lydia."

"So, you'd have to be a dutiful wife and sex slave?"

Natalie snorts. "A fairly good summary... Yes. And I'd rather get my bikini line waxed daily than be at Lydia's beck and call."

I can't help but laugh.

"Now." Natalie points to the sad-looking rollaway bed in the corner. "Can you please step to the side because I need to work out how to get into that monstrosity without killing myself?"

I hold up my arm. "No. I'm going to sleep in it, Natalie. I always loved camping as a kid. Nothing like being out in nature -"

Natalie stares. "Except we're in a hotel with a beautiful bed. No sane person ever loved camping. I'm going to sleep there."

"That makes absolutely no sense at all."

"Are we really fighting about this?"

"Yes." With brut determination, I push her out of the way, race over, and slide under the industrial strength covers onto a long, skinny pad. It takes a few attempts to get in there. "You'll have to carry me."

Natalie just blinks. "Carry you? Are you for real, Mia?" Her hands go to her hips. "Okay, whatever. Enjoy your indoor camping vibe, then." She turns and hops into bed, crawling beneath the fluffy covers, and I'm secretly envious.

I wriggle around and try to get comfortable, but it's impossible. Spindly springs pierce my spine, hospital sheets strapping my body down like spandex, and the whole contraption is incredibly noisy. Even when I breathe, it creaks.

"I can hear you squeaking from here," she says ten seconds later.

Unsurprisingly, my voice comes out tinny too. "It's this damn bed. It needs oiling."

"It needs to be read its last rites," Natalie grunts and pats the space next to her. "Come into this bed, then."

"No."

"Mia. Are you always this difficult?"

"Only when I skip my morning coffee."

Dammit.

I rip back the covers with all my strength and hop up, the bed snapping shut like a Venus fly trap.

I scream.

"Oh my God!" Natalie sits bolt upright. "You could've lost a limb!"

A moment later, she starts to laugh, like really laugh.

I shuffle across the carpet, stubbing my toe on the corner of the bed. "Argh!" I hop on one foot. "I'm glad you're finding the fact that I almost died so amusing. PS I also just broke my toe. I should receive danger pay for this trip."

But this just makes her laugh even more, and soon I see the funny side of it too, snorting along unflatteringly through my pain.

Eventually, we settle down, and I lever myself into the bed. "Okay, well, stay on your side," I warn.

Natalie laughs. "Mia. This bed is the size of a spaceship."

"Mmm."

Regardless, I grip onto the side of the mattress. Unfortunately, every sense is heightened, and I can feel every sensation. I try to breathe without making a sound, my mind racing like a caged hamster on a wheel.

Oh, God. I'm in bed with my boss.

So, so worse than her having a shower.

Oh, shower. Fuck, now she's naked again.

Naked. Bed. Boss.

I hate my brain.

Natalie sighs. "It's been a long day."

Yes, it feels like it will never end. Sleep so far away it's not funny.

She goes on. "We should probably get some sleep, you know. Big day tomorrow. Can I turn off the lights?"

"Uh-huh."

There's a click of the light switch, and I scowl, even though she can't see me. Is she kidding me right now? How can she possibly sleep?

I feel her roll onto her side, and I wonder if she's facing me.

God, why does it even matter?

"Goodnight, Mia," she says.

I emit a silent scream. "Night."

After fifteen minutes of chewing my bottom lip, the suspense is killing me, and I ever so stealthily roll over.

Natalie's facing me, and even though I'm studying her in the darkness, it's her smell that hits me first. Jasmine and soap and gorgeous woman.

Her dark hair still damp from the shower.

Those inky long lashes dark against classical cheekbones.

That perfect groove etched above her full lips.

That -

One eye suddenly peels open, and I startle.

"What?"

"Nothing," I squawk.

You might be a bit hot, that's all.

"I just can't go to sleep on command." I blink at her. "Can you talk to me?"

"What?" Natalie scrunches her face. "Next, you'll ask me for a bedtime story."

"Okay, thanks for the chat." I roll onto my back.

"Well, now you have woken me up."

I hide my grin. "So, you want to keep talking?

"Yes."

"Tell me something about you," I say, smiling this time.

"I hardly know you, Mia."

"Me?" I throw my arms wide, almost slapping her in the head.

She glares at me.

"Sorry. . . . Anyway, I'm an open book. Twenty-seven. Grew up in Ocean Beach with my mom, dad, and evil sister, Janet. My mom passed away from an aneurysm when I was nine. Dad remarried Mimi a few years later, and I adore her. Favorite color is blue, like your eyes. I'm a Libra but on the cusp of Scorpio, so will sting if provoked. Sneakers over heels any day. Tacos over bagels. I have a pen obsession nobody knows about, but I seem to be telling you. Oh, and I love animals. Maybe even more than humans. Which you may have already worked out."

Natalie nods slowly. Her eyes find mine, and I see her soften. "I'm really sorry about your mom. You were so young to lose her." She reaches out for my hand, and for some reason, I let her take it.

"Hurts whatever age," I reply, and we share a sad smile. I roll to face her. "Why do you dislike your dad so much?"

Natalie goes to speak, then stops. "Long story."

"Okay then -"

"He cheated on my mom and, when she was on her deathbed, moved his stripper girlfriend into our home. I've never forgiven him. Plus, he is a serial pervert. Oh, and a shit father. Succinct enough?"

"Oh, God. He sounds like an asshole." Natalie looks at me, and I say, "Sorry."

"No. Don't be. He *is* an asshole. I hate that we are related."

"Definitely explains why you aren't close. I'm glad your mom ran over his toe -"

Her head lifts from the pillow. "You heard about that?"

I nod. "Yes. First day. Office seems to be well-informed." I pause and say softly, "I'm sorry about your mom, too."

Natalie gives me a weak smile. "You know, even though my father was in the picture, it only ever felt like the two of us. He never wanted a daughter in the first place, so I was fully aware that I was a disappointment from the day I was born.

I was home-schooled because I was bullied pretty bad in high school. My mom was my best friend. What my father did... well, I will never understand. We're just built differently."

I nod. "I can't believe you're not more messed up. That's just awful."

"Oh, I'm damaged goods. More than a few dents and dings," she says with a laugh. "I should come with a warning. I trust no one. Not even the coffee machine."

"Holy crap. That *is* serious."

Natalie smiles, and it feels like a warm, lazy kiss under a gorgeous sunset. "You like your stepmom?" she asks.

"Got lucky, I think. I love her. Mimi is nothing short of an angel. We baked cookies together." I blink, my eyes hot just thinking about her. "I even told her I was gay before my dad. She was always in the garden, pruning something, and used to come in with leaves and twigs in her hair. I helped her pluck them out while my sister huffed in the corner, setting fire to my things."

Her eyes go wide.

It's true – Janet was some sort of mini pyromaniac.

When I ate the last piece of Mimi's cheesecake.

When I wore her stupid pink tutu as a joke and then slipped in the mud.

When I took a photo of her on the loo with my FAKE toy camera.

Boom. There went my belongings. Usually teddy bears and dolls, but anything was fair game. Obviously, I'm not going to go into detail with Natalie. I don't want her to think Janet is a total psycho.

I sigh. "Only happened a few times. My sister can be a real sh-... piece of cake. We don't exactly get along. Sometimes I wonder if we are really related. Do you have any siblings?"

"No. I'm an only child."

"Really? I figured you were the oldest."

"Why?"

"Smart, driven, bossy... "

Her laugh spreads warm across my skin. "I walked right into that."

"And I take it you're not any closer to your stepmom these days?"

"No, I can't stand Ronnie. She's just a gold-digger and usually heavily self-medicated. Probably needs to be around him. I used to get these images of her swinging around a pole, upside down and naked, entertaining my smarmy father. Thankfully, I managed to flush those out of my brain fairly quickly."

I think we both realize we are holding hands and finally pull away.

My mind still trying to work out the physics of being upside down *and* naked on a pole. How did she not faceplant? Instead, I say, "Sounds like they deserve each other."

She nods. "True. Two shallow souls."

Despite Natalie not wanting to talk, we soon start chatting about our childhood, bad fashion choices, and past relationships.

She tells me how she used to let down her mom's tires so she didn't have to go to the office and how she had braces so large it looked like she swallowed train tracks, and I tell her how I endured unfortunate haircuts during my youth. Firstly, a bowl cut after Jenny Jackson put gum in my hair in third grade and then a sad-looking mullet until freshman year because Janet told me mullets were cool.

Natalie tells me that although she's always busy with work, sometimes she's lonely. Her best friend, Kyra, moved to Hong Kong around the same time as her divorce, and she finds it hard to make genuine friendships. On occasion, she even misses liking people.

I tell her how my love life feels doomed, I think, to make her feel better, and how the longest relationship I ever had was one year and four days with investment banker, Jenny Rialo, who went to prison for embezzlement. She also drained my account in the process when I stupidly gave her my pin number.

Perhaps it's the slippery time, well after midnight, where you feel safe to tell your secrets, but something about this conversation feels organic. Both our voices are starting to sound croaky, and when there's a brief lull in conversation, I realize I don't want this conversation to end.

"Please don't be hard on Joan about this... arrangement. She really thinks of you as a daughter. She stresses about you a lot -" When our eyes meet, I notice Natalie is giving me an odd look. "We have lunch on Tuesdays at the Lotus Dumpling bar."

Natalie narrows her eyes. "I thought she had a secret man." There's a pause, and she frowns. "You stole my cat and Joan."

I start to laugh. "Natalie... "

"There's a clear pattern emerging. Seems you're far too likable, Mia."

"I'm just trying to make a good impression."

Natalie frowns. "Then please stop trying."

I squeeze her shoulder, laughing. "Natalie! She adores you. You'll always be her favorite."

"And that's exactly what people stealing your things say to make you feel better." She grunts, and I giggle into my pillow. "Now that we've established that you're a professional thief, can we please go to sleep?"

I can't help but grin into the darkness. "Uh-huh. Good-night."

She shuffles onto her side. "Night, Mia."

I roll over and eventually fall asleep with a big fat smile on my face, knowing a whole lot more about Natalie Dalton.

* * * * *

When I wake in the morning, Natalie is still asleep.

Unfortunately, not one part of me is. Everything from my waist down is raging. It doesn't help that her top is twisted halfway up her body, offering a peek of smooth, tan skin over taut muscle. Maybe I'll just stretch out my foot, touch her with a toe and see what happens -

Her eyes snap open, and mine slam shut.

"Jesus, Mia. You need to stop doing that."

I scoff. "What? I literally just woke up!"

Half an hour ago.

I peel my eyes open and feign a yawn. My voice comes out thick. "How did you sleep?"

"Amazing," she replies, adjusting her arm under the pillow.

Liar, liar, pants on fire.

She has bags the size of Jupiter under her eyes.

Oddly, this brightens my mood. Why should I be the only one to suffer?

My head feels heavy, my legs like lead, but even so, the prospect of spending the day with Natalie sends a jolt of adrenaline surging through my veins. I stretch out on the giant king plus sized bed. "First day in paradise!"

"Can you please lower your level of perkiness this morning?" Natalie grumbles and brushes her hair away from her face. "I have a contract negotiation with Hardins at eleven, which I would like you to attend so I can introduce you. And I thought we could take Jeremy Perkins from Seven Peaks out for lunch at one-thirty."

"Oh, no. We have a team-building exercise at the same time."

Her brow creases. "What? No. Count me out."

"I've already signed us up with Helen, the event coordinator." I smile, and she rolls her eyes. "We have to go. You might even have fun. Bauer Media will be there. Don't you want to stick it to our competition?"

Natalie nods warily, sensing a trap. "Mmm. Well."

"Probably just be something like team quizzes. So yes? It'd be great PR."

"God, you're like a dog with a bone... Okay," Natalie mutters, then throws back the covers and flings her legs off the bed. "But I need an extremely strong coffee first. Let's have a double shot latte on the balcony and discuss the contract negotiation."

I grin, and my mood improves considerably as I follow her, staring at the back of her messy head.

CHAPTER THIRTEEN
MIA

Natalie's utter look of contempt says it all.

About twenty of us are milling around the marshaling area at the edge of a forested area. It's steaming hot, and the sky is full of dull, humidity-laden clouds. We've been divided into small groups and assigned a team color. The two of us, along with Lydia, and some random young guy called Marvin, make up the blue team.

"Yay! Dream team!" yells Lydia, emerging from a wooden hut in a blue tank slash short combo. She weaves her way over through a sea of colors and excitedly waves her arms above her head.

Natalie hides behind her hand. "Oh, God. Please save me."

"Stop grumbling." I yank at her sleeve, and she batts me away like I'm an annoying gnat.

"Why would I be grumbling? Lydia's in our team, and I look like a smurf!" she whisper-hisses, and I desperately hold in my laugh.

She continues to glare.

"What? It brings out your eyes," I reply with a tiny snort, and she looks like she wants to flatten me.

"You told me we would be indoors doing quizzes. Quizzes! Not sloshing around in a mud pit with bugs and, you know... mud," replies Natalie, her hair starting to curl in the humidity. Something ominous flutters between her eyes, and she slaps herself. "Ow! What was that?"

"Natalie. It's a team-building challenge, and what can I do if they've had an unseasonal amount of rain?" I discreetly pluck a mosquito the size of my hand from her back and dispose of it outside her line of vision. I refocus on her unsmiling face, and my stomach flips. God, even grouchy Natalie is beautiful. "Anyway, don't worry. It will be a piece of cake. We just have to work out how to get all four of us through this obstacle course."

Okay, this time, she is definitely checking out my breasts.

"Eyes on the prize?" I ask, feeling bold.

"As if," Natalie scoffs, but a quirk on her lips soon quickens my pulse. "What's going on with your top? Looks like you put it through the wash again."

I slap her arm. "They ran out of larger sizes! It wasn't deliberate."

Natalie pushes me away, and I have to hide my smile, turning my attention to Marvin.

"Marvin!" I yell, but he's just daydreaming and looking out to sea.

"Why does he look familiar?" mutters Lydia.

"Hey, Marvin!" hollers Natalie.

Still, no response.

God, there's always one. What the hell?

"Martin!" screams Lydia, almost bursting my ear drum, and he runs over with his spindly legs and shag of black hair. The guy is tiny.

"What the f… " I cover my ear, glaring at Lydia, and she shrugs.

To make matters more interesting in this challenge, the co-ordinator has just announced over the speaker that we need to assign a handicap to each team member – whether it's losing your sight, hearing, touch, or ability to talk.

Natalie murders me with her eyes. "So, piece of cake, huh?"

"Uh-huh." I nod unconvincingly.

Shit.

Regardless, Natalie is a total boss and immediately takes charge. Marvin is muzzled with a cloth wrapped around his mouth, and Lydia is blindfolded. I'm fitted with noise-canceling headphones, and a marshal ties Natalie's hands behind her back.

There was absolutely no mistaking a mischievous glint in Natalie's eyes when she tightened Lydia's blindfold. Given her lack of vision, she basically has to go along with whatever is decided. Thankfully for me, I'm an excellent lip reader, so I'm not too stressed about it all.

We shuffle over toward a clearing, and a moment later, the buzzer blares overhead. The first obstacle is traversing a ten-foot-tall wooden fence. There are a few rungs up near the top, while the bottom half is a flat wooden panel, so it's impossible to climb without getting a boost. Only one person is allowed to roll underneath.

"Right. Short guy first. Marvin," Natalie commands, and I tap his shoulder. Natalie tells him, "We're going to fling you in the air, so latch onto a rung and then swing your body over to the other side. Okay?"

But Marvin just gives her a blank face.

"Oh." Lydia decides to chime in and swipes at the sweat beading her forehead. "I just remembered Martin is our marketing manager's nephew. Richard must've brought him along to the conference. He's from Mauritius and wanted to get some work experience. You know, get his foot in the door in the media industry. Unfortunately, he doesn't speak any English."

"What? How did you only just remember this? And it's Marvin, not Martin," Natalie hisses.

Lydia snaps, "It's a big company! Far bigger than yours."

I see Natalie's cheek flinch, but she remains cool. She looks at Marvin, does some weird facial movements, and starts bobbing her body since her hands are tied, but to be honest, she kind of looks like she's having a seizure, so I interject with some simple up-and-over hand signals. He gives me the thumbs up, and Natalie just gives me a look.

Natalie instructs Lydia and me to lock our arms together by holding each other's wrists in a basket-weave pattern, and Marvin jumps up on our hands. "Now. On the count of three. One, two, three!"

Weighing not much more than a paperweight, we fling Marvin into the sky with surprising force. He does a bit of a mid-air tumble, whacking his head on the fence, and crashes to the ground on the other side. We all hold our breaths when he doesn't move for a few seconds, then cheer loudly when he springs to life with his hands in the air.

"Jesus. The guy was almost knocked out," I shriek. "How do we not have protective padding?"

"Lydia. You're next," orders Natalie, ignoring my concerns.

"What? No. I'm the tallest," she whines as she stumbles off course, flattening a saw palmetto.

"And least fit, so you need more help to get over," Natalie replies, and I cover my laugh at her cheeky grin.

"Shut up, Natalie," huffs Lydia as I jog over to her side, dragging her blind ass back to our group. "Are you questioning my stamina? I can go all night -"

"Stop it, you two!" I yell. "And we need to hurry up! We're already falling behind."

Natalie and I crouch down, and Lydia crawls onto our shoulders, and to be fair, it's the right decision for her to go first. She's a heavy bag of bones. We stand shakily, and thankfully, she manages to swing herself over the top first attempt and drops down onto the other side with a loud thud, skidding on one foot. "Ow, my freaking ankle!"

"You're next, shorty." Natalie grins at me, and I roll my eyes. "By a mere inch," I snip.

"Hurry up. Get on top of me."

It's hard to take her seriously, and I'm definitely smirking.

She tilts her head back. "My shoulders, Mia. Dammit. Same deal. I'll give you a boost, then swing over. I'll roll under and meet you on the other side."

I end up making it to the top of the fence with my biceps screaming as my sneakers scramble for grip and then jump onto the ground. However, I seem to lose my footing just as Natalie stands, and I stumble forward into her chest. I'm not sure what overcomes me, but I give one breast a gentle squeeze.

Natalie blinks twice. I have to say I'm starting to enjoy these startled looks on her face. "Did you just manhandle me?"

Yes, since you like to leer so much.

I put one hand behind my ear, pretending not to understand.

Natalie exhales loudly. I think she says, "so deliberate."

"Can you two stop flirting over there and hurry up! I'm up to my eyeballs in mud and have an itchy hoo-hah," Lydia shouts, facing the wrong direction. Her face is pink from the heat, and she's glowering at a palm tree.

There's a round of snickering, the loudest coming from Marvin. None of this seems lost in translation.

"Come on, Smurfette." I grin brightly at Natalie, and she shoots me daggers as we trip through mud thick as molasses. I pause to spin Lydia the right way.

"Okay, team." Natalie seems to collect herself. "Our next challenge is a tunnel so straightforward." She deliberately knocks Lydia sideways with her hip, and she flops face-first into the mud.

It has her squealing. "What the hell was that?"

Natalie's eyes lighting up like Christmas. "You got hit by a swinging log. Just part of the obstacle course. You're doing great!"

Lydia tries to get to her feet, but it's not that easy, falling over several times, and she ultimately decides to stay on her hands and feet. I see Natalie turning and snorting with laughter, and this sets Marvin and me off in hysterics.

Thank God Lydia's blindfolded, and there's no access to a mirror. Because Lydia is a sight – she looks like a swamp rat. Her hair is matted. Mud thickly smeared over her body, and I think I even spot a scary-looking neon green bug on her shoulder.

"Crawl over here, Lydia," Natalie instructs, trying to stay straight-faced. She guides her with her leg over a prickly bush, and laughter starts building inside me again. My boss is the devil. "Now, the tunnel is narrow, so single file everyone. Marvin, you go first. Lydia." Natalie looks at me, but I motion for her to go next. She shakes her head. "No. I don't trust you. After you, Mia."

"But I -"

"No. Go." She nudges me with her shoulder, and I laugh. Well, I wouldn't trust me either.

Halfway through the very dark and claustrophobic tunnel, Lydia yelps, "I'm stuck."

"What happened to your stamina?" grunts Natalie, and I can't help giggling into Lydia's rear.

"I'm going to knock you out, Natalie. So, help you, God," replies Lydia in a clipped tone.

I push her spongy ass as hard as I can.

"Oh, hi there, Mia. Thanks for the boost. Can you feel how strong my glutes are?"

Natalie grumbles behind me.

"I need another push," chirps Lydia. "Squeeze a little harder this time."

God, get me out of here.

When I emerge from the tunnel, Marvin is back staring out to sea while Lydia is staggering around on all fours, going nowhere fast. I quickly see that our final challenge is a sack race, but there are only two sacks, meaning we need to pair up.

Crazy laughter bubbles inside my throat, and I immediately latch onto Marvin, who grins at me as we rush over to a sack.

When I briefly glance over my shoulder mid-hop, I see Natalie shoot me a glare, and I wave cheerily back as she struggles and bickers with Lydia inside a very small sack.

I start sniveling next to Marvin, who is deceptively lithe and athletic for a small guy. We reach the finish line in a matter of minutes, collapsing on our hands and knees.

Natalie and Lydia take far longer.

"Lydia, what the hell is wrong with you? How hard is it to jump at the same time?"

"Shut up, Natalie. Your ass keeps knocking me sideways."

"Better than your boobs hitting me in the face."

"That's it. You're dead!" Lydia deliberately rams her, and they tumble out of the sack and into the mud. "My marriage proposal is officially off the table!"

"Hallelujah! Because I'm about to fucking kill you!"

Natalie chases a squealing Lydia, and Marvin and I double over, laughing. Tears streaming down my face, I stealthily whip out my phone. Just as Natalie launches on top of Lydia, I take a photo. There's no way I'm not going to hell.

Unsurprisingly, the dream team finishes last.

CHAPTER FOURTEEN
MIA

Sometime later, I'm safely back in the confines of my own room.

I've had a long steaming shower, exfoliated the crap out of my mud-soaked body, and thrown my sneakers in the trash. And even though I'm in my pajamas, sleep is just not happening.

Truffling through the mini-bar and counting the one hundred and eight ceiling tiles doesn't help either because I can't stop thinking about Natalie. Seems all the looks, banter, and deliberate groping on my part have now turned a seemingly innocent crush into a full-blown infatuation.

I know I'm here for work.

I know.

But it's impossible. There's something addictive about our interactions. Being with Natalie feels like an extravagant luxury, even when she's coated head to toe in mud. It's not one I'm sure I deserve, but one that I would love to last a bit longer. Now, I'm wondering if she's thinking of me.

Dear God. I slap my hand over my eyes.

I need to think of an excuse to see her. What can I borrow from her massive suite? Blender? Too weird. Plush robe? Too creepy.

Think Mia, think!

Right, that's it. Either way, I decide I'm not going to be contained by these four walls and slide out onto the carpet, whipping off my pajamas. Hopping into my shorts, I crash into the dresser and then bounce back onto my mattress, where I slip on my shirt. I toe on some flats and rush to the door, ripping it open, only to find Natalie standing there in a white mini-dress with her hand poised like she was about to knock. With a neckline dipping down to accentuate her smooth, soft neck and collarbone, the white fabric clings to her breasts.

Natalie looks like heaven and hell, gift-wrapped.

I hold onto the door for support. "Oh, hey... "

She drops her arm and gives me her trademark slow smile. "Hi... "

My stomach twists. Her voice does things to me. Her presence setting me alight.

Obviously, I say something stupid, "You look clean."

"Shower helps."

I nod slowly.

When she starts blinking those dangerous sapphire eyes at me, I know I'm in trouble. "I wanted to know if... "

"If?" I manage.

Her eyes fix on mine with unmistakable intent, and I'm trapped in her gaze. My breaths coming out in shorter and shorter gusts. All I can hear in my ears is static.

Wait.

Is she... Are we...

Oh, fuck it.

I lunge forward, grabbing her by her dress. My mouth crushing down on hers, claiming, demanding. I kiss her passionately, recklessly, as though it's the only kiss that matters. We wrestle each other and stumble inside, door slamming, and bounce off a small table.

Tongues twining, lips bruising. Her back hits the wall, my hips pinning her there.

There's no room to breathe, but oxygen is suddenly the furthest thing from my mind. My breath is hers, and her mouth. Oh my God, her mouth. It's like crushed velvet. The feel of her lips, the pressure, and that perfect angle. Stars explode behind my eyelids, and my longing transforms into a staggering hunger.

She's drowning my moan with these kisses that just melt you to the bone, and my hands are all over her body, desperately craving friction. I'm scraping my teeth down her jaw, sucking at her neck, and she starts yanking at my shirt, buttons scattering on the carpet.

It's all happening so fast, but it can't be any other way.

"If you don't get out of that dress, I'm going to destroy it." My voice rough with need.

A second later, white silk pools at her ankles, and my nails rake over her toned arms, back, stomach. Natalie's firm and hot everywhere. Licking, nibbling, I can't get enough of her skin. We tease and playfully bite at each other's mouths. I memorize all the sounds she's making because she's right here with me. She feels it too.

I hook my finger beneath her bra, flicking off one strap, then the other. I kiss her shoulder, my tongue trailing along her collarbone.

"Mia," gasps Natalie.

I remove her bra. "Mmm... "

"Once. Only once."

I nod. "Uh-huh." I'll agree to anything at this point.

Her nipples hard against my palms, and I give them a squeeze.

Natalie groans. "Only because -"

I mumble against her mouth.

Now. Here. I don't care.

What the hell is going on?

I was never really one to make noise, now I can't shut up. My vision is just swimming, a series of dots, and she's breathing as hard as I am. My bra falling somewhere between us.

"So beautiful. So perfect," she murmurs, running her fingertips along my taut breasts, and a visible shudder runs through me. I love the look on her face when she sees my bare skin, but I love even more how greedy her mouth is on me. I hiss in a breath. Her tongue flicking at my nipple, sucking, then trailing a path up between my breasts.

Our lips crash together again, and I'm grabbing her ass pulling her toward me. Her skin on mine feels like being kissed to the deepest corner of my body. "God, Natalie," I groan.

"I know... " She lets out a shaky exhale, fingers slipping beneath my elastic, pulling my underwear to one side. Her long index finger smoothing along my slick center, and finally to where I want her the most.

A deep moan escapes from the depths of somewhere I never knew existed, and I'm digging my fingers into her back. She traces the same path, over and over, along my entrance to my clit and back again.

"Please." My voice wrapped tightly around the single syllable, and I push her head down, down, down. She spreads me open, and I cry out at the first sensation of warmth. Hands fisting her hair, she presses closer. Her breath feels like bursts of fire, the flat of her tongue sure and possessive. "Mmm. More..." I whimper, and her moan vibrates through me.

I'm desperate now, wanting everything she is offering. Tiny tease of teeth, her words muffled against me. Her fingers pushing inside, tongue circling in perfect rhythm with my sounds. Driving me absolutely crazy.

The woman moving insistently between my legs is nothing like my together boss, and I think I'm in a bit of shock about how wrong I am about Natalie Dalton.

I'm close. *So close.*

I pant and writhe against her mouth, riding the edge of my climax, not ready for it to end, holding back enough so we can keep going. The pressure of her tongue quickening, my stomach grows tight, and everything around me starts fading into black.

Grappling for her with hands and nails, I only get one word out, "I'm" before an explosion hits me, splitting me from the inside out, and I shatter like crystal against her lips.

My breaths echoing off the walls. Too loud, too fast.

Lost in aftershocks, air barely cooling my fevered skin. Natalie holds me still, one arm wrapped tightly around my left thigh. She slowly pulls her fingers from me, and presses a warm kiss to my clit, my hip.

When I finally open my eyes, the blurry shape of her forms in front of me. She cradles my face, deepening the kiss with her hands on my face, sliding into my hair and around my neck.

"You don't know how crazy you make me," Natalie groans, but I think I *might*.

Because I am lost to everything, but her and this. The ragged sounds of our breathing, the heat permeating every inch of my body, the intensity of her kiss.

I feel her own impatience, fingers clutching at my skin, hips tilting into me, and I shove her underwear down until it's a tiny pile at her feet. My fingers slip between her thighs, and I love how she jerks underneath my touch.

Lips and teeth all over her mouth and jaw, we move toward the bed. The back of her legs hit the mattress and she crawls back onto it. Her eyes glassy, unfocused, she's biting her lower lip.

Spreading her legs wide, I kiss the inside of her knee. The other. My lips drifting over the insides of her thighs. Below me, hips rock up, urging. I bend forward to slowly lick her clit, warm and sweet. "God, yes. . ." she moans, the sound reverberating through my body.

My mouth open and sucking, devouring. Tongue gliding over her, and inside. Her taste destroys me, sliding around my mouth, in my head. Our moans mingling and filling the room.

She's licking her lips, her legs close around me. "*So* fucking good."

I'd smile, but my mouth is busy. Turns out I like compliments from my boss.

My fingers easily slip inside her, and I feel every last muscle of hers clench around me.

"Oh, shit. . . " Natalie twists her body closer. Her hips start rolling, slowly at first, then faster. "Don't stop."

So, I don't.

Deeper. Harder. Whatever *she* wants.

"Mia – Fuck," she pants, and her words become a breathy moan.

Her little sounds, trembling thighs, the twisting of her fingers in my hair – I'm aware of it all. Shivering, her movement starts faltering, growing jagged. Her back arching from the mattress, she cries out as she comes. The sound echoing off the ceiling, and I feel her pulsing all around me. She stays like that for a long moment, gasping for breath.

The room just ticking in silence.

We're sweaty and messy, and Natalie looks absolutely perfect. Her blue eyes burning into mine, warming me on the inside. Now by her side, we share a lingering kiss, and I relish how soft and swollen her lips feel.

Natalie smiles, half covering her eyes. "You know. . . I actually showed up at your door hoping to take you out to dinner."

I laugh into her shoulder. "I think I prefer this."

"Mmm... " She laughs too.

Kissing her fingertips, I say, "Thought you might be mad at me after the whole team-building debacle."

"Oh, yeah. That was *fun*." Natalie goes wide-eyed.

A laugh escapes me. "The wrestling at the end. . . an unexpected highlight."

Rolling her eyes, she says, "Do you blame me? Sharing the sack with Lydia -" She stops mid-sentence.

I try to hide my grin. "Not the first time."

Natalie chuckles. "Oh, I see what you've done. You're good."

"Well. . . " I smile, then run my finger over her cheek. "Now, what do you think the board would say about all this?"

Her lips brush my ear, I shiver. "That they hired you to elevate our profile, not to sleep with me and give me orgasms."

"The orgasms are free of charge." I push her hair over her shoulder and draw lazy circles over her chest.

Tilting her head and wearing a smile, Natalie murmurs, "How very generous of you." I giggle. She presses her face into my neck, arms curled lazily around me, and groans. "Ugh. The board. Please do not bring those grumpy old men into the bedroom."

Fingers running down her spine, I give a small laugh and say softly, "Hey. You're in control. If you're not happy, change things. Veer off course."

Obviously, I'm not just talking about work here. I want her to veer into my arms because when I'm with Natalie, my heartbeat is chasing hers. I want to leave fingerprints all over her skin, her body. I want to get lost in conversation where words come easy and then go back to the bedroom and use none at all.

I think Natalie is able to read between the lines. Her brows pulling together for a beat. "Mia. I'm not a great partner. I work too much. I can be selfish."

But I'm not sure if it's her or me she is trying to convince because the Natalie I know is amazing. Still, I can't wrap my head around any of this right now, so I press up against her, warmth flowing from her body into mine. I decide there and then that there's nothing sexier than lying beside a naked Natalie Dalton. I'm not even sure I'm the same person I was an hour ago, but I don't dare say it.

"We need to get up early," I sigh.

When I glance up, Natalie's eyes are fixed on me. "Yeah, busy day ahead. We should go to bed soon."

"Soon?"

Give me an inch. I'll take a mile.

Her lips part, and my eyes lower, stomach squeezing. She bends to kiss me again, lips pulling at mine. God, her kiss feels like a drug. "Why do I feel like we could do this all night?" I say, whispering into her mouth, and she moans in reply.

Seriously, how does this feel so good, so soon?

So familiar yet completely new. Too much, but somehow not nearly enough.

It doesn't take long until we're tumbling around in the sheets again, fighting for dominance, for skin-on-skin contact. Natalie seems to know exactly what I need, exactly when I need it, and we fall into an easy rhythm.

It's late when we collapse into each other exhausted. Natalie's expression is disarmingly open with a softness that scares me to my core, but I can't look away, and for a while, we just stare at each other. It's like we both know we only have tonight and want to hold onto this, whatever it is, for as long as we can. And I don't know if it's just me, but the more I'm told I can't have something, the more I want it.

I've always needed more than skimming the surface, always needed depth. Perhaps that's why my relationships have all been such a disappointment. Either way, I know I have it with Natalie. I can't help but feel no matter what we've told each other, we both know that this is more.

In the dark while in her arms, I find the beat of her heart and lose mine.

And I know that I'm not ready for this to end.

* * * * *

I feel drugged, pulling me up from somewhere heavy.

Hands moving over my body. Bare breasts pressed against my skin, and all around me, I feel softness and curves. The feeling of warmth pushing rhythmically against my thigh.

I'm dreaming – at least I think I am until I feel fingernails digging sharply into my back.

My eyes fly open.

They may take a while to adjust to the darkness, but one thing's clear - Natalie is grinding against me. Dark hair fanning over my shoulder, breaths brushing against my neck, the slick heat of her against my skin.

Holy crap. Is she even awake?

She's making noises, but I'm not sure.

Something about seeing her this *way* makes me crazy. The need to feel her. Touch her. Kiss her. I trace the outline of her face, the line of her jaw. Her skin smooth along her cheeks.

All the while, I feel her moving, wet against me.

Beneath the sheets, I run my hand up her bare thigh and hear a feminine sigh. "Natalie?" I whisper, placing a warm kiss on her shoulder, her neck, and softly palm her breast, her nipple pebbling under my touch. Still technically a one-night thing, right?

I smile against her skin at her moan, and this time her eyes pop open, glazed yet filled with heat. "Oh... Sorry. I must've been dreaming -" she says, looking a bit embarrassed.

Don't be.

I cut her off with a kiss because is she joking? I've had fantasies like this, waking to a beautiful woman doing that in the middle of the night.

Mouth to mouth. Breast to breast. I stretch into her, pressing my bare skin into her curves. Rational thought all but disappearing. She's warm and wet all around me. Her tongue slides across mine, and she nips at my lip. I love the feel of her tongue on my lips, the feel of her lips on my tongue.

Natalie pulls my hair to one side, her teeth all up and down my neck. My hand slips under the covers, and this time it's my turn to moan. Soft and slick under my fingertips.

Our mouths only a breath away from each other, I work her in slow, deliberate strokes.

I know I've never had *this* before, this unspoken understanding of what's happening.

Unable to draw my eyes away from her face, I gasp sharply when she pushes her palm against me and grip her forehand.

Natalie is dragging her teeth over her lip, and I dip my fingers inside her, stroking her from the inside out. She moans, getting closer and closer, and pushes her hot mouth into my neck. "Mia -"

She cuts herself off when her mouth finds mine, already searching for hers.

And suddenly, we're both *there*.

My fingers pumping inside her; I'm riding her palm, hard, desperate for release. Natalie gasps, her body clamping down around my thigh and my fingers. I'm grabbing the back of her neck, urging her to kiss me harder, touch me. Heat pooling low in my stomach, it starts pulsing through my whole body, and I'm going to come. I need to come with her. "Natalie... "

"Now." Her lips part in a sharp cry, and she catches my mouth in a rough kiss, and I'm right there with her, heat exploding between my legs and ricocheting through every part of my body. Coming so hard I can't even speak.

Still trembling in each other's arms, I can barely open my eyes. Instead, I place a warm kiss at the base of her throat, hopefully conveying what I can't say with words.

＊ ＊ ＊ ＊ ＊

The morning is a total blur.

There's been so much activity I'm not even sure it's the same day. All I know is that I'm wildly disoriented in a tussle of sheets and tangle of limbs with a Natalie-sized lump beside me, and I'm very, very naked.

It takes me a moment or two to realize that we're upside down at the foot of the bed. Right, my bed. Not hers. Our pillows are bunched up near the headboard. I'm also so wrecked that I can barely move. We've only slept in tiny bursts of sleep, not that I'm complaining.

A stupid grin quickly fixes on my face, and I pull the sheet up to cover it.

I mean, I know it was just sex, but Natalie and I crossed an invisible boundary last night. Something about it felt strangely intimate, like she stripped me down and put me back together. I'm not ready to untangle myself from her just yet. Not when everything feels so fucking perfect.

Unfortunately, the stupid alarm has other ideas and starts blaring not long after.

Natalie startles. "What -" She sits bolt upright, head swinging left and right, then blinks in confusion. "Hang on. Why are we -"

Shrugging, I say, "No clue."

"Right. Morning, Mia." She's dragging a hand over her face, and then she looks at me, equally muddled. Her hair is sticking up all over the place. "It is morning, right?"

"Yes. I think so," I half-laugh.

Her head immediately whipping over to the red digits on display. "Oh, God. I'm so late... Sorry, I... " She gently unhooks my leg hitched over her thigh, and slides to the edge of the mattress, disentangling from the sheets. She fumbles for the light switch and floods the room. When she glances back at me, I read her eyes. "Mia -"

"I know." I cut her off because I don't want to hear what she has to say. I know it was purely physical, she doesn't like me. But why does that make me feel sad? Suddenly, I'm feeling a bit fragile. I force a smile to my lips. "It won't happen again. It's okay. You can go."

I think I see her flinch, but I roll on my back because eye contact right now feels akin to a smack in the face. Something appears to have changed overnight. In every touch, every kiss. And I'm not sure I'm ready to deal with it.

"Um... " Natalie pauses like she is going to say something, but then I feel her body rising up and pushing off the mattress. I hear her pick up clothes from the floor and get dressed, the soft sound of her zipper filling the room, and wow, this feels so weird.

I squeeze my eyes shut because I don't want to watch her leave.

"I'll see you later, then?" Natalie says a moment later.

"Sure," I reply, looking at the ceiling. "See you."

I hear the click of the door, and she leaves, the scent of her still very much on my skin. My stomach twists with an immediate dousing of cold *Holy hell, what have we just done?*

CHAPTER FIFTEEN

MIA

I can't see her anywhere.

Sure, the breakfast networking event is busy, but not so busy that Natalie could just vanish into thin air. Honestly, she's going to act like this now?

I weave through pockets of people, moving from one end of the room to the other, but Natalie isn't here, and I'm worried. Of course, I'm concerned for the welfare of my colleague. Absolutely not on a personal level or anything to do with what happened hours earlier.

Look, I'm not going to lie. I wasn't expecting pillow talk, but when she left so abruptly, it stung. That brief hesitation, I thought she might want to stay or ask to have dinner together. Perhaps I secretly wished she had. Stupid illogical heart always trying to mess me up. I should know better.

I head to the food table and grab a grilled cheese sandwich, a blueberry scone, and a coffee. Make that two coffees. My body aches, and I've not had nearly enough sleep. I can still feel Natalie's hands and mouth on me. Hear her voice in my ear, taste her kisses. I knew sex could be like that, I just never thought it could be like that for me. Last night comes back to me in scattered flashes.

Her face as she tore my clothes from me.

The sight of her nipping at my breasts.

The shape of her mouth when I moved between her legs.

Distracting, to say the least.

I wait and wait, even do a bit of mindless networking between these pesky flashbacks. An hour passes, but still no Natalie. Heat starts pouring into my chest like hot wax, and I feel anger bubble up inside me.

When the event finishes, I catch the elevator straight to her floor, knocking on the door.

Nothing.

I can't shake the feeling that something feels off, so I go down to the front desk and get a keycard to her room. On my return, I swipe and open the door slightly. "Natalie?"

Still nothing.

I push through and flick on the light.

Oh my God.

Natalie.

Curled up in a tight ball on the carpet in a white cotton robe.

"What the hell are you doing down there?" I gasp.

"So hot," she croaks.

"Oh, shit," I mutter, rushing forward into her suite. "You're sick?"

"No! Don't come near me," she yells, and I stop. "You should go."

"Absolutely not. You look like… regurgitated death," I say gently, teasing. Upon closer inspection, Natalie really does look sick. Her hair is damp, and she's pale and clammy.

Natalie laugh-groans. A mild bout of embarrassment coloring her cheeks. "Did you break in?"

"No." I shrug. "Just told them, you know, you were my wife."

Her eyebrows lift.

"Honeymoon suite and all." I gesture with my hands. "Also, informed them that you are prone to bipolar outbursts, so sometimes you need your own space. Hence the separate rooms."

She rolls her eyes, and I grin.

Bending down, I ask, "On a scale of one to ten, how bad is it?"

"Like a thousand," she replies with an expression of absolute misery.

"Why didn't you call me?"

"You were at the networking event. Working."

It's my turn to roll my eyes.

"You should stay away," she warns.

"Did you forget what happened last night? And this morning?"

Natalie averts her gaze.

"Well, if it's a virus. I most likely already have it too. I should take you to a doctor."

"I'm not going anywhere."

Ignoring her weak protests, I fling her arm around my shoulder and help her to her feet, then to the bed. I press the cool back of my hand against her clammy forehead. "God, Natalie. You're like a million degrees." I rush to the bathroom and run a washcloth under cold water, and skitter back, pressing it against her skin. "Any other symptoms? Vomiting?"

"No."

"Pain?"

"Everywhere."

"Diarrhea?"

Natalie opens one eye. "Really?"

"What? I'm trying to work out if you need to go to hospital. Maybe an IV drip or something would help?"

"I told you I'm not going anywhere."

Stubborn ass.

I exhale loudly.

Natalie is sweaty, disheveled, and her hair an absolute riot. Yet somehow, she's completely adorable. Maybe I *am* coming down with a virus.

"Just really tired," she sighs, defeated, and I get two glasses of water. I watch her drain both, then refill and repeat.

I wait for her to slide under the covers and slowly recline, then tuck them around her shoulders like Mimi used to do when I was a kid. "Well, you should get some rest." I brush her hair back, which feels oddly intimate because she's my boss but seems okay, given that we slept together.

Natalie gives me a sleepy nod. "Thanks. What would I do without you, Mia Andrews?" she murmurs. Every whisper makes my skin prickle from head to toe, and I feel a wave of tenderness as her lashes sweep over the dark shadows underneath her eyes.

"That's okay." I bite my lip and look up at the clock. I've already missed the lunch session. Taking a deep breath, I go to stand. "I'm happy to leave if you want, or I can stay -"

"Stay," she says, reaching for my hand, and I settle back down on the bed with a small smile.

"Okay. Well, as soon as you fall asleep, I'm going to the pharmacy to get you a few things."

"You don't need to do that."

"Don't worry. I'm already mentally drafting a list of ways you can repay me."

She smiles. "I'll honor every one of them."

"I know... That's one of my favorite things about you."

Oh, God. What am I doing? I know all of this is a bad idea. I should be running for the hills, but I just can't seem to make myself. Looking at Natalie, so peaceful beside me, something creaks to life in my chest.

Something that I've been searching for my whole life.

* * * * *

Poor Natalie sleeps almost the entire day.

It's close to six in the evening. The sun is starting to sink, painting the sky a dusky pink, and I'm sitting in a lounge chair on the balcony with my laptop burning into my thighs when my phone starts dancing on the small rattan table. It's a message from Amy.

AMY: Are you alive?

ME: Oh my God. Amy!

AMY: Mia. Did you have sex with Natalie Dalton?

How does she -

ME: I can neither confirm nor deny.

AMY: !!! OMFG!!! Priya, the psychic, had a hunch about you two!

ME: You're obsessed with Priya, the freaking psychic. You should go out with her.

AMY: I am tonight! Going to that new Korean spa for a scrub down ;)

ME: Did she predict that?

AMY: . . .

AMY: Tell me everything!

ME: God, I don't know where to start. We were put in the honeymoon suite! The HONEYMOON suite! With ONE bed. Well, I had a camping bed which almost killed me, so Natalie invited me into the main bed –

AMY: Fuck off! Honeymoon suite with the boss! An invitation! This story just gets better and better!

ME: Wait. We didn't sleep together then.

AMY: Why not?

ME: Because we got separate rooms.

AMY: ARE YOU OUT OF YOUR GODDAMN MIND?

ME: Hmm. It doesn't make much sense, does it? Anyway, then she knocked on my door, and it happened. A few times.

AMY: Unbelievable. Wait till I tell Priya.

ME: Do NOT tell Priya. We're being discreet.

AMY: Sorry, I already told her. She says hi!

For fuck's sake.

Suddenly, there's a click of a door, and I drop my phone in my lap. Natalie shuffles into the living room, freezing when she sees me.

My heart melts because sleepy bed-headed Natalie is just something else. Stripped down without her suits, just her basics, she looks... I don't even know, but I think I might hate her a little for it.

Natalie almost looks like she wants to rub her eyes to see if I'm really there, so I give her a little wave. She blinks, and I think she mutters, "Shower."

When I hear the water running, I pick up the phone and order her a pumpkin soup and bread basket. Also, some minestrone, chicken noodle, and quite a few other types of soups I've never heard of.

What?

Natalie is a complicated woman. I want to make sure I cover all the bases.

CHAPTER SIXTEEN

NATALIE

"Wow. I feel like a new person -" I walk out into the living area, drying my hair with a towel, and notice she's not on the balcony. "Mia?"

I pad through the suite, checking each room, but Mia is nowhere to be seen.

Great.

I stop dead in my tracks. "What on earth -"

Blinded by an assortment of silver on the kitchen counter-top, I march over to about one hundred bowls and cloches. Is this room service? I lift one cloche, then another. A myriad of soups in all different colors. It goes on and on.

What is this?

It's like a soup buffet. There's also a massive breadbasket. Enough food to feed a small village. Mia must've ordered food before she left. I tear at a buttery croissant and sigh because it's very sweet, but where the heck is she?

Out of the corner of my eye, I see my phone screen flashing on the coffee table.

MIA: Lydia popped by while you were in the shower. Apparently, you had a dinner reservation with her and Charles from Maxitron tonight? After much consideration, I decided to go in your place. You know, to make an appearance! I won't be long. Debrief later!

PS Don't forget to eat your soup/s xo

I groan audibly and snatch a spoon, tasting some moss-green concoction, and stuff a stiff slice of sourdough into my mouth, but my brain has been hijacked.

"What the fuck is happening to me?" I warble through a mouthful of ancient grains.

I need it to un-happen.

Despite my strict instructions to snap out of it, I soon start pacing the honeymoon suite with the occasional stop at the buffet.

Back and forth.

Back and forth.

I think I'm going to send myself mad. While I've apparently recovered from my virus, this nauseous feeling sits in my stomach because why is she taking so long? And exactly how long constitutes making an appearance? An unfamiliar burn of jealousy starts to take over as the hours tick by.

I eat my body weight in soup, but it's okay because I've burnt it off with all my laps. I stack the empty bowls and silverware on a tray by the front door and gently rub my temples. Stomping out to the balcony, I try to let the soothing sounds of the ocean calm me. It doesn't work. So, I lie on the bed and then on the couch, my phone beside me. I don't know what to do with myself. I stare at the ceiling for thirty minutes, at the carpet for another thirty, when that horrible feeling starts cursing through my body again.

So, so stupid. Mia's just doing her job. Actually, my job. She's going above and beyond. Saving the day, I tell myself. Absolutely nothing to worry about. I'm in total control.

Ten seconds later, I text her.

ME: *Hi. Just me. Everything okay? Waiting patiently for a debrief?*

Patiently being the operative word.

No response.

I stare at my phone, willing it to beep.

Come on!

The urge to fling it across the room almost overwhelming.

I startle when it beeps a moment later.

MIA: *Out the front. Keycard not working.*

I rush to the front door, tripping over a hazardous pile of empty cloches, and make an absolute racket, almost headbutting the wall in the process. Fuck's sake. I just need to break my leg now to top off this stellar trip. I clamber to my feet, whipping open the door.

That's weird -

"Boo!"

"Aaahhh!" I jump, clutching at my chest.

Mia springs up from around the corner, grinning from ear to ear, her blonde hair loose and shiny.

"Are you like five years old?" I scowl at her, but it's impossible not to register the tiny black strappy dress clinging to her body. Heels so high I fear for her ankles.

"Yep," she smirks, and I snatch her keycard, glaring at it. "Using your room's keycard on my door. Well, that always works."

"Whoops. Must've mixed up my two keycards. Perhaps I should just stay here, then." Mia barges past me like I'm in the way.

Who knew she had so much sass?

Unfortunately, I really like that, too. I also notice her dress is backless. Great. Not wearing a bra either. Just what my stupid brain needs.

I rub my brow in frustration. "Are you inebriated?"

"You mean drunk?" She turns to me, her breasts rising up and down in her dress. Focus, Natalie, focus. "I mean, it's a possibility. Technically, I had one glass of Tempranillo, but I don't know how many times they refilled it because it always seemed full. Carlos, the waiter, was incredibly efficient." Mia stumbles into the couch, trying to unstrap her heels. "These things are killing me, by the way. A thank you would be nice."

I roll my eyes. "Thank you... What happened to just making an appearance? You were gone forever." I stare at her, everything else melting in a fuzzy background. A wild urge to grab her and kiss her almost overcomes me.

"Well, one thing led to another." Mia blows a blonde lock of hair that flops over her eye. "Miss me, did you?"

I suppress a smile, but I don't know why I bother because she always seems to be able to read my expression. "I was just seeing if you were okay," I say eventually. I hear myself, faltering and weak like a church mouse. What is happening to my mask? Oh, God. I'm pathetic. "How was Lydia?" The question slips out before I can shove it back in my throat.

With a shrug, she murmurs, "She was, you know... friendly."

I turn to the wall, closing my eyes. "Of course, she was."

"Only chatted about work, really."

She is lying.

"Mmm."

"Hey. I had to smooth things over with her after your epic meltdown at the team-building event. She was still pissed at you. Anyway, I think I fixed things. Said you messed up your hormone stabilizers again. Basically, they even out your mood – "

My eyes fly to hers. "You what?"

Her smile turning sharp at the corners. "Don't worry. She bought it." She jabs me in the nose with her finger. "You're in the clear."

My lips thinning in irritation. I'm not often lost for words, but I am now.

"Oh, and I convinced her to give us her family fashion account," Mia adds, and I go wide-eyed. She gives me a playful curtsey. "You know, the one you've been trying to win unsuccessfully for the last two years."

"What? How? Tell me you didn't... "

Mia scoffs loudly. "I showed her my portfolio, Natalie."

"Only your portfolio?"

"Yes, my portfolio!" I secretly love the glare she pins me with. "And I pitched an idea to partner with some influential vlogger slash fashionista friends that I have on YouTube who are really on-trend at the moment. She loved it. I also got her to sign our standard letter of intent. You know, before you put your foot in it, and she changes her mind." Mia picks up her iPad and shows me our online portal with Lydia's signature.

"I rang Joan on my way to dinner, and she ran through protocol, so I thought I'd take the initiative and just get it done. Obviously, we can nut out the finer details with Lydia at a later date."

I hunch over and start to laugh. "I mean... I just.... Who are you, Mia Andrews? I've completely underestimated you."

Mia is fast becoming one of my favorite people. Not only does she make me feel high as a kite, she also makes me feel like the world's biggest moron all at once. An impressive feat by any means.

She winks. "Your mistake, not mine."

"Your mind is a fascination."

"Better stop before you catch feelings." She smiles, and it's the kind that makes my heart turn over in my chest.

"Never going to happen," I reply with zero conviction.

"You know, I'm not sure why we got an extra room. Seems rather wasteful," Mia calls out from the bathroom.

I tilt my head back and sigh.

Still, she has a point. We've hardly spent a second apart. I've never met anyone quite like Mia. Something about her completely addictive. Honestly, how can one person simply have it all?

Suddenly needing fresh air and rational thought to permeate my clouded brain, I step out onto the balcony. Night has consumed the sky, the blanket of stars above reminding me just how small and insignificant I am in the big universe. I collapse into the lounge chair, absorbing the lingering humidity, and listen to the thrum of the waves. It doesn't drown out my thoughts, however, which are beating in my head over and over.

I hear Mia approach and turn to find her standing there, barefoot, with a pointed stare. She's scrubbed off her makeup, left only with lip gloss and flushed cheeks. Perfection. I literally can't take my eyes off her.

Mia arches her brow. "So, are you going to thank me properly?"

"And how do you propose I do that?" I ask, already fearing her answer.

Her eyes trip down my face and stall on my lips. I thought that might be the case. Then she walks over, swinging a leg over my lap, and straddles me. This close, I feel the last vestige of self-control washing off me. She places a hand over my heart. It's beating like crazy. I hate that she affects me like this. Hate that she knows it. Either way, I force my eyes on to Mia's, waiting for her response.

Her dilated pupils almost darken to black. She drags her finger down my top. "Well, this would be a start," she says in a soft, low voice, and my heart drops into my stomach.

With her dress bunched around her waist, she squeezes my torso with her thighs. It's paralyzing. I can't catch my breath, but I can feel hers.

My fingertips trail down her throat. I press a kiss over her pulse, feeling the beat against my lips. "Tell me what you want."

"This." Her hand skims over my jaw, angles it so our noses graze against each other, and then she kisses me, pushing my lips apart, tongues tangling in an inferno of desire. "Touch me," she begs into my open mouth.

I hear myself groan, and she takes my hand, dragging my fingers up the inside of her thigh until they are brushing against her, touching her, right there. I suck in a sharp breath. She's warm and wet as the ocean. "Soaking," I murmur, and she moans.

She draws back, biting my chin, my cheek. Her lips brushing the shell of my ear. "And before you ask, I wore underwear to dinner... This is just for you."

My voice raspy. "Are you trying to give me a heart attack?"

"Maybe." Her eyes twinkle mischievously, and I can't help laugh.

I catch her bottom lip with my teeth, and tug down the front of her dress. When I wrap my mouth around her nipple and suck through the delicate lace of her bra, a moan spills from her throat. My fingers slide down over her clit, barely dipping into her. I stroke her soft at first, slowly, then speed up until her breath catches.

As much as we have been discreet, at this point, I don't care if a cruise ship with a million leering passengers on deck sails by. I just want her. Tonight, I want to see her let go. I want it so much I can hardly breathe.

Around my fingers, she ripples. Her dark eyes turning hooded and glazed, while her breaths turn to soft pants. "Need you, Natalie... " Spreading her legs wider, she slowly sinks down all the way on my fingers and we both groan. She does it again, her pace quickening.

What is she doing to me?

Circling a thumb over her clit, both of us look down at where I'm touching her. "Do you know how good you feel?" I mumble. She swallows a moan. Her eyes roll closed; head starts tipping back. Heat crawls up my skin, and I grip her hair so her eyes meet mine. "You're ruining me, Mia."

Rolling her hips, she pushes further into my hand. She flicks her tongue against my lips and whispers, "I hope so."

Our eyes never break contact. She rocks over me, forgetting herself, losing herself. Her mouth hovering over mine, lips so close I can feel their shadow. I kiss her hard, demanding the feel of her.

Mia pulls back, only far enough to gasp, "Want to hear me?"

"I want the whole resort to hear you," I murmur.

Shit.

What am I saying?

Hands sink into my hair at the nape of my neck, and her hips falter, trapping my fingers deep inside as she rocks wildly against my palm.

"Oh, *God...*" Mia breathes, biting her lip.

Over her shoulder, I see an elderly couple chatting and walking along the footpath toward the ocean. I don't want to give them a heart attack. My free hand flying over her mouth, I hear her curse, breath ragged and hot on my skin. I hide behind her body while continuing to work her, pushing even deeper. There's no way I'm stopping. Not now.

Eyes fixed on my face, I feel her body tighten. She lets out a muffled cry, perhaps the sound of my name, and she comes in a series of tight spasms. Her face flushes red, and everything feels electric. She kisses my palm, and I slow and still, gently removing my fingers.

Pliant, and boneless, she slumps forward on my chest, and I wrap my arms around her. My mind is an absolute mess. The only thing I know for certain is that I want her. More of whatever she has to give. More of us together. How can tomorrow possibly be the end? I can't even bear to think about it.

I kiss the damp skin between her breasts. When I pull back, her lips find mine, and we kiss and kiss under the inky sky until I forget all my worries, forget everything.

Right now, nothing else existing beyond our postage stamp next to the ocean.

CHAPTER SEVENTEEN
MIA

I wake in the morning to the sound of the tide washing along the beach. Oh, and to Natalie rambling about pineapple and ferrets.

Even though she talks nonsense in her sleep, it's hard not to smile when she's curled on her side, her arm still draped over my shoulder, my hand pressed against her stomach. It's also hard to ignore the pulse between my thighs and bite marks covering my body.

Life really doesn't get much better than this.

Blinking, I adjust to the bright yellow sun streaming in from the window, warming my skin where it cuts across the bed. I watch it bathe Natalie in a peach-hued light, and something wraps around my heart, growing tighter the longer I look at her.

Memorizing her profile, I lightly trace her cheek with my finger. Her chestnut hair against the stark white linens, eyes closed but fluttering in a dream, perfect full lips slightly parted and ready to be kissed.

For days, I've been living on a cloud, and now, I'm hyper-aware of this end to what feels like a fairytale. There's even a painful twinge in my chest, and I know I'm in for a crash landing when we get back to San Diego.

Why?

Because this feels like *something*.

Underneath Natalie's fancy wrapping is a kind and gentle soul that feels so strangely connected to mine. Our time together has been nothing short of a revelation. I breathe in, storing every memory. Every one of her curves and dips, every small hollow. I start replaying our conversations and reliving every touch. The way she stared at me when I spoke. A million sparks lighting up her face.

No one has ever looked at me like that before.

No woman has ever made me feel the way she did.

None have ever been quite like Natalie.

Just a few more minutes here with her...

She mumbles something in her sleep, hooking a smooth leg over mine, and moves closer. When my alarm buzzes for the third time, I gently extricate myself from her grip and slip out of the bed to shower.

When I reenter the room, it's obvious we've officially slipped back into work mode. There's no chatter or affection, and Natalie is having problems looking at me.

A weird fog hanging over us.

How can we possibly go back to normal after *this*?

Natalie huffs when she sees my lip gloss smeared on her collar and disappears into the bathroom, grumbling along because she can't seem to find her right heel either. Meanwhile, I have to undress and dress again because I'm accidentally wearing her bra, which is making it difficult to breathe.

When I'm fastening my sleeveless cream silk blouse, Natalie is zipping up her black gingham pencil skirt and muttering under her breath.

I smooth down my crop pants. "Still complaining?"

"Of course," Natalie replies, staring at the ground, and I roll my eyes.

On impulse, I ask, "You up for breakfast by the pool before we go to the airport?"

"I suppose," she mumbles.

I smile quietly to myself. Even though this is the 'end,' we'll share one final meal in paradise.

"Well, I'm ready. I just need to get my bag from my room," I say, and Natalie lifts her head, eyes skirting the length of my body, then quickly back up. A trail of heat follows that path, and my heart begins to pound. My stupid nipples also salute her through my top.

Natalie closes her eyes at the same time as my hand flies to my chest.

I try not to laugh, but this is awful.

In an effort to avoid me, Natalie spins around and knocks into the sideboard, then rams her suitcase into the door on the way out. I fare much better, my knee only collecting the corner of the bedpost.

Unfortunately, it doesn't get much better in the elevator on the way down. A group of ten or so middle-aged line dancers wearing 'I love Tennessee' t-shirts decide to squeeze in on the fifth floor, and we end up plastered against each other in the far left corner. Natalie is against the back wall, and I'm wedged in on the side. Our own luggage actively conspiring to fence us in.

Natalie keeps her eyes fixed on the polished mirror doors. "This is like a nightmare," she mutters.

She is *not* wrong.

Every exhalation is tickling my neck, and she definitely cops an overhead view of my breasts which, given the slight height difference, seem to be pressing directly into her nipple line.

Oh my God.

I can feel her heartbeat. I try to find the words, but it's drowned out by her rhythmic thud. My vision starts graying at the edges, and when my gaze briefly flits down to her lips, Natalie mouths a hostile "Don't."

Suddenly, manic-type laughter bubbles up inside me over the sheer absurdity of the situation, and she rolls her eyes for like the hundredth time this morning.

I never thought I'd see the day when Natalie Dalton was rattled, especially by *me*, but I secretly love it. I also can't explain this free-falling happiness I'm feeling around her.

All I know is that I don't want it to stop.

CHAPTER EIGHTEEN

NATALIE

"Are you going to stop sniggering, Mia?"

We make our way onto the terrace where flowering pink hibiscus climb white walls and sit down at a wooden table next to the infinity edge pool sparkling under the sun. A waiter gives us menus plus a complementary basket of pastries and a bowl of vibrant summer fruit.

"It's just. . . " Mia shakes her head, still laughing.

"You went out of your way to make things uncomfortable for me back there. And why are you wearing a new top? It's practically see-through," I hiss.

"Are you talking to my boobs again?" She's smirking, her long, loose blonde hair spilling over her shoulder and lifting in the wind.

"Yes. Partly. . . Fuck -" I groan, momentarily slapping a hand over my eyes, and begin to hear my heartbeat in my ears. "Just stop doing whatever you're doing," I say, voice strained.

I'm feeling everything I don't want to. I'm hot and sweaty. My mouth is dry, my words a jumble.

"Which is?" Mia folds her arms against her chest, pushing her boobs together.

She's doing this to torment me. She *has* to be.

I wave my hand in front of her body like that should answer the question.

"Poor thing. Should've really let me return the favor last night, but you were so insistent on taking care of my needs." Mia leans back in her chair, fixing me with a mischievous-as-hell smirk, and I sigh. "You know, you're pretty cute when you're flustered," she adds.

I roll my eyes. "I swear I will relocate you to the Kalahari Desert if you continue to push me."

Mia has a hand over her mouth, laughing silently. She pauses, then lifts her chin defiantly. "Do you want to have sex instead? Over there in that striped cabana lined with plush pillows?"

Stupidly, I glance over, pausing for too long, and then snap, "No!"

When I turn back to Mia, she's still looking at me.

"No!"

Mia holds up her hands. "Okay, okay. Just thought an orgasm might help your raging stress levels."

My eyes drift down to the table, the tip of her little finger curled against mine. I snatch it away like I've been burned. "Yes. I can see how incredibly helpful you are being right now," I say with a thick layer of sarcasm and grab a pastry from the basket. I sink back into my chair, my stomach churning with frustration because her touch is everything. Not many things feel this good these days.

"Your butt looks amazing in that skirt, by the way." Mia makes a grabbing motion with her hands. "Just perfect."

I sigh loudly, feeling tension present in every single muscle. "Please shove a custard tart or whatever the hell this Danish thing is in your mouth and stop talking."

Her grin looks as though she can hear what I'm thinking, but this time, she listens.

Thank God for that.

The waiter returns, and Mia orders eggs benedict. Obviously, I'm not hungry, but at least I've put this conversation to rest, so I'm able to finally tilt my head back and let the serenity of the ocean lapping the shore wash over me.

Not two minutes later, a grating voice asks, "Natalie? Is that you?"

I grit my teeth, and when I open my eyes, an extra large head with close-set eyes is looming over me and blocking out my sun. Even her silhouette is annoying.

"Lydia. Hey." Far too close. I can smell the bacon she had for breakfast. My head snaps back down. Hoping to make her rack off, I say, "We're heading to the airport shortly, so see you next -"

"Oh, wonderful!" She adjusts her ridiculous sun hat over her chignon at the base of her neck. Her plunging canary yellow top cuts way past her vast cleavage. "We must be on the same flight. I'm heading to San Diego instead of back to San Francisco to see my folks. I'll hitch a ride in your cab, then." I'm really about to lose my shit right now. "Hey, Mia. Love your blouse." She gives her a wink. "It's really flattering, you know."

Of course, Mia is all bright-eyed and teasing smile. "Thanks. Natalie loves it too."

I kick her under the table. I hope it hurts.

She throws me a dirty look, and I fake a broad smile.

"I suspect she might. We are all one team here, Mia." Lydia waves her mosquito-ravaged arms around, and I deliberately recall her time on the obstacle course. It temporarily lifts my spirits. Turning to me, Lydia studies my face and says, "I'm glad to see you're feeling better. Diarrhea can be oh-so taxing. Especially away from home."

"I did not have di -" I break off.

Well, there goes my mood.

Out of the corner of my eye, I see Mia start snuffling, and I'm this close to stabbing her with my fork. Married, bipolar episodes, hormone stabilizers, diarrhea. Turns out Mia is quite the storyteller.

"Keep up the fluids. I'm sure Mia was a wonderful nurse. Mmm, yes, well. Nurses, don't get me started." Honestly, I don't know if I hate Mia or Lydia more right now. And Lydia doesn't shut up. "You know, Mia was a wonderful stand-in. Answered all the tough questions like a pro. Hardly missed you at all."

Lydia slaps my arm, and I jerk forward. "Joking! Mia's quite the hire, though. Even convinced me to give Dalton Media my family fashion account." She squeezes Mia's shoulder, then leaves her hand there. I try to freeze it off with my eyes. "Hang on to her, or I'll steal her. I promise you that. I could teach her a thing or two."

Oh my God.

Just leave.

Suddenly, I feel a foot working its way up my leg.

Startling, I look over to Mia. No way. She wouldn't dare, but the devious glint in her eye tells me otherwise.

When the wayward foot reaches my thighs, I jump in my seat, hitting the table, and my stupid pastry spectacularly launches off my plate and torpedos into the pool.

"Oh, my." Lydia looks at my sad floating breakfast and then at me. "Are you sure you're okay?"

"Medication has made me a bit jumpy, that's all," I reply a little hoarsely.

"Pepto-Bismal or Imodium? Just so I avoid it in the future."

Honestly, what is this conversation?

"Mia?" I narrow my eyes at her.

Let her struggle with her lies.

"Whatever the strongest stuff available is," Mia replies smugly. "The name is right on the tip of my tongue." She clicks her fingers, looking beyond amused.

"Oh. You mean Lotronex. For when things get diabolical." Lydia pauses and makes some weird baby noises. "Oh, poor little Natalie."

I can't take it anymore... I'm almost at breaking point.

"Yes! That's it!" Mia practically leaps out of her seat.

I murder her with my eyes. I'm going to kill her. I'm just trying to work out the most efficient way to dispose of the body. She's only petite. She'll fit in my carry-on luggage.

"Right. Well, the three of us should arrange a night out on the west coast and hit the gay clubs." Lydia zeroes in on Mia like a predator, and the only thing I want to *hit* right now is her. I deliberate the pros and cons of her meeting the same aquatic fate as my pastry.

Naturally, Mia claps her hands together excitedly. I wouldn't expect anything less. "I'm always up for a bit of fun. The more, the merrier, as far as I'm concerned." She gives me an annoying grin. "Count me in!"

"Wonderful! Me too!" chortles Lydia.

And yay! Just freaking yay.

"Well. I'll let you two get back to your breakfast, then," Lydia says as the waiter arrives with a plate of food. She gives Mia a lingering smile and leans into me, whispering, "And stick to solids, Natalie." My life officially sucks. Lydia points off in the distance like I could give a shit where she's sitting. I hope it's far, far away. "I'll just be over there under that small palm tree with the red bow. Grab me when you're ready."

I squint out to the azure waters, lying through my teeth. "Uh-huh. Will do."

"Toodles! See you soon," she says gleefully and trots off in her strappy Saint Laurent platforms.

Leaning forward with my palms on the table, I whisper-hiss, "Brilliant stunt. Bravo!"

"You started it. I probably have a bruise now!" Mia replies wide-eyed, and I snap, "Put your shoes back on and keep your exploratory foot out of my -"

Lydia's back.

Mia and I still staring fiercely at each other from across the table.

"Oh, here. I'd thought I'd save you the trouble." Her long fingers drop the waterlogged pastry, and it makes a splat noise on my plate. "Bye now!"

"Brilliant, thanks," I sigh and mutter under my breath to the tan-colored congealed goo, "Because I'm really going to eat you now."

Shaking my head, I push my plate to the side, and a blackbird divebombs my hair. "Shoo! Get off!" I yell, and Mia continues to chuckle behind her hand.

I think I'm making her day.

"Ah. Such a great trip for *so* many reasons." Mia wipes tears from under her eyes, and chirps, "You know, Lydia's nice! I like her."

"Lydia's nice. I like her," I mimic because clearly, I've lost my mind. "She's a vulture and all that sexual innuendo! Oh my God!" I gag dramatically. "She's only being nice to you because she wants to get in your pants."

"Well, right now, she's being nicer to me than you are," she states, pointing her index finger at me, eyes widening in a challenge. "And you *were* in my pants. More than a few times!"

A vise grip clutches my stomach. Oh, I remember. I rub my eyes because I'm starting to feel the mother of all migraines coming on.

"Here. Eat the rest of this, grumpy," Mia grunts and slides her plate of eggs benedict across the table. "You've barely eaten anything the past few days. You can't survive on air."

When I look up, she pokes her tongue out at me.

Honestly, I'm at a total loss for words. I'm completely and utterly out of my element with this woman.

Picking up my knife and fork, I shovel some ham, egg, and English muffin into my face and chew in silence.

"The hollandaise is unreal, right?"

Mia has a point.

"It's good," I mutter, and she grins.

I feel her unabashedly studying me. Obviously, I'm tense.

"Natalie. Are you happy?" Mia asks a minute later, her words hanging in the salt air.

I furrow my brow and give her a weird look. "What?"

"I mean, at work. This constant power struggle with your dad. Isn't it soul-destroying? All that money and power really worth it?"

I put my fork down. "Dalton Media is a very successful business."

Mia stares at me for the longest time, trying to find something I don't quite understand, and I'm hoping this is the end of life's big questions. "I guess I'm just asking if that is what you really want. I see glimpses of someone else outside work. I didn't even know you had a sense of humor until this trip."

"Good to know." I roll my eyes. Why is this woman suddenly making me question my purpose? It's not like I throw myself into work so I don't have to think about the emptiness in my life. I dab my lips with my napkin. "What makes you think I'm not just another ruthless executive?"

Mia throws a blueberry at me, and I catch it with my mouth. "Easy tiger," she huffs.

So, shoot me. I'm on edge. I want to be cool and calm, but I don't know how.

I also briefly entertain lobbing Mia head first into the pool so I don't have to look at her, but then she'd be soaked wearing that sleeveless cream fitted top, and oh my God, that's even more to wrap my head around.

I wriggle around in my chair, hit with an unfamiliar ache. Ugh.

Apparently, there's no way to extinguish this attraction. What exactly is it about this woman that makes me feel this way?

She's also still looking at me for an answer.

I count down from ten before answering, "Look, I'm hardly the type to go off sailing into the sunset and start knitting now, am I?"

"I'm sure Georgia would like that," she smirks with small lines of laughter in the corner of her eyes, and I tilt my head back to the sky, willing the torture to end because this day is starting to feel like four years.

Unfortunately, her smart quips only make me like her more.

* * * * *

Originally, I planned to sit in the front of the cab to the airport so Mia couldn't hypnotize me with her face, and body, and damn shirt. But given that Lydia insists on joining us, I make a point of sitting right up beside Mia and shove Lydia and her lecherous eyes up front instead.

While Lydia natters on about herself, Mia and I are both quiet for the ride to the airport, our eyes fixed on the sun-bleached road. Unfortunately, I feel every breath, every movement, every squeak of her leather seat.

Mia completely surrounds me.

When her skin brushes my sleeve, I pull my arm away. And when my leg accidentally touches hers when we launch over a speed hump, she edges closer to the door. Not even a glance my way.

The mood continues on the plane, and there's no conversation. Just silence so thick I want to cut it with a knife. We stow our bags, take our seats.

Mia is scrolling through work emails on her phone, and I've just done up my seat buckle when I notice something dark and ominous on my shoulder. "What is -"

"Poo," she practically shouts.

"Huh?"

"Remember the blackbird? Parting gift for being so pleasant this morning. Too bad he didn't drop it on your head," Mia snaps, and I scoff. Her head whips back around the other way, angrily fighting to get a sleeping mask onto her face while I'm left to deal with this disaster.

I hate my life.

My control is fraying. I take a deep cleansing breath. Then another.

There's a tap on my shoulder, safely away from the bird's deposit, and I turn to a thirtysomething mother across the aisle who looks like she hasn't slept all year. I'm momentarily distracted by the pink pacifier in her mouth (not hers) and a bald-headed baby hanging off her right boob, but then I notice that she's waving a wet wipe at me.

Oh, thank God for that.

Smiling, I say, "Thank you. Really appreciate it." I remove the disgusting lump on my shoulder as best I can, but end up smearing it instead. Oh, whatever. I fold the wipe over and crankily shove it into the sick bag in the seat pocket.

Such a perfect way to finish this trip.

Thirty thousand feet in the air with a five-hour flight ahead, and I'm sandwiched next to a woman I can't have, smelling like bird shit.

I'm just grateful that Lydia is seated in business, and our company is tight, so we're in economy. I'm also grateful that Mia has that stupid mask on so she can't see me inadvertently glancing at her every five seconds like some dopey puppy-dog intern.

I curse under my breath. My brain is swiss fucking cheese.

This wasn't supposed to happen. It was only a few days. What the hell is wrong with me? Everything I'm doing is so out of character. I've become genuinely stupid around her. Since when did I take up shin-kicking under the table?

Mia's not even my type. Yet it doesn't seem to quell my need to be near her, the niggling desire to know her better. I've lost control of my mind and am clearly unable to make a rational decision around this woman. Our time together playing out like a movie reel every time I shut my eyes.

And I feel something – a connection.

Something that I was unsure I'd feel again. It's been two years since my divorce when Lara just up and left me one day. It took me totally by surprise. She wasn't exactly delicate, telling me she didn't want to be in a loveless marriage any-more. She took our dog, Lola, a sizeable chunk of the savings and moved overseas the following week. I didn't even fight her.

Perhaps I would've picked up on it if I wasn't working so much, traveling less overseas, been at home more. Or perhaps I just didn't love her the way I was supposed to. I mean, I cared for her and enjoyed her company, but that knock-you-out-of-the-park kind of love? I don't think that was ever us. Not at the beginning, not ever.

I think two lonely souls just gravitated to one another and then settled. I might've even pushed for marriage because my mom was sick, and I wanted her to know that I'd be okay.

I felt like a failure when Lara left me. I turn my mom's ring that I wear on my right hand. I often wonder if I failed her too. Perhaps if I could've persuaded her to leave my father earlier, maybe she wouldn't have gotten sick.

As for Mia, it's clear she has reignited something I thought was long lost. I glance down at my watch. Surely, we're halfway to San Diego by now. . .

It's been twelve minutes.

For fuck's sake.

My eyes clamp shut.

Despite all my protests, I eventually turn my head left, my gaze gliding over her face. How can Mia be so calm when I'm not? It's madness. Madness! I'm the cold, clinical one. This just isn't who I am.

Frowning, I notice that she starts to shiver. Goosebumps prickling her skin while tiny, pale hairs on her arms stand on end.

Ignore, I tell myself. This is the same woman that wanted the bird to aim for my head, and I put my foot down on the vortex my mind wants to suck me into. I can't go there. I clutch at the armrests and concentrate on an old episode of Seinfeld, which is playing on the screen, but it's pointless.

The more I try *not* to notice, the more Mia shivers. I ball my hands into fists and internally reprimand myself. I'm not sure what is happening to me, but it's very annoying. Somehow, Mia has done the impossible and gotten under my skin.

I last another ten seconds before I cave and flag down a flight attendant with a French plait to get a blanket. I cover Mia's body and sigh, but thankfully she soon drifts off to sleep, which means I can finally get some rest too.

Closing my eyes, I tilt my head back into the seat. I'm almost asleep when I hear her mutter, "Stupid cashmere sweater."

I shouldn't be smiling, but I am.

CHAPTER NINETEEN

MIA

When we emerge from the elevator with our luggage, Joan launches out of her seat like her ass is on fire.

"Hello, you two," she calls out cheerily, feigning innocence. "How was your trip away? Room up to your standards?"

"Your meddling was well and truly noted, Joan." Natalie rolls her eyes, briefly pausing to scoop up messages from her desk. "Please collect your severance package on the way out."

"You're so funny," Joan chuckles and gestures to the messages. "An urgent inquiry from a potential investor on top of that pile, IT problems on the bottom... Hang on, what on earth is on your shirt -"

"Don't." Natalie holds up her hand, marching through the front door. "I'm getting changed right now!"

I try not to smile, but a flaming blush must give it away because Joan starts grinning ear to ear when she glances at me. I even get a wink when Natalie is out of sight.

When I enter the office, I steel myself to be calm and repeat my mantra.

Don't tell anyone. Do not tell a soul.

Don't tell anyone. Do not tell a soul.

"Hi, Mia!"

I jump into the air. "Hi, Theo!"

God, not discreet at all with my gymnast leap.

Ugh. Great start. I slide my luggage into the space between my workstation and the wall and plop down in my seat. Right, I just need to bury myself under a mountain of designs today so I don't put my proverbial foot in it. I straighten a pile of papers into alignment and switch on my computer.

"How was your trip?" Theo perches himself on the edge of my desk and straightens his thin, black tie.

Why? Why must he do that today?

"Great, thanks," I answer, poking around in my pot of pens. "Conference was flat out. Meetings, meetings, meetings. No private time to do... anyon-..anything! Very productive."

Oh, just shut up.

"Okay," he says, bemused, and Kayley floats by. "Hey, Mia! Great to have you back. The human headshots have been superimposed on those cattle for the Bergman campaign. Bit weird, but you know, whatever the client wants, right?" She shrugs, smoothing her bangs to her side, and then whispers, "What's up Natalie's ass today? Looks like she might murder someone... Hopefully, Margot, but you know."

"No sleep... She's completely zonked. Because she was so flat out in Florida. Massive trip. No other reason." I cough to cover my squeak.

Honestly, I am my own worst enemy.

Kayley looks at Theo, Theo looks at me, and I can't look anywhere but the carpet.

Argh. Go away.

To diffuse suspicion, I have no choice but to make small talk with my team. I ask Theo about his night out with a Peruvian magician while Kayley tells us all about her daughter Ava's baptism, where the pastor tripped and almost drowned Ava in the baptismal font.

Somewhere during this conversation, I also vaguely accept an invitation to drinks later this week, which I now need to come up with an excuse to get out of. Brilliant. Anyway, I'm just grateful I didn't let the cat out of the bag and relax when Theo and Kayley finally disperse.

My thoughts soon drift to Amy, who has been unusually quiet. I wonder how her date with Priya went. Snatching my phone from my bag, I text her.

AMY: Still with her. Won't let me leave.

ME: You haven't been home in three days?

I'm not sure if this is good or bad?
Who is this Priya character?
A few dots appear, then disappear.
Alarm bells ring.

ME: Amy!! Do you need help? Is this a hostage situation?

AMY: Don't think so, but she is tying me to her bed :)

I snort a laugh. Okay, thank God for the smiley face.

Sighing, I place my phone on my desk. Well, I need to get out of this fug somehow. Finding yet another reason to procrastinate, I wander to the kitchen to get a coffee, only to find Nancy crouched over, blitzing a cheesy enchilada in the microwave.

"Hey, Nancy."

Nancy lifts her head. "Hi, Mia. How was your trip -"

No, not again. I start jabbing the buttons of the very loud coffee machine. "Sorry. What?" I pretend to not hear her over the combined noise of the appliances. Suddenly, someone bumps my hip, and I don't turn around.

I don't need to, to feel her presence.

Closing my eyes, my heart rate goes from resting to racing. As Natalie shuffles past in the cramped space, I unwittingly breathe in her citrusy perfume and am smacked with a naked memory of her. My treacherous face starts getting hot again.

"Sorry," Natalie stammers, and I almost knock her cup off the counter when I try to spin my way out of there.

An hour later, we cross paths in the copy room.

"When did this office become so small? I feel like you're stalking me," I snap, snatching my campaign printouts.

"I feel like I'm in a two-by-two cell. You're everywhere." Natalie stares straight at me, and it hits me between the thighs. She stalks off and seems to forget all about her quarterly cash flow report.

I'm such a swirling mess of feelings. There's only one thing left to do, really. I rush back to my desk and book that boring Advanced Microsoft Excel course I've been putting off for over two years.

Looks like I'll be out of the office for the rest of the afternoon and this time, I'm actually happy about it.

CHAPTER TWENTY

MIA

I've been in a detached daze since Florida.

Something in me has changed.

I'm sick. Heartsick. And it's not good.

Being in such close proximity to Natalie at work and not being able to touch her is making me crazy. Tuesday and Wednesday fly by. I get a nod as I pass her in the hallway, and it's not nearly enough. Thursday, and with no more offsite courses left to book, I do the only sensible thing I can think of – I phone Joan, telling her I'm under the weather and will be working from home.

No way I am overthinking any of this at all.

Which is why when I hear a knock on the door close to six in the evening, I absolutely do not leap over the couch and almost wipe out on the rug, then stop dead and wonder for a full ten seconds if I should change out of my old yoga shorts.

Whatever.

I whip open the door, only to catch her walking away.

My hair hanging, damp, and limp on my face. "Natalie?"

She turns around, and when our eyes meet, it's like an electric shock, only nice. "Oh, hey. Sorry, I know it's late."

If I think time away from the office would dampen her impact on me, I am sorely mistaken. I stare at her, my heart in my throat. Her ocean-blue eyes glimmer, her cheeks red from the evening wind, and her chestnut mane a perfect mess.

Natalie stares right back at me. "Joan mentioned you weren't feeling very well, so I thought I'd check if you were okay. Was worried you caught my bug?" She holds up a paper bag. "Brought some soup, Gatorade, Advil... Lotronex?"

I'm smiling. "Oh, ha-ha. For when things get diabolical... Right, I deserve that."

Natalie takes a small step forward. "Are you okay?" she asks, and I go all fuzzy inside.

"Yeah." I wave my hand around. "Just a migrainey thing."

"I've been working you too hard?"

Not hard enough.

"No. I just get them from time to time. And thank you, it's nice of you to check up on me. Do you want to come in?"

Natalie hesitates. "Sure. For a minute. Here." She hands me the bag, and we pad inside. I drop the bag on the small table. Turning around, I raise an eyebrow. "So, tell Miss Dalton. Do you make house calls to all your sick staff?"

She opens her mouth and then gives me a slow smile. "Only the ones that have met Fabio."

"And how many have done that?"

Her eyes fix on mine, leaving me nowhere else to look. "One."

My stomach flips, and I edge closer. "I see," I say quietly. "So... did you really miss me that much that you needed to see me?"

Natalie tries not to smile. "Mia..." she says softly. "The conference is over."

My heart sinks.

What happens in Florida, stays in Florida.

Natalie reaches forward, pushing a strand of hair out of my face, and my whole body becomes electrified.

"Honestly, you can't say my name *and* touch me."

She quirks an eyebrow. "The combination?"

"Deadly," I say, basking in the warmth of her closeness.

"I don't know what I'm doing."

"Good. Either do I."

We stare at one another.

Too close.

Too intimate.

Just a little bit longer of whatever this is.

"Mia, maybe I should -"

Suddenly, she grabs my head, kissing me hard, and everything seems to fall away. I hear her keys drop, her bag, and then it's just the two of us.

She's digging her fingers into my hair, and I mirror her, gripping her hair, fisting it wildly. Our kisses are teasing, then rough, coming together and pulling apart, tongues sliding against each other. We slam into the arm of the couch, and I spin us around, pushing her up against the wall. Grabbing each of her hands, I raise them above her head.

"*God,* " Natalie breathes. Her leg wrapping around my waist, her heel digging into my back.

"I want you," I whisper, tugging frantically at her shirt, reaching under, cold hands on warm skin. Her breath shudders, and I can't help but smile against her lips, relishing these small chinks I'm finding in her armor.

It's scary how much I've been wanting this. Wanting her to want me. Years of subpar when this is how it was supposed to be. Better than anything. A small voice in my head is getting louder and louder, telling me I will never get enough of this.

Natalie twists into the hem of my t-shirt, the other hand grazing up to my stomach, beneath my breasts, making me shiver. As I planned on binge-watching tv, I am not wearing a bra. She groans. "Habit of not wearing underwear?"

My tongue running along her bottom lip. "Trying to save you time."

"How considerate."

"Always." I grin, and she pulls back, looking as unhinged as I feel. "Flatmate?"

"Has a date. Less talking. More action." I bite her shoulder through her shirt.

Natalie smirks, sliding both hands up my front, fingers barely tracing the slope of my breasts in a non-touch tease, and I whimper. She is most definitely doing this on purpose.

I see her devilish smile and I choke out a laugh.

This time, Natalie palms my breasts and when her tongue flicks over my aching nipple, just once, I gasp and lose it, dropping between her thighs.

"Mia... "

It sounds like a warning, but I don't care. I'm never in control, not around this woman.

I. Need. This.

"I think about you all the time," I say, pushing her skirt up along her thighs and ghosting my lips over the thin fabric of her panties. Natalie sucks in a deep breath, reaching for my hair. My pulse is thumping in my ears. I flick my tongue until the fabric is thick with wetness. "This."

Her head crashes back against the wall, and she lets out a tortured groan. Some thug next door pounds the wall twice.

Natalie tries to pull me up, but my hands grip her hips in place. I'm kissing and nipping at her until she is soaked right through. Her head moves restlessly against the wall. "Mia. Off. I -" The neediness in her voice sends a jolt straight between my thighs. I yank the satin straps down over her legs, needing them gone and nothing between her and my mouth.

Arching against the first touch of my tongue against her skin, her voice rings out around the room and definitely through to our neighbors.

She opens her legs wider, asking for more, and I feel the way she trembles as she gets closer, reaching for something to hold on to. The legs of the couch scrape against the hardwood floor, her spiky heel pressing into the wall. When my eyes move sideways, I catch her reflection in the mirror, teeth biting into her lower lip, and oh, fuck -

A key is rattling in the front lock.

We have exactly four seconds to make it to my room.

* * * * *

We break my bed.

Mind you, it isn't sturdy.

189

Creaking from the sagging box springs should've been a pre-warning, but we were a little preoccupied. The legs snapped, the mattress now sitting on the floor.

Her lips firm on mine, and her perfume like a warm blanket around me. Let's be clear when I'm naked, Natalie Dalton owns me. But there's no way I'm telling her that.

I whisper against her mouth, "Well, that's a first." Her face creasing into a gorgeous smile. "You know, I'm glad you showed up here uninvited, even if it was under the guise of 'concerned boss'... "

Natalie replies with the same bunny ears. "I was a concerned boss. But I admit I also wanted to see you and... "

I kiss her neck, tasting the faint salt of her sweat and mine. "Break the bed?"

She chuckles. "I can't bear full responsibility for that."

"Really?" I poke her in the shoulder. "Pretty sure it started to creak when you flipped me around like a rag doll down the other end."

Our eyes meet, and we start laughing. Natalie's nose crinkles up when she laughs, and for some reason, this makes it even funnier. "Looks like a relic from the eighteenth century," she gurgles.

"Ha-ha. Okay, true," I snort. "Was never going to last, but still."

Honestly, my head feels like a marshmallow. Dreamy and soft. Whatever this is between us, it's more than chemistry. It's magnetism. A scientific force.

"So, somehow, we ended up naked again." I press my face into the hollow of her neck, trying to hide my smile. Natalie tilts my face up, her features blurring out of focus. "It's *definitely* a recurring problem."

I kiss the tip of her nose. "And I'm *definitely* not complaining."

"Do you think Amy heard?"

"She had a date with Priya at six thirty. Probably just forgot her purse or phone."

Natalie lets out a long sigh. "You know. You're pretty amazing, Mia Andrews."

"Right?"

"Humble too." Natalie rolls her eyes, and I grin.

She kisses me with unexpected tenderness. Soft and raw, and everything it shouldn't be, silently agreeing not to ask each other any difficult questions.

When we finally break apart, I'm wrapped around her like a vine, her hand running up and down my back. This is new for us, her in my apartment and in my bed. I *really* like it.

I see her take in my magazines piled high on the dresser, clothes scattered across the floor, my nude dress hanging on the wardrobe door, and necklaces dangling over my reading lamp.

God, stop looking around.

She plants small kisses on my collarbone. "Your room is very homey."

I feel my face flush. "Obviously, I wasn't expecting visitors."

Out of the corner of my eye, I spot my time-of-the-month underpants, so when Natalie pulls back, distracted by photos on my corkboard, I lean over the side and stuff them under the mattress. Nobody should be subjected to those, only me.

Natalie points. "Is that your mom on the horse with you?"

"Uh-huh."

"She's pretty. Same spectacular smile," Natalie teases, and I smack her playfully. She looks closer at the picture. "And I'm guessing Janet is the frumpy one sitting in the dirt. Her ice cream cone is empty, and oh look, the ice cream is on her knee."

"Very perceptive," I say with a laugh.

Natalie pulls me into her, trailing her lips along my neck.

"Stop kissing your way out of trouble. You still owe me a bed."

She kisses my nose, my lips. "I would never do that."

"That's exactly what you're doing."

"It's working, isn't it?" she asks smugly, and I smile into another kiss.

I hate it when she's right.

* * * * *

When I sneak out of my room to grab some water, I startle when I spot Amy and Jules sitting on the couch with their arms folded across their chests like a pair of scary parents.

"Jesus. You scared the shit out of me! What the hell are you two doing?"

"I think that's fairly obvious," snips Jules.

"Amy. You're supposed to be on a date with Priya!"

"Change of plans. She had a last-minute chanting session with some guru that's almost as big as the Dalai Lama. Can't remember his name."

Amy's wearing one of her edgy New York outfits and Jules, her activewear. She has also had a haircut. Half her hair is missing.

They both look serious, but Jules starts to smile. "What are you doing, more importantly?"

"Having a good time?" Amy grins, dangling Natalie's keys from her index finger.

God.

Here we go.

"I suppose," I reply, trying to keep my tone neutral.

Jules sniggers. "We thought we heard an earthquake? The walls were shaking. There was a loud bang and a lot of screaming."

Amy loses it first, then Jules falls about laughing on top of her.

I roll my eyes. "Oh, ha-ha." Then I whisper-hiss, "The damn bed broke, okay!"

Unfortunately, they burst into a howling fit of laughter that vibrates off the walls.

"Sssh!" I whack them both, but they're still clinging onto each other and carrying on like idiots.

Amy wipes away tears. "Wait, she's still here?"

"In the shower," I say quietly.

A cheer erupting so loud, it can be heard from the moon. Honestly, these two wouldn't know how to be quiet even if it bit them in the ass.

"Stop! Amy! Jules! She'll hear -"

They share a glance and lunge forward, pulling me toward them.

"She smells of sex."

"Positively reeking."

They're poking me, laughing, and I'm giggling, trying to slap them away. "God, let me go!"

Eventually, they do.

"You really, *really* like her," assesses Jules.

I shrug casually. "Just enjoying the ride."

"Oh, I bet," sniggers Amy.

"Is that all you think about?" I huff. "But yes, that part is good too."

Jules considers me through narrow eyes. "Your face is still red and has yet to return to a human shade."

"Beyond curable," smirks Amy

"Lost cause," Jules nods gravely.

"Would you two just quit it?"

"No!" They both start laughing.

I smack each with a cushion. Hard -

"Hi Natalie!" they beam brightly, and my head jerks up, face flooding with heat.

Natalie looks as fresh as a daisy, unfairly beautiful. She's also back in the same clothes she was wearing when she arrived and gives the pair of them a smile that would melt ice cream in your palm. Certainly, not one they deserve. "Hi, Jules."

"Hey, Natalie," replies Jules as a smile spreads across her face. "At least you have an acceptable excuse for missing spin class. I'll give you a pass this time."

"I was *planning* on going," Natalie says sheepishly. "And you must be Amy?"

I love that she remembers her name.

Amy nods like she's in a hypnotic spell. "Hi. Yes, I'm Amy," she says robotically as she visually drinks her in. Two red spots appear in her cheeks, and I hear Jules snicker.

"So, what did I miss?" Natalie asks, and something in the air changes when our eyes meet across the room. Then she does something completely unexpected. Something very un-Natalie. She walks to my side and reaches down, lacing her fingers with mine like it's the most natural thing in the world.

Warmth spirals up through my fingertips, crackling along every inch of my chest. A simple act meaning more than she knows.

I bump her shoulder, and she bumps mine. "Hi."

My friends most definitely register whatever the hell is happening because Amy starts grinning like a maniac and asks her something she never ever asked my ex, Nadia, the whole time we were dating.

"Natalie, do you want to stay for dinner?"

CHAPTER TWENTY-ONE

MIA

Friday morning shoots through my window, slicing my room and, eventually, my face.

Oh, God.

I make shapes with my mouth, but no other words come out. My head also has a pulse, and I want to kill it. I can practically hear my headache.

A few hideous moments later, I reach out and tug at Natalie's sleeve. "Please just let me die in peace," she groans.

"What happened last night?" I croak. "I can't even remember having dinner. Were we roofied?"

Natalie wraps my Ramones t-shirt over her head. "Can we discuss this at another time when I'm not actually dying?"

I glance left and right. "Where's my phone?"

"Probably wherever your pants are." Her voice muffled through my top.

I drag myself up to a seated position. "Good point."

"Natalie. Why are you wearing Jules's black satin leggings?"

Her head snaps down. "What?"

To be fair, they *do* look good on her.

"Is that freaking Janet still banging around in the kitchen? Tell her to shut up!"

We go wide-eyed and peer over the edge of the mattress.

Amy is burrowed in a mound of washing, groaning like a fragile animal preparing to take her last breath. Her hair is everywhere. There's a grumpy crease across her forehead, one of my red sports bras casually draped over her eyes, and she's using a few of my sweaters for blankets.

I giggle into Natalie's shoulder.

This is catastrophic.

"I won't be coming over for dinner again. Just so you know," says Natalie sternly with her eyebrows drawn together, and I burst out laughing. She starts shaking her head. "For one, I'm sleeping on a mattress on the floor with an apparent wedgie. I'm not even wearing my own pants!" she adds far too seriously and squeezes her eyes shut like she is just focusing on breathing.

I laugh and laugh. Why is this so funny?

"At least you're wearing pants," I reply when I collect myself. "Where are mine?"

"What are all these voices?" grumbles Amy. "Go away."

"Amy!" I half-shout, and she startles.

"What the fuck?" My bra sliding off her face. "Why am I in your room?" She clocks Natalie, light dawning in her eyes. "Jesus. Did we have a three-way? Why do I always forget poignant moments?"

"What? I don't think -" I look to Natalie, and she shakes her head. "No. You took a wrong turn. You were crawling -"

"Crawling?" Amy scratches her head, squinting.

"Oh my God! What happened last night!" I yell-groan.

I look for my phone to piece together the evidence, but I can't see it anywhere. "Where the fuck is my phone?" I ask, slightly more exasperated.

Natalie's alarm starts beeping, and we all scream at it.

After a few failed attempts, Natalie and I eventually stagger out of bed with the last of our motor skills. I'm tugging my t-shirt over the hem of my underpants with one hand and pulling my hair into some sort of shape with the other, while Natalie is still smarting about her pants.

We stumble into the living room, arm in arm, stooped over like we're a thousand years old, and find Jules flat on her back on the couch in a deathly sprawl. Her new hairdo is matted to her forehead with God-knows-what while her mouth is so far open that I can count all her teeth.

"Jules?"

"Huh?" Her head jerks up and then crashes immediately back down. "What the fu... Oh, hi. Oh, God. My cranium." Pale-faced and drawn, she squints. "Since when do I have flat-mates?"

"You stayed over," I confirm.

"What? That would explain my screaming brain. Apparently so obliterated last night, I was unable to make the five steps to my front door." Jules points to Natalie accusingly. "You. Compadre. You're wearing my pants."

Natalie limply raises her arm. "And you're wearing mine!"

"Jesus. I thought my pants must've shrunk in the wash. Size 0. Makes sense," snaps Jules. "They're cutting off my circulation, by the way!"

"Well, get them off!" I instruct. "Did we play freaking strip poker last night?" Natalie gives me a blank look, my eyes widening at the carnage before me. Cushions, clothes, and broken tortilla chips strewn over the floor, two tubs of ice cream upside down near the door, dozens of half-empty glasses and bottles resting on every service.

We are *animals*.

Suddenly, I get a vision of Natalie cartwheeling across the floor. "Wait. Did you -"

"No," she cuts me off.

"You don't even know what I was going to ask."

"The answer is still no," she says, staring straight ahead.

She totally did. I grin. My very own gymnast.

"Christ." I flap my arms around. "How did we get so shit-faced?"

"The short Italian man with the cat in a diaper dropped by. Blame him. Marco, Matteo. Something with M," replies Jules.

"Mario? You mean, our landlord?"

"Uh-huh... Help." Jules is struggling to remove Natalie's pants. I yank them down over her hips and peel them off, one leg at a time. "Once he had a hint of a gathering, he raced upstairs and rejoined with a very, very large bottle of absinthe he got duty-free from Aeroporto di Roma."

"And we ran out of rosé, so... "

I turn, and Amy is crawling into the living room. "Do *not* ask me to stand." She's wiping smudged mascara from under her red eyes, then dry heaves a couple of times. Her suede top is a nice shade of green. Very similar to the color of her face. "It's impossible."

I take a brief moment to breathe in through my mouth, out through my nose so I don't throw up either.

God, I hope this story is funny in a couple of years.

"Last I remember, we were all sitting around getting on like a house on fire," quips Jules.

She gasps, and so do I.

"Fire!" I rush into the kitchen, having a vague smokey flashback from last night. There's a huge black stain on the ceiling above the cooktop visible from Africa, and the charred remains of something animal-like that I can't make out in a baking tray. Chicken, Turkey… Oh my God, please don't be Mario's cat.

I plaster my head to the cool counter and close my eyes. "Tell me Mario didn't leave Lorenzo here!"

"No. He dropped him home because he needed another diaper!" Jules yells back.

I feel a huge sigh of relief, and when I walk back in, I say to Amy, "We need another tin of paint."

Her head drops between her four legs. "That ceiling is exhausting."

"Appears the night disintegrated rather quickly," Jules concludes. "When did we get so old?"

Natalie removes her leggings and changes into her pants.

"I can't believe Mario was here to bear witness to… " I wave my hands around to my friends. "Oh my God, he is going to kick us out on the street!"

"Hopefully, we'll be in luck, and the absinthe wiped his memory, too," says Amy with forced positivity.

"Yeah, hope -" I break when I spot a foot.

It's human and very hairy.

"Mario," I gasp and point. "He's in the cat castle!"

Natalie grunts. "Does he not know that's for cats?"

Suddenly, Mario sits bolt upright, a fluffy catnip-scented mouse dropping off his bare shoulder, and we almost jump into the roof. He's sans shirt with more hair than a gorilla wearing only a pair of gray suspenders, face so pale he almost blends into the white backdrop of the palm tree wallpaper.

Mario clocks our half-dressed bodies, his bed in the cat castle, and coughs up what looks like an orange furball.

Ever so slowly, he blinks and blinks again, then in broken English, says, "No absinthe. I can not… Ever!" And collapses flat on his back within the castle walls.

Yes, Mario. I think we can all agree.

* * * * *

The morning is a mess.

An endless search for our belongings and a mad scramble to get showered and changed, but eventually, we're ready to go to work.

For a break in tradition, Natalie is wearing one of my dark, fitted shirts and also my underwear. Which is kind of hot now that my brain can semi-register it.

She decides to pick up two extra-large coffees from the coffee shop where we first met (her sentimentality is not lost on me), and we head to work in her car.

Hoping to feel human soon, I take a large gulp and press my head against the cool, buttery leather, closing my eyes. "Sorry to have derailed your morning routine."

Natalie smiles. "Hey, I turned up unannounced -"

My eyes spring open. "And seduced me. Yes."

We start laughing, and she reaches across, squeezing my hand.

"Things really took a turn for the south." Natalie pauses, and her eyes flick from the road to me. "I need to watch my words with you."

Caffeine slowly bringing my brain to life, I say, "Far too much sexual innuendo at this hour. You should probably get it all out of your system before your important meetings. Do you want to pull over?"

Natalie smiles over the steering wheel. "Think I should just focus on the road right now... And sorry, I keep forgetting to pick up that damn cat castle. I'll organize a courier today."

"Whenever is fine. Besides, it's handy having extra accommodation. I'm actually glad Mario had somewhere to sleep," I say with a giggle, and she rolls her eyes.

Things feel like they shifted up a gear this weekend. I'm not sure if it was Natalie showing me that she cared, staying at mine, or meeting my friends. But somehow, I can't help feeling excited.

Natalie gets an incoming call and frowns. "Sorry, I need to get this. It's my father." She presses a button. "Hello?"

"Natalie. Where the hell are you!" booms a voice over the speaker. "Did you forget you need to be on this conference call for the Gardenia deal?"

A pang of sorrow slices through me, and I instantly hate him for the tone he takes with her. Her father is some piece of work.

Something dark flashes across her face. Something that's always there with *him*. "I'll connect in a few minutes. I'm almost at work."

"Do you have any idea how bad this looks? I don't know what's gotten into you lately, but this reckless behavior is a disgrace. Hurry the hell up!" he yells, and there's a visible flinch in her cheek, followed by a click of the receiver.

He's gone.

I squeeze Natalie's hand, but she is as still as a statue, eyes firmly fixed on the road.

Privy to that conversation, the final piece of the puzzle appears to fall in place. Even though Natalie runs the business, she remains in a gilded cage with her father. Spacious but, nonetheless, locked, and much like a prison. Her father is slowly killing her. Something I think she already knows.

Her phone rings and rings, and we eventually pull to a stop in the underground parking lot of the building. Natalie looks down at the screen with a grimace and says, "I need to go."

My heart constricts because the more time I spend with her, the more I want, and I don't know how to stop feeling this way. I know she doesn't want a relationship, but I can't help but feel we're halfway there.

Leaning across, I cup her face and kiss her gently.

When we pull back, her eyes search mine, and I feel like Natalie has so much to say but chooses to stay silent. "Wait a few minutes and come up?" She traces my cheek with her finger, and I nod, and then I watch as she leaves the car and walks away.

My heart sinks a little, but my brain gives me a gentle slap and gets me into the office.

It takes me a while to get into the groove because my head is still in the clouds from last night, but by lunch, I'm far more relaxed. Natalie has been holed up in the boardroom, so I guess I'm not as distracted as I would normally be.

I've just had a meeting with Theo and Kayley about an upcoming project when Theo stays back to talk about his new boyfriend, Charles, whom he met in a panic room.

"Well, the stress of it all brought us together." He happily spins around in his chair. "My cousin, Kylie, brought him along, and I didn't know him from a bar of soap. But it appears fear and the need to escape really got things moving. Quite literally. He was squeezing my leg. I was squeezing his hand. You get the picture."

Theo and I start firing skittles into each other's mouths, and I giggle. "Great way of initiating contact."

"I know, right? Normally, it takes me a few dates to get so much action!"

Suddenly, I see smooth lines of an expensive suit in my peripheral vision, and my head snaps around just as a red skittle bops me on the head. And as if the office has suddenly become vacuum-sealed, all noise comes to an abrupt stop.

"Team looks like they are having fun," smirks a tall, polished woman in tailored pants. Her stiff white blouse buttoned up to her neck.

Oh, shit.

One breath in, one breath out.

Natalie is standing amongst a group of professional-looking people wearing "Visitor" badges, and I feel sets of appraising eyes casting judgment. More than a few of them chuckle.

"Hi," I say with a squeak, and a frown settles on her face, so deep, I can't even make out her eyes. My stomach sinks. Relaxed Natalie is gone.

"Mia. I need that design update for Schofields emailed through to production by close of business." Her voice is stiff, like she's talking to a stranger, and I'm not going to lie. It hurts.

All the same, I nod, and they walk past. I watch as they wander down the aisle, conversations end, keyboards start clacking, and online shopping windows close.

"Freaking journalist tour of the office." Theo chews nervously on a pen cap. "I missed the reminder in my calendar."

As did I.

Dammit. Why didn't Natalie mention this in the car? And just like that, I go from floating in the air to wanting to bury myself six feet under.

After lunch, Natalie strides past with her head down, phone pressed to her ear, and then she just disappears.

In fact, she doesn't return to the office, and even though, I get a sparkling new bed delivered the next day, I don't hear from her at all.

CHAPTER TWENTY-TWO
NATALIE

It's Thursday, and I'm finally back from San Francisco after confidential talks with investors for my new business.

I pretended I was in town meeting with Lydia to avoid arousing suspicion. Well, I did meet her for one brain-frying hour, but the rest of the time was dedicated to organizing financing and drafting contracts.

I shut my office door, kick off my heels, and scrape together nearly two hours to plow through urgent items relating to Dalton Media. Setting up a new business *and* running this place means my batteries are almost empty. Working almost seven days a week, I'm exhausted, but I have no choice but to push through.

Just after midday, my door clicks open, and I sense an annoying presence.

I don't need to look up to know it's my father, so I don't.

With my head down, I ignore his babbling for the most part and only engage when I see fit. "No, for the last time. Charlie Chen will not be CFO," I say, still typing. "He's currently under investigation for fraud."

"I'm not sure if you're just dim-witted or what?" My father has always had a way with words. Luckily, I'm immune to them. "If he quits, we'll lose those multi-million-dollar contracts with Epsom. What happens then?"

"Our reputation will improve because we'll eliminate a bad seed. One down, a few more to go. Stop hiring shady characters."

He snarls. "You won't get a cent from me, Natalie."

"Good. Now that you've finished chastising me, can I get back to running the company? I'm very busy."

There's a pause, and just when I think he's about to leave, he says, "Miss Andrews. Quite the delectable little creature, isn't she?"

I stand so abruptly that my chair skids back, banging into the wall. So, now he's got my full attention.

He's rubbing his chin, resting a hand on the glass wall. One look at him standing there like a tourist in a gift store, and I know he is practically undressing her with his eyes. He revolts me to my core. My own father.

He turns and laughs. Like actually laughs.

I grit my teeth, and my pencil snaps in half. "Get out now."

"Ah, and there it is." He starts wagging his finger at my broken pencil, smirking. "Your Achilles heels. Thought so when I saw the photo of the two of you in the paper. Nothing wrong with having an eye for beauty."

My stomach churns. "I am nothing like you. Touch her, and I'll kill you," I growl.

There's no way I'll let him make work another hunting ground. No way.

He walks over to my desk, hands tucked in his pockets, and leans in, smelly sick. "You don't think I'm scared of you, do you?"

"You should be."

"You've always been your mother's daughter," he snaps, and I'm this close to hitting him with the entire contents of the stationery cupboard.

I throw him a glare, soaked with repulsion. Words exploding from my mouth bitterly. "And you've always been a garbage human. Out of my office now, or I'll have you escorted."

He holds up his hands, grinning wolfishly. "On my way. Need to pick up my suit for the charity ball with Miss Andrews tonight. I'm always up for a challenge." His voice quiet and menacing. "Bet I can crack her in forty-eight hours."

With one final wink, he waltzes out the door.

I snatch the phone. "Nancy. I need you to make some urgent reservations."

* * * * *

Since there's zero chance I'm going to enjoy this conversation, I decide to get it over with.

I've hardly been in the office, so I haven't seen Mia since last Friday. Still, I *know* I've consciously put some space between us.

Drowning in responsibility and outside noise, I'm struggling to cope with everything on my plate, and I don't know how else to deal with it but to take a step back. Even if it's the last thing I want.

Staring out the window, I take a deep breath and then turn when I hear her approach. Although I've done my prep, I'm not remotely ready for her sailing into the boardroom.

Her hair is up in a messy knot that young women seem to love, and she's wearing a gorgeous rust-colored wool dress that clings to every curve. Her poise is calm, chin up, and in complete contrast to me because, honestly, I feel like I'm disappearing into the floor.

"You wanted to see me?" she asks cooly.

Yep, definitely not too happy with me.

"Yes, Mia. Please take a seat," I say, deliberately avoiding her eye. I need to remain clinical, but everything about this, the formality, feels weird.

Mia picks a seat halfway between me and the door – somewhere safe. Even I'm edging toward the wall for safety.

I swallow my emotions before I face her, the blonde expanse of the meeting table between her and me. But when I meet her eyes, something pinches in my chest. "There's a client in Montana, the Bergman account, and I need you to go."

I see her shoulders tensing as I speak, and silence descends in the room.

"But isn't that the crazy guy that lives in the shed?" she asks, spine erect, hands demurely resting in her lap.

I cock an eyebrow, still standing up. "Larry Bergman. Yes. He operates his organic crop farm business from shipping containers on his ranch."

Mia seems to regard me with suspicion. "But that's Margot's account? And hardly adds anything to our bottom line."

I suppress a groan. "Yes. You'll be taking her place," I say, clipped. "Your flight leaves tonight. You'll be gone for two days."

"*Two* days?" she echoes so skeptically that I stare at her. "Can't we just arrange a zoom meeting? And why me?"

I rub my brow. "Larry wants a new landing page for his summer campaign. It's simple. You have design experience, and she doesn't."

"Surely, Margot can just speak to him and take some notes. You realize she's going to go ballistic?" Her eyes darkening with annoyance. "I also have the Gottlieb charity ball with your father tonight at City Hall. I even bought a dress that cost an arm and a leg. He's already made arrangements to pick me up from my apartment."

He knows her address. I bristle. "Give the receipt to Penny in Accounts today, and you'll be reimbursed immediately."

Mia pauses and then narrows her eyes. "And this has nothing to do with... *us*?"

Of course, I'm sending her away on purpose.

"No." I look away before her eyes swallow me whole. "Take the rest of the afternoon off and go and pack."

"But none of this makes sense." Mia isn't buying any of it; that's clear from her stony expression. "Don't treat me like a baby."

"Don't act like one," I deadpan.

Our eyes meet and hold. Seconds tick by, she doesn't waver, and I sidestep the squeeze of emotion in my throat. "Dammit, Mia. You're going, and that's final. You have no say in the matter."

"Charming. You should work in marketing."

"Luckily, my talents lie elsewhere."

Mia crosses her arms. "I prefer you out of work. You appear to have had a complete personality transplant from the last time you were in my bed."

I rub my forehead and snap back, "I was fine before you came along and confused everything."

And with that single line, I've exposed myself.

"Oh, then it *absolutely* has to do with us." Mia sits there with a face like thunder. "So, now that you're finished with me, you send me to bumfuck nowhere to free you up? What for the next one?"

I force myself to meet her eyes. "I'm the boss, so I'm pretty sure I can do whatever I like."

Biggest dick line ever, and I'm cringing the moment I say it.

We stare at each other in terse silence.

"Great," she says with a layer of sarcasm. "Are we done?"

I nod.

Mia shoots up from her chair and storms out, but not before I hear a very audible "Asshole."

I grip the edge of the table, closing my eyes while my stomach twists with regret.

Somehow, I've managed to screw things six ways to Sunday.

CHAPTER TWENTY-THREE

M I A

Irritated? Of course, I am.

Yes, we agreed it would be a one-time roll in the hay. Okay, well, a few rolls.

Yes, I knew that feelings would inevitably rise up and smack me in the face.

But no, I wasn't expecting her to go out of her way to ignore me or to send me to Montana in place of Margot to meet some freaking cowboy.

It's surprising Margot hasn't confronted me yet, but I know it will happen soon. After an hour of banging on the keyboard at some spreadsheets, I decide I need a break and head to the bathroom.

A figure immediately springs up behind me in the mirror. "Mia."

Obviously, I startle. When I see her thunderous face, it feels like a scene from Fatal Attraction. "Jesus, Margot."

"Don't Jesus me," she says with a spiteful sneer and angrily crosses her arms against her camel-colored designer dress. "You think you can just waltz in here, daggy as hell, not giving a care in the world. Everybody listening to you. I've been here for years! You didn't even go to college. God, look at your shoes!"

Huh?

I look down, perplexed. What's wrong with my shoes? Sure, they were a bargain, but...

"I turn up here every day trying to be seen, and then you go steal my account!" Her chin dancing like Jell-O as she fumes. "Spread your legs for the boss, did you?"

Hmm. Well, this is awkward. So many things I could say right now...

Instead, I focus on keeping my stare strong. Margot is so enraged it would be frightening, but for the fact, one of her eyelashes flutters to the ground a moment later.

For God's sake. The woman is falling apart.

Against my better judgment, I bend down and retrieve it. "Here." I slap it in her hand. "Has it ever occurred to you that my life hasn't been all unicorns, Margot? I'm insecure about everything. Everyone has shit they go through. We are all just trying to do the best we can and put a smile on our faces. I've got to where I am because I work hard and try to be a decent human. Maybe try it sometime! And I happen to like my shoes!"

Rant complete, I spin on my heel and leave Margot to reattach body parts.

I just don't get it. Surely Natalie knew this would send Margot into a tailspin and put an even larger target on my back. What game is she playing at?

Natalie's been aloof since she stayed at mine. I know she's struggling with work. Maybe it's just too much for her, maybe I'm too much. Regardless, I miss our usual banter. Her work emails have been short and strictly professional. Not even a selfie on my new bed elicited a reply.

I've never cared about someone with such heated abandon, and I thought that she hadn't either, so what's changed?

It can't be the freaking skittle incident. I mean, not my finest moment, but surely, not a reason to ice me out. I have no idea. Maybe Natalie *is* that fickle.

Oh, my head.

Unfortunately, Natalie is as easy to read as a blank sheet. New anger icing the scalding attraction that consumes me. Then it hits me, she has the ability to knock me over, and I don't like it one bit.

Thankfully, Amy agrees to meet me for a drink at the hole-in-the-wall Irish bar diagonally across from work because I need to calm down before my flight tonight. Even though the menus look like they are printed from a back-office computer, they do great prime rib sliders and three-dollar shrimp tacos, so I'm sure we'll stress eat a few of those too.

"Thank you so much for meeting me," I say to Amy, who is totally rocking a biker jacket and short red textured skirt.

We push through the sticky wooden door into a dimly lit space. It's crowded, bustling with a four o'clock rush.

"Any excuse to leave work early. Plus, those tacos have my name all over them."

I grin, and we weave around a wall of people.

"So, what's doing with Natalie?"

"Honestly, who knows? I'm such a mess trying to work out all these different signals she's giving me. I know she cares on some level. She's also under a lot of pressure. I mean, she never made any promises, but -" I stop dead. "Oh, hell no." My eyes spot Natalie sitting at the bar, and a new bullet of anger pierces my gut.

"What?" Amy asks, following my line of sight. Her eyes widen. "Oh, shit."

I'm already pissed off at her, and when I see the waif-like woman in a black leather skirt and a skimpy top next to her, throwing her head back and laughing hysterically at something she said, my vision turns red.

My mind immediately jumping to conclusions. She's been distant, and now, she's sending me away because she's moved on. Really? My heart is throbbing in my ears. I hate the fact that she affects me so much.

"I wouldn't if -" Amy grabs my wrist, and I throw her hand away, charging over like a psycho, my fists balling like angry stones.

"Sweetheart." I run my hand down her spine. Natalie startles, her head snapping around, and I curse the traitorous zing that skyrockets through my blood when our eyes meet. "Aren't you supposed to be 'working'?"

God, I love a good air quote when I'm irate.

The woman next to her slowly stirs her martini with a skewer of olives, and I make a quick assessment. She's beautiful and blonde with sparkly sapphire eyes and a sunkissed tan. She's also younger than me.

I hate her.

Natalie's lips pull tight into a flat line. "Sorry. Do I know you?" she asks with a flash of annoyance in her voice.

I laugh. "Sweetheart. You're too much. God, you have one... " I pick up her neon yellow cocktail and take a swig. "Pina Colada with an umbrella?" Is she kidding me right now?

"And you forget the most important person in your life. Your wife."

"Oh. Ha-ha. Very funny." Natalie turns to the woman, who is halfway through choking on her olive, and whispers behind her hand, "You know, she has the wackiest sense of -"

"Your wife?" The woman finally splutters.

"Uh-huh. That's me!" I nod as Natalie corrects, "My cousin."

The woman visibly recoils, but eyes still drift over Natalie's cleavage.

Seriously? That's not a deal breaker?

I'm going to chop that designer dress into a thousand pieces.

"Wait." The woman narrows her eyes at Natalie. Thank God, I think the penny has finally dropped. "You married your cousin?"

Not the brightest spark.

The Scandinavian-looking bartender cleverly backs away while Natalie swings her legs around, swiveling on the stool. She pins me with a deathly glare that promises a slow, drawn-out end to my life that most likely involves suffocation and torture devices to render me mute.

"Our divorce papers are currently being drawn up by the lawyers," Natalie clarifies.

I yank her toward me with surprising force and step between her legs. I strategically pin her hips down so she can't move *or* kill me. "Papers haven't been signed yet. This is our last shot, and boy, are we going to give it our all!"

The woman eyes us suspiciously. "How long have you been together?"

"Six months," Natalie says just as I say, "One incredible year."

"Engaged for six months, married for six. She's always forgetting important dates because she has a thing for ditzy models who wear leather, frequent Irish dive bars, and have nothing between their ears." I glare at the woman, but she just blinks. The not-so-subtle dig missed entirely. God, some people are slow. "Anyway, that's why we're getting divorced."

"You cheat?" asks the woman.

Natalie's head whips my way, and she points. "She started it. When she asked our Brazilian housekeeper, Carol, and her partner if they wanted to have group sex. Carol was so mortified that she quit the next day. Then she moved on to our hairdresser, Zara. She's relentless." Natalie whispers to the woman, "See, she's into the kinky stuff." Then looks up at me brightly. "Isn't that right?"

I'm pretty sure my eyes glow red at this point.

The woman puts her glass on the bar. "Oh, God. You two have some serious issues. I think I need to go home, lie down, and purge my mind of this entire conversation."

I wrap my arm around Natalie's shoulder with crushing force, hoping to leave a permanent mark, while the woman slips off her stool and rushes away. She glances over her shoulder with a look of apathy, then disappears.

"So, I take it you're a bit pissed off?" Natalie asks.

A dry, sardonic laugh bursts out of me. "Is that really a serious question?" I ask, eyes flashing with temper, and give her one final wide-eyed glare before turning away, whipping my curtain of hair over my shoulder.

"Mia, wait."

Her voice drifts after me, but I don't stop.

I merely give her the middle finger over my shoulder and stalk off into the night.

CHAPTER TWENTY-FOUR

MIA

My trip to Montana turned out to be a total waste of time, but I could've told you that.

The highlight was riding Clyde the Shetland pony. There were two lowlights: The first, listening to Larry Bergman sing and play guitar around the campfire, and the second, his wife Lynette forcing us to applaud, which only encouraged Larry to continue long into the night.

Of course, there was radio silence from Natalie, but a call from Joan post-pony ride on Friday seemed to lift my spirits when she told me that Natalie had been in a particularly dark mood since I left. My legs were a bit wobbly at our run-in at the bar, but it was kind of liberating seeing her stupefied face.

I arrive back in San Diego Saturday afternoon with a fresh determination not to think about Natalie and her cold shoulder, the hussy in the bar, sending me to hang with a tuneless cowboy. Shit. This is going to be harder than I thought.

The fridge doesn't offer much inspiration, so I hurtle downstairs to the corner store and get a tub of Kit Kat flavored ice cream.

Spoon in hand, I park myself on the couch, wearing my slouchy track pants and worn t-shirt, and mindlessly eat my way through the entire tub. All the while, staring at my phone and willing it to light up, torturing myself in the process.

When I'm done with that, I try to listen to a podcast, but the upbeat voice irritates me, so I quit that too. With my Netflix queue empty and absolutely nothing left to do, I log in to Tinder, swiping left and right until it gets too depressing to carry on.

What an incredibly productive afternoon of nothing.

God, what did I do before Natalie?!

Grabbing a cushion, I yell into it and then throw myself back onto the couch. I must doze off because I'm woken by my phone buzzing from within the cushions. Amy lighting up the screen.

AMY: *Don't get mad.*

You should never lead with this line. I'm automatically on edge.

AMY: *I have someone you should meet. Like a distraction.*

ME: *Amy. I'm not going on a date.*

AMY: *Not a date. A mere meeting of minds. Bronte's café across the street in like fifteen minutes!*

ME: *???*

AMY: *She's single.*

ME: *That doesn't work anymore!*

AMY: *Apparently, she's cute, funny, and has a JOB.*

ME: *Apparently??*

AMY: *She comes highly recommended through a friend of a friend of an acquaintance.*

ME: *ABSOLUTELY NOT!*

AMY: *She has pets.*

ME: *. . .*

AMY: *PETS! Are you listening, Mia? Not one, but multiple P-E-T-S!*

ME: *Keep talking...*

AMY: *Two cats, one dog, and a bird.*

My fingers hover over the message. Maybe I do need a distraction. At some point, I also really need to say no to Amy.

AMY: *I'm going to take your silence as a yes.*

ME: *Ffs. Okay.*

Clearly, not today.

I look down at my outfit and make an assessment. Put on jeans and keep the t-shirt but add a bra and some deodorant.

AMY: *Yay! And don't even think about wearing your loungewear! Or your Target tennis shoes!*

My head swings around, checking the roof for surveillance. What the fuck?

I groan loudly.

ME: *Okay, okay. I'll be there soon.*

AMY: *Boom!*

With great reluctance, I tear myself away from the sanctity of the couch and go to my room to get ready. Even though I'm alone, I complain the entire time and vent to my spiky cacti (amazing listeners).

Seven minutes later, I splash some water on my face, brush my teeth, and intentionally bypass the mirror on my way out.

* * * * *

I'm back.

Amy is hoovering with a chicken nugget dangling from her mouth and startles when she sees me, flicking off the vacuum. "What are you doing back so early?" she asks and seems to swallow her nugget whole. She launches into a coughing fit. "It can't have been half an hour. Did Melissa not show?"

"Amy Buchanan. Bend over."

She drops the vacuum and covers her butt. "No. I'm scared."

I walk toward her. She backs up toward the hallway. "Mia… "

"How the fuck could you not tell me that Melissa walks around with a parrot on her shoulder all day?" I fling my arms in the air.

Her cheeks dot with pink. "What all day?"

"So, you knew about the parrot on the shoulder?" I almost shriek.

Rather than distract me from Natalie, this calamitous meet and greet has just galvanized the fact that she's exactly what I'm after.

"Wait." Amy blinks. "She turned up with the parrot to the actual café?"

"Yes."

"Ha!" A laugh bursts out of her, and she slaps her hand over her mouth. "Sorry."

"It's a pet-friendly café. Willy, the parrot, repeated everything. I thought I was going mad. By the twenty-minute mark and listening to a repeat of her very bland life story from said parrot, I was out of there, but not before the parrot called me a shithead. Harry, Janet's husband, is the shithead! Not me!"

Amy is snorting with laughter in her sleeve. "I love everything about this story."

I roll my eyes. "Melissa was a crap conversationalist, by the way."

"Maybe that's why she brought the bird," Amy counters and wipes away tears.

I stare at her. "Really?"

Amy starts giggling. "Come on. It's a little bit funny," she says in a quiet voice and then holds her thumb and index finger together. "Just a teeny bit?"

Now I'm glaring, but my lips twitch slightly. "You're starting to become an annoying flatmate." I edge closer, and she shuffles back. "And you still need to pay, Amy."

"No. Okay. Mia. No! Whatever you want. I'll bend over. Please just don't tickle me." Amy screams before I even touch her. "Last time I peed my pants. I had ten glasses of water today. TEN. It won't be pretty. Please. You wouldn't be so cruel."

"Mmm. I think I would." I start to run, and she swivels, sprinting barefoot down the hallway. "Mia! No!" This time she screams like a banshee. Honestly, I wouldn't be surprised if the police turned up.

Either way, I've latched onto her leg, and Amy Buchanan is going down. Whether or not she pees her pants is entirely up to her.

CHAPTER TWENTY-FIVE
NATALIE

Everything has changed.

Everything is different.

I'm not joking. Mia has ruined me.

My mind a thick, white fog. I've barely slept this week. Even fantasizing about being in her apartment with the broken bed slash futon and crap all over the floor.

Because despite being a world away from what I'm used to, I felt an aching sense of belonging. There I was away from pretension, away from my father's web, and away from the ghosts of my past that have always defined my life.

First time in a long time, I remembered what it's like to be human. Someone who can feel, laugh and just be.

Mia has given me a glimpse of what is on the other side of my prison walls, and now it's all I want. I've fallen for her, despite not wanting or agreeing to be. She clawed her way into my heart. There, taking more and more space, until nothing was left but her.

"This is all your fault, Fabio. Things started to go haywire when you two started hanging out," I end up venting to my cat, but I know my anger is sorely misplaced.

Either way, I'm completely useless without her.

Sleep. Work. Stare.

Not even an endless supply of coffee will snap me out of my reverie. So, I submerge myself in digital strategies, IT-recommended upgrades, and people I don't give a shit about, but that doesn't help either because I'm back to thinking about the woman who wanted to stab me between the eyes in the bar.

Obviously, Mia jumped to conclusions. Her last-minute trip to Montana had nothing to do with the fact I was chatting with that woman. I was actually waiting for my lawyer, who was running late.

Now, I can't get that interaction out of my mind. Go fucking figure. She haunts me through the day and comes for me at night. Feelings start rioting through me because, without her, my life has reverted back to monochrome.

I'm still processing all this when Joan runs her customary scan over me. We're waiting in the seated area of Dr. Yip's surgery for her monthly check-up. "What's wrong, Natalie?"

"Nothing," I grumble, and she levels me with a look. "Well, maybe the raw fish taco I had for lunch," I offer lamely.

"No." Joan waves her hand over my face. "Whatever that is, it's not indigestion." Suddenly, she grips the armrests of her chair like a toddler. Her knuckles start to turn white. "I won't go in."

"Oh, for God's sake. Here we go again with the threats! You're unbelievable." Her cat-like eyes burn into my temples. "Ugh, I'm sure you can work it out," I huff, flicking off imaginary lint from my sateen pants.

Joan visibly relaxes. "Mia... " She starts grinning like a cat that swallowed a canary. "Well, well, well. That's why you're moodier than ever. She's gotten to you."

"Happy?"

Her eyes, bigger than saucers, glow at me. "Immensely!"

"Well. Look at me now. I haven't slept in days. I've been joining Fabio in his witching hour. Not quite flinging myself against the walls yet, but I tell you, I'm not far off!"

Joan rolls her eyes. "Oh, such a drama llama. Are you really complaining?"

"Of course!" I nod, then scrunch up my face a second later. "I don't know... No," I sigh. "I sent her to Montana. My father was going to hit on her at the ball, and I just couldn't bear... "

"Oh, I see. Ronald had his dirty little pincers out again."

"Yes, but my delivery to Mia was off. I think because I'm stressed but also because I miss her. You know, I've been so busy with work and trying to get things moving with my new business. And the whole thing with Mia has been affecting my judgment so badly. I've been forgetting things and making mistakes. Everything was going too fast. So, I thought that some space between us might help, but now I'm even more of a mess! All I can think about is *her*. If I'm honest, it's a total clusterfu-" I pause, and a lady in a print dress with pineapples whips her head to me.

"Sorry," I mouth, and then whisper to Joan, "You know what I mean."

"Yes, a total clusterfuck. I know," she practically booms, and the pineapple woman rolls her eyes at both of us.

I give Joan a wide-eyed look.

"What? I'm not a thousand years old, you know." She shakes her head. "I see the way you look at her. The way she looks at you. Plus, Fabio adores her. He doesn't even pee in her shoes."

"How do you know?" I tilt my head back. "Oh, right. Your lunch dates."

"Uh-huh. Well, Fabio has peed in all your exes' shoes. I think Mia's a keeper, and you're blowing it."

I drag my hand down my face. "Tell me what you really think."

"You're complaining about a connection people search for their whole life. You know, the course of true love never did run smooth, Natalie. Life's too long to live with regrets. Why can't you run a business and love Mia at the same time? Just get more organized, delegate if you're getting overwhelmed. Stop trying to prove to the world that you can do everything. That's what you have staff for, right?"

I look over, and I think I even go red. "Yes?"

Joan's certainly a chatterbox today, and from all the surreptitious glances I'm coping, it appears we have quite the audience.

She continues. "Maybe she's just opened your eyes to what you truly want."

"Which is?"

"A partner that is *finally* your match. Someone that makes you want to be a better woman. Oh, and to wholly remove yourself from your father's grasp once and for all."

"Can you please stop being so wise?"

Joan chuckles. "Like the young people say. Time to pull your head out of your ass, Natalie."

"Joan!" I gasp, and a single man with a paunch snorts a laugh. I lean into her. "What is going on with you today? You're out of control."

She giggles and reaches across, squeezing my hand. "The moment Mia walked in wearing your sweater, she changed you. It wasn't profound but gradual. In the way, you started smiling more. In the way, you softened around the edges. In the way, work became less important. This isn't something you'll just get over. Make it right with Mia. I mean it, or she will walk away. She doesn't know you sent her away to protect her. From her perspective, you don't care. She'll start dating someone else. Probably not someone with a parrot on their shoulder again, but she *is* a staunch animal lover, so -"

"Parrot?" Joan shuffles in her seat, and I narrow my eyes. My mind working very quickly. "Joan. Did she -"

"No." She cuts me off sharply, then shakes her head and hands and basically her whole body. "Oh, stop getting distracted from my point! Natalie, you can have the life you've always dreamed of. As far as I can see, everything is there for the taking. Sometimes you just need to be brave and go for it. Plus, unfortunately, I love you like my own and want to see you happy."

I frown at her, but I know I'm absorbing every word she's saying. "What would I do without you, Joan?"

"Honestly, I shudder to think about it."

I start to laugh, and Joan grins wider, still.

Once Joan is given the all-clear by her doctor and a new script for blood pressure medication, we head back to the office. She's right. I've been treading water during my time at Dalton Media. No more dilly-dallying. I'm fast-tracking the life

I want and setting an actual deadline to get out of here. But first things first. Mia.

I do as I'm told and pull my head out of my ass, ordering a big bunch of exotic flowers from boutique florist, Amethyst, in East Village, and click through the cards. Definitely not the colorful Macaw. Suddenly, I have a hatred for all birds.

I know the flowers are not enough, and we need to have a proper conversation, but it's a start because, right now, I miss everything about her. I miss how she smiles almost all the time, even when she's sleeping. I miss her warmth which melts the icy chill that sometimes enters my heart. I even miss sparring with her and, oddly, her poking her tongue out at me.

Who knew that could be so endearing?

But most of all, I just miss her presence.

It's staggering how quickly and how fiercely I've fallen for her.

Somehow, when I am with Mia, I feel more like myself than I ever have. I used to be so serious, and she brings out a playfulness that I'd long forgotten I had. Who knew cartwheeling across a living room would be my new party trick?

My eyes catch on a headline of a paper sitting in my tray. It appears to have been strategically placed on top of a stack of urgent marketing reports. Honestly, Joan will be the end of me.

I snatch the paper and let out a long breath.

Could Dalton Media CEO Natalie Dalton and senior designer Mia Andrews be the new dream team?

There's a picture of the two of us at that stupid team-building event in Florida. I'm covered in mud and sticks like some grotty gutter rat living under the subway. Seriously, they couldn't publish a better photo?

Of course, Mia looks breathtaking. She's beaming at me, and I can't seem to tear my eyes away from her. Hang on. This was right after she intentionally groped me. Thank God they didn't take a shot five seconds earlier. I look closer. They've captured something that I'm not quite ready to see. I actually look happy. I'm smiling from the inside out.

I sigh audibly and put the paper down.

Mia's the sole reason for the constant ache in my chest. She is also offsite today, visiting clients in LA, while I've just decided I'll be in San Francisco for the rest of the week. The finish line almost in sight, and this time, nothing can stop me.

Still, I already know there won't be a minute that passes where I won't be thinking about Mia. Or this damn photo.

* * * * *

On Monday, the moment the air pressure changes, my stomach flips, knowing we are coming to land at San Diego airport, and I'll be seeing Mia in the office.

I haven't heard anything about the flowers, but I wasn't expecting to. Either way, it feels like an eternity since we have spoken.

The sky is overcast, with rain threatening as the cab enters the city. I ask the driver to drop me off a couple of blocks from the office so I can grab a latte from my favorite lunch spot. Soon, I'm draining my cup and urgently shouldering my way through the human traffic in the Gaslamp Quarter.

Just as I approach the entry of our shiny metal tower, a car pulls up. The rear door flings open, and I spot a black high heel, followed by a shapely calf.

I'd recognize that leg anywhere. Like always, a thrill zings up my spine, my skin prickling at the sight of her. Mia steps out onto the sidewalk in a short deep blue wrap dress that flows around her like some aura. Her blonde hair is pulled back in a ponytail, wisps of hair escaping and framing her jawline.

She disappears inside, hair swinging behind her, and I break out into a run across the marble floor. I squeeze in through the closing elevator doors, and her body visibly tenses. Her expression remains fixed, looking straight ahead.

"Hey... How was your weekend?" I ask, moving beside her as the cart jolts into action.

Her cheek flinches. "Busy," she replies stiffly.

I raise my eyebrow.

"Shredding your flowers," Mia scoffs. "And yes, you were an ass."

I feel my mouth twitch.

Wow, I've missed this. Well, at least I know she read the card.

The red numbers creep up on the display.

Three.

Four.

Five.

I need more time.

"What about you? Sending anyone else to the back of beyond so you can have dates with blonde Barbies?" she asks saucily, and I roll my eyes.

Honestly, this woman will be the death of me.

"I was meeting my lawyer, Jo Crawley," I reply. "Supposed to sign some papers today, but she's heading to Portugal, so we arranged to meet earlier. I had a drink at the bar because Jo was running late. I don't know who that woman was."

Mia eyes me skeptically. "Likely story."

"It's true. Joan will verify. Besides, I seem to have a thing for mouthy women with back-breaking beds who like to do strange role-plays in public settings."

"Too bad they hate you," she quips.

I chuckle, and I swear I see the hint of a smile as the elevator dings our arrival. She walks into the office, head straight and shoulders back, with noticeably more sway to her hips.

One hundred percent taunting me.

Despite her sass, that interaction certainly lifts my spirits. And as measly as it was, I think it will be enough to get me through my tedious afternoon with the company accountant.

CHAPTER TWENTY-SIX
NATALIE

The last couple of weeks have been a blur, but Friday morning, I have total clarity.

I walk into the office knowing exactly what I need to do, and funnily enough, I've never felt more at ease.

I've got board members calling me non-stop. Twenty-two messages. Most are retired executives who know a company is only as good as its leadership, and they're probably even more concerned about whom my father will put in my place. Obviously, there are a dozen less pleasant messages from my father himself.

But it only strengthens my resolve to get the hell out of here. I am selling my share of the business, my resignation effective immediately. Sure, I forgo some generous benefits, but I can't be here a day longer. Not for my sanity and not if I want the life I've always imagined.

Today is going to be the day I bury what remains of my relationship with the man that despises me only a little less than I despise him.

"Morning, Nancy," I practically whistle while I pick up reminders and callbacks.

Nancy's head snaps up, reading glasses askew. "Morning, Natalie. Here's your daily schedule and some news bulletins. You have a noon lunch with Jorga regarding renewing his contract, a two o'clock with Shelley Black, and a briefing with Legal at four."

"No, not today. Please cancel all meetings and clear my schedule." I tap her shoulder, feeling lighter than I have in years.

"Oh, okay." Nancy pauses and lowers her voice. "Should I arrange a security detail? Or perhaps a pre-emptive restraining order against your father?" she asks nervously, slipping one hand straight into the candy jar.

Joan and Nancy were the only ones that were given a heads-up about my resignation because I didn't want to risk sabotaging the company I was preparing to raid. But now, with everything in place, I'm ready for the dominos to start falling.

"No. It'll all be fine," I reply calmly. "And I'd like to chat with you after my father leaves. Say Bert's café across the road?"

"Okay... " Nancy says slowly and looks down at her diary. "But he doesn't have a meeting penciled in today."

"He'll be here shortly," I say simply. "Oh, have you seen Mia this morning? I wanted to have a chat with her."

Nancy looks at her screen. "She's offsite at the Bauer Media networking event. Not sure if she's coming back into the office."

"What? Oh, okay. Thanks." I smile, but my stomach turns over because I wanted to speak to her privately about my news. I guess our conversation will have to wait. Our last interaction in the elevator certainly gave me a bit of pep in my step, and I'm determined to show her how I feel and make things right. "I'll be in my office if you need me, Nancy."

Five minutes later, I hear a commotion and look up from my desk. Just as I expected, my lousy excuse for a father is storming across the floor with Ronnie trotting on her heels to keep up, breasts bouncing every which way.

I brace myself for the onslaught as the door swings open, shuddering on its hinges, and my father explodes into the room.

"Good morning," I beam.

His laugh is mirthless. "I don't think so!" he spits.

"Before you start motoring on. Here." I stand and shove a letter in his hand with my demands.

A short while later, he's practically combusting. "You stupid fool... You... Have you lost your goddamn mind?"

"No," I reply with measured patience. "Don't think so. Our business model is passe. Time to go in a new direction."

"By skinning the company of all its resources?" he barks, face swelling with anger.

"Only the good ones," I wink.

"Natalie. You're playing with fire. I will destroy you," he warns. "I know the best lawyers in the country, and trust me, I know how to play dirty."

"Mmm, you certainly do, but not this time," I say, knowing that this whale-sized sex scandal I've unearthed has just nailed his metaphorical coffin. My clown of a father, a PR disaster of his own. "Plus, if you don't agree, I'm going straight to the press. Seems Ronnie is pretty open after two bottles of wine and a greasy slab of pizza. Isn't that right?" I glare at her, and she smiles with her ill-applied lipstick.

Oh my God, she thinks it's a compliment.

I pick up a file and snap it open. "I have the name of all your floozies plus… " I chirp. "Compromising photos. Surprisingly vigorous for a seventysomething-year-old man. Some of these moves are outrageous. The media would have a field day. But seriously, dick pics? A little low-brow and crude. Even for you." I lean forward in a whisper, "You know, this might just sink your beloved IPO."

"They came onto me!" he stammers.

"The pictures definitely look that way," I say sarcastically. "What woman could resist Ron Dalton in all his glory?"

I probably do need that restraining order Nancy offered me because if looks could kill, I'd be dead on the spot.

"Oh, and I also stumbled across undeclared millions in an offshore account. Wonder what the IRS will say about that?"

My father points at me with a stubby finger. "You… you… goddamn." He paces back and forth in the small room and then hurls a chair between us which has Ronnie shrieking.

For a second, I marvel at the irony. My father cheating on my mom. His meandering all but costing him his share of the business. I suspect Ronnie will also leave him and take him to the cleaners. Looks like we've come full circle.

I hide my hands which are shaking by now. My face still impassive as stone. "I know it's a bit late, but consider this my anniversary present to you." I pat his shoulder and wink at my stepmom, making my way to the door. "Thanks, Ronnie. You have no idea how much this means. After eight years, I can finally repay the favor."

My father's face almost snaps in half, and he tries to put an arm on my shoulder. "Wait, right there, young lady!"

I shake him off almost violently. "Do *not* touch me."

He shoots me a dirty look. "I want to have the honor of throwing you out of here personally. No way will I let you remove any of our property."

I force myself to jerk my chin up. "I have legs. I don't need you. And you can keep all of it."

For *now*.

Once his lawyer reads the letter of demand, they'll see that I'm bringing most of the resources with me, including the staff.

I turn and, finally, I'm able to walk out on my life at Dalton Media without looking back, without any regrets.

CHAPTER TWENTY-SEVEN

MIA

Something isn't right.

This weird dread has been at me all day. When I return from the networking event, I see Natalie leaving with a smile so big, she's practically skipping out of the building. Naturally, she didn't see me, but her sunny disposition only adds to my unease.

Conversation floats around me in the elevator.

'Company is heading in a new direction, but we've been kept in the dark... '

'Apparently, she's been working on a top-secret venture for months... '

Things get even stranger in the office because everyone's quiet.

Everyone except Margot.

She's whistling and doing some weird shimmy dance, which goes entirely against the grain of who she is.

My stomach starts churning, and I crack. "Okay, will someone tell me what's going on?"

Margot slides across on her ten-inch heels, dropping one shoulder. "Oh, your lover has left. Like for good."

My heart stops inside my chest.

"Natalie resigned. Looks like she's heading to San Francisco to take up a new post at a second-tier marketing company," Margot says with a flip of her shiny blonde hair. "Probably shacking up with Lydia Longman too."

"Stop spreading rumors," snaps Nancy at the same time as Theo says, "Put a cork in it, Margot."

I excuse myself.

It hits me in successive churning waves, and my mind starts racing. This is permanent. She's moving to another city. I'll have a new boss. She will meet the woman of her dreams, that isn't me.

Why the fuck did I tell her I shredded her flowers when they're sitting on my desk in my room in full bloom!

Oh, God.

I squeeze my eyes shut against tears and hunch over, latching onto my desk since my legs can't seem to do their job.

"What the hell is wrong with you? Cramps?" Margot asks crudely.

I inhale a jagged breath, running a shaky hand through my hair. "No, nothing."

"Well. Can you act normal and do some actual work? That's what we pay you for."

She really thinks she runs this place. Well, not today, Satan.

I try to think of a smart reply. "Fuck off, Margot."

Sometimes you don't need to be that smart.

When I look up, there is muffled laughter from the office floor, and Nancy is wearing an all-chocolate smile.

"God, who's going to take over now?" asks Kayley chugging her iced Americano.

The front door slams open.

"Surprise!" a voice trills.

The wicked stepmother?

There is a collective gasp, and all chatter in the office comes to a deafening halt. Blood drains from my face and pools in my ankles. Nancy and Theo look frozen with fear.

"How is everybody this fine morning?" Ronnie flounces into the office wearing a white pantsuit, sheer white blouse, and gold-studded stilettos. Her hair is big, and makeup is trawled on, and she is battering her eyelids to anyone that glances in her direction. There's a bento box in one hand and a shiny new briefcase in the other.

Briefcase? The mind boggles.

Still white as a ghost, Theo quips, "It's definitely a prop."

"And empty," adds Nancy.

When her office door closes, I'm lost in a blur of comments: 'Oh, shit, no,' 'My life is over,' 'I'm throwing myself into the Pacific.'

Some of them seem very dramatic but no more than Kayley, who is seated in the brace position with her head over her knees.

Jesus.

Natalie's office door swings open. "By the way, I can hear you, you little turds. I'm just supervising today to ensure no one slackens off. But I might be your boss soon, so you know. . . behave!" She flashes an insincere smile, and the door slams shut.

"Did you get a waft of her on her way through?" Theo whispers behind a manila folder.

"She smells like a VAT of wine," replies Nancy out of the side of her mouth. "Give it one hour, and she'll be shriveled up like a grape behind her desk."

Kayley crosses her fingers, still in the brace position. "Here's hoping."

"I didn't realize you guys liked Natalie so much," I say quietly.

Nancy upturns the candy jar on her desk. "Everyone dig in. Natalie was firm but fair."

Theo starts picking out the yellow peanut M&Ms. "Yeah. She turned this company around. She also gave me time off when my fiancé left me at the altar."

"She's far less terrifying than people make out. You know, she's organizing a three-tiered cake for my wedding," says Nancy crunching down on a hard-boiled candy. "I think everyone needs to calm down. She will look out for us, one way or another."

But Nancy's sage words barely register, my world spinning on an axis. I think of our last interaction again in the elevator when I didn't want to look at her and chance showing what was behind my eyes. Perhaps I should've. Regret filling me with tears.

My day following this bombshell seems to capitulate instantly.

When all my printouts from the latest design journal get chewed up by the copy machine.

When I try to submerge myself in the latest financial report, the network crashes.

When I reach the foyer seeking Joan's warmth but find it cold and empty. Not even the San Diego skyline can pick me up because, of course, it's fucking raining too.

Just when I think it can't get worse, Ronnie staggers toward me, bleary-eyed. She inadvertently knocks over Nancy's prized lucky bamboo plant along the way and drops a big cardboard envelope on my desk. She taps it twice. "Congratulations, darling."

It appears I've just been fired.

CHAPTER TWENTY-EIGHT

MIA

My world becomes black for a moment.

Walking down the street in a daze, swollen gray clouds hover over me, and a car horn blares when I almost stumble in front of it.

This can't possibly be real. It can't...

How did my life suddenly implode?

I look up, staring at the ashen sky.

Natalie. Gone. My job. Gone.

My eyes stinging beyond belief at the realization. Having never been fired before, I'm not sure of the exact protocol, but one thing's for sure, I won't be going back. Still, my work ethic and motivation were always the one thing I could count on to pull me through tough times. Take that away, and I'm just an empty shell with no purpose. I know I can get another job, but right now, it feels like a body blow.

Raindrops start mingling with tears, and I sob, strange sounds coming out of me as I skid along the pavement in my rubber-soled shoes. Some people give me a wide berth, others ram straight into me. But I am so numb, disembodied. I don't even clock their abuse.

Down at the subway station, a large hand yanks me through the doors before I am crushed to death, and frankly, it's a mystery how I get home in one piece, but I do.

Hot salty tears continue to pour out of me as I hide Natalie's flowers in the bath. Out of sight, out of mind. Then I hurl myself on my bed and soak my pillow.

I see a missed call from Natalie on my phone, maybe two, but to be honest, I'm so sad, so angry. She is the absolute last person I want to talk to. Especially when she looked like the world's freaking happiest person this morning. Such a stark contrast to my current state that I can't help but hate her a little bit.

I get that she was happy to be leaving but San Francisco? All those recent side trips shrouded in secrecy. Of course, now it makes sense. She was setting up her new life that didn't involve me. Did she just string me along the entire time? Why didn't she tell me? Did she know I was getting fired?

My head is a total muddle of thoughts and emotions.

I roll over, clutching my pillow, and cry because all I want to do right now is pass out and sleep off this nightmare.

* * * * *

The blue sky does little to coax me out of bed the following day.

Strangely, neither does a hot cup of coffee. I am broken. I'm in such a fug that when I try to get out of bed, I just end up collapsing back down. I try to read a book, but words keep slipping like they're falling off the page. It's impossible. Trying to concentrate on anything right now except how shitty I feel.

Drawing my blinds, my room plunges into a gloominess that matches my heart. Hello, darkness. It's been a while. The self-pity is crippling.

I doze in and out of consciousness, losing all sense of time. I only get out of bed to pee and to feed on sugar. I might also check on my flowers in the bath.

All I know is that when I eventually wake, I'm scratchy-eyed and miserable. Candy wrappers all over me and under my duvet.

I'm prying my eyes open with my fingers when there's a knock at my door. "Enter at your own peril."

The door opens, and I shield my eyes from the light.

"Hey, hey -" Amy startles. Her nose is sunburned, and she's wearing a coral necklace. "Holy crap! When was the last time you brushed your hair?"

"Huh?" I reach up and pat my head. My hair is like a pile of hay. "Oh, right... What day is it?"

"Monday."

Shit. The weekend went fast.

Amy frowns. "I just got back from Cabo with Priya. Remember I told you we were going away?"

I nod slowly, wiping melted choc chip cookie from my hands. "Have fun?"

"Yeah... " Her eyes laser scanning my messy cave. "What is... how long have you been holed up in here?"

"Since Friday."

"Friday?" Amy shrieks and rushes over, tripping over a bag of flaming Cheetos and then an empty box of tissues. "Mia! What has happened to you?"

"Natalie happened to me," I choke. "She quit, moved to San Francisco. Oh, and I also got fired."

She inhales sharply. "What?? All in one day? Are you – . . . Hang on, that doesn't make any sense."

"Amy. . . "

"I saw the way she looked at you. She wouldn't just ditch you. She cares. Maybe she doesn't want to, but it's there -"

I cut her off. "Natalie's gone, okay? And so is my job."

"Did you speak to her?"

"No. I had a few missed calls on Friday but seriously? I saw her leaving the building, so happy, she was practically spinning around on the mountaintop like Fraulein Maria in The Sound Of Music -"

"Fraulein Maria?"

"Doesn't matter. Point is, Natalie was happy without a care in the world, and look at me. . . " I kind of screech, gesturing to my hair, chocolate-stained body, and bed of tissues. "And she really thought I would want to talk to her on the way to the airport? What to wish her bon-fucking-voyage?" My voice starts to crack.

"Hmm. Right." Amy sighs, settles on the edge of my bed, and plucks a candy wrapper from my elbow. "I see. Rough week, then. Nothing on Tinder to distract you?"

Amy and her *distractions*.

"Only just looked," I grimace. "I did get one message from someone called Andrea."

"Does she have a parrot?"

I swat her shoulder. "Shut up."

Amy grins. "And?"

"It just says hello, and there's a picture of a massive rack of boobs. Not even nice ones."

I groan, and she starts to laugh.

"Honestly, I don't think it would matter if Angelina Jolie rocked up for dinner tonight naked, riding a white stallion. Being with Natalie Dalton has ruined any future romantic liaison."

"Sounds quite dire. So, why don't you tell me what *actually* happened? From the start."

Amy, for all her theatrics, really is a great listener. She shakes her head and nods in all the right places.

"So, did you ever tell her how you feel?" she asks softly.

"No," I say with a squeak.

"You're totally in love with her."

"Mmm." I nod, starting to tear up. I guess it feels good to admit it to someone, even if it hurts. "Last night, I stared at my phone until it died, then listened to Celine Dion love ballads on repeat. I also watched The Titanic." I find a crumpled tissue in my bed and blow my nose. Falling in love is so tragic. No wonder it makes people depressed. "I just need a few days to get over it. Maybe a week. Tops."

I'm a big lying liar.

"Oh, you're totally in control." Amy widens her eyes. "You know, you didn't seem that upset with Nadia."

I lift my head from my pillow, my hair a static halo of frizz. "Nadia, who? Natalie was everything I've never had before, and it just feels so. . . so unfinished. I even kept her flowers because I *actually* thought -" I break off.

Amy rubs my back. "Okay."

"Plus, I really loved her cat. Nadia didn't have a Fabio."

"Oh, that's the clincher."

And I tell myself that I'm not going to cry, even when my bottom lip wobbles.

Amy wraps me up in one of her amazing hugs, and when she pats the back of my head like Mimi used to, it's the pat that does it. I bury my face in her shoulder and cry and cry, and she gives me an even bigger squeeze.

Eventually, I pull back, and Amy disappears into the bathroom. "Sorry. This will have to do until I go to the store." She wipes my face with scratchy toilet paper. "Look, life always has a way of working things out. Try to look at the positives. At least you won't have to see Satan's minion again."

"Huh?"

"You know, Margot."

"Yeah, good point."

Amy ruffles my head. "Now, you are going to get up, and I'm going to cook you my world-famous spaghetti bolognese with extra cheese."

"Can we have chocolate too?" I ask in a small voice.

"Hell, yes! A whole slab." Amy winks, and I smile. She shuffles across the carpet to the door. "But you're also going to have a long hot shower because, holy hell, you stink."

I laugh through my salty tears, wiping them away with the back of my hand.

You can't put a price on the value of an honest friend, and finally, I find some energy to roll out of bed and head straight for the bathroom.

* * * * *

The next morning I'm not woken up by the usual shrieking of my alarm but by the sun streaming in.

At first, I think, what a beautiful day, and oh, how beautiful the birds sound, and then with a horrible smack in the face, I remember what happened.

My anger about my sacking has all but faded into the background, and there's only one thing on my mind. One person. I miss her like crazy.

Amy is working from home today, but she spends most of her time floating in and out of my room like an angel with trays of cupcakes and cookies. Not only am I heartbroken, but now I'll also die prematurely with type two diabetes.

I also refuse to leave my bed. When she tries to extract me, I tell her in no uncertain terms that I'm staying here forever. Well, it's not like I have a job or somewhere to go. She can't argue with that point.

At the moment, my biggest plan for the future is takeout pizza (definitely no pineapple) and watching reruns of Friends.

Amy also ends up bailing on her dinner date with Priya so she can hang with me on the couch. Did I mention she's an amazing friend?

We eat an indescribable amount of crap and watch The Secret and then a billion episodes of Tyler Henry connecting with the dead. I'm starting to think Amy might be in love with Priya. Suddenly, she has a thing for all things mystical. Not that I'm complaining, I could use a bit of spiritual enlightenment.

I might also secretly will a ghost to chase Natalie all the way back to San Diego.

The next night, three shadowy figures appear at the foot of my bed in what appears to be a very scary nightmare. I only asked for one ghost, not three. This is *exactly* why you shouldn't mess with the spirit world.

I try to blink them away, but they're still there. "Jesus Christ!" I rasp out loud. "Am I dead?"

"You will be if you don't get up," says the tallest figure. "We're staging an intervention."

"Going to a party in one hour to snap you out of your gloom," the middle one snaps.

The other one viciously flicks on the bedroom lights. "Get up!"

Definitely my evil sister.

"Oh my God! This isn't a dream!" I cover my eyes and say defiantly, "And there's nothing wrong with getting sleep."

"Except that you've been hibernating like a bear for a week. Get up!" Amy throws clothes and shoes at me. "Put these on, then Jules will sort your hair and do your makeup."

"Since when did you get so bossy?" I snap and give her my most brutal glare, which, to be honest, is... not that brutal.

"Since you became my mopey friend. Up!"

Naturally, Janet rips the duvet off me. I practically see the joy in her eyes.

"Get her out!" I yell at my friends.

"No. Not today!" Amy protests. "Every other occasion, yes. But today, Janet stays. We need the extra muscle."

It appears my pity party has been usurped by a pack of henchmen.

"Move it! Move it!" yells Janet with army authority.

"I hate all of you," I spit.

Amy claps her hands in excitement. "Excellent. Have a shower, and see you in the living room in ten minutes. If you don't, Janet has personally offered to bathe you."

The door slams shut, and I scream into the pillow.

* * * * *

"Stay still!" Jules commands, spraying what feels like an entire can of dry shampoo in my hair.

"It's not that dirty!" I cough through the fumes.

Jules throws me a glare, ruffling my blonde tresses. I batt her hand away, and Amy shoves me in front of the mirror, examining their handiwork. I'm all smokey eyes and red lips.

"Super hot!" Jules grins.

"A femme fatale!" Amy makes a strange animal noise, and I think Janet murmurs, "Satisfactory. Just."

I pluck my spray-on jeans from my butt and lift the deep V of my strappy silver top. "I can't believe I'm listening to you guys."

A few minutes later, I'm shepherded out of my own apartment building in kitten heels that are viciously pointed and guaranteed to slice my toes off within the hour. The trio thrust me into the backseat of a dark car, where I end up wedged between Amy and Jules in a BFF sandwich, so I can't escape.

I fasten my seatbelt, scowling. "Hang on. Who's driving?"

"Janet," they chorus.

"No. No. No. She's a maniac." I try to move, and they pin me down.

"She can't be that bad," says Jules, and Janet hops into the driver's seat.

"Ready, suckers?" With one final crazy-eyed glance over her shoulder, Janet guns the engine. "Hold on!" She raises a fist in the air, only to knock over a trashcan and be stalled by a red light, all of us jerking forward against our seatbelts when she slams on the brake.

There's a collective scream, the windows fogging up with our heavy breathing.

"Oh my fucking God!" I shout with my heart beating wildly in my chest. "We'll be lucky if we make it out alive."

"Someone shut her up!" hisses Janet.

Amy covers my mouth, and I try to bite it. "Quit it!" she snaps. I send her a FU with my eyes.

Somehow, even with Amy's hand slapped over my mouth, I still manage to grumble the entire way, but it falls on deaf ears, and when we arrive at our destination, I am plucked out of my seat and shuffled inside like some sort of precious cargo.

"This is *so* unnecessary." I bat my sister's pincer-like claws away, only to have my alleged best friends frogmarch me inside.

Okay, this behavior is extreme. Even for my friends.

What in the ever-lasting shit is going on?

CHAPTER TWENTY-NINE

MIA

Before I know it, I'm sitting on a couch in an empty room.

If this is a party, it's the worst one I've ever been to.

No decorations, no atmosphere, and, unbelievably, no people.

Even worse than my birthday party in the seventh grade, when Mimi chucked everyone out because Liam Black and Simon Martin were smoking pot in our treehouse. I was so embarrassed that I told Mimi I was quitting high school immediately to join the Roland Brothers circus -

Suddenly, the door slams open, making everything in the room jump.

Including me.

And my heart nearly stops. After not seeing her for close to a week, her presence hits me like a wrecking ball.

"Hey..." Natalie says breathlessly.

I'm so rattled I can barely reply and fold my arms, protecting myself. "Hi..."

We are a safe distance apart, but I can still feel electricity bouncing off the walls.

Her hair is plastered all over her face, and dark circles bloom under her bloodshot eyes, and I wonder if she has been losing sleep for the same reason as me. She is also barefoot but strangely looks like she jumped into a swimming pool which makes no sense at all.

Somehow, she is still the most gorgeous woman I have ever seen, and that annoying cord of longing pulls from my throat to my stomach even though I'm mad at her.

We just stare at one another.

Natalie inhales deeply, slowly. "You look beautiful," she says.

Ugh.

She pushes her hair out of her face and plucks her tight white shirt from her chest.

Definitely not looking.

"You're shivering," I quietly counter.

"I can't feel my toes or fingers, and I can't hear in my left ear, but I'm okay." My eyebrows lift. Her eyes, blue and brooding, bore into mine. "My Uber ran out of gas, so I had to run a few blocks. Then my left heel snared in a grill, and a fire hydrant exploded on Huntley Street, pummeling me with water. It's been a rough trip across town."

I cross my arms defiantly because no way will I fall for that sob story, but I kind of want to dash home to get her a towel and a change of dry clothes. I'm also curious about the fire hydrant. That's quite impressive. How on earth did she manage -

No, I mustn't digress. Shaking my head, I ask, "What's this all about? It felt like I was a prop in a military operation."

"Janet thought it necessary."

"Janet," I parrot.

Of course. Who else?

"Sorry, I was desperate," Natalie winces and closes the distance between us. "I know you're probably mad at me."

"Mmm. Let me see. You ignore me, send me to a ranch with a loon, and quit without a word. Oh, and I get my ass handed to me on a platter by your stepmom. Why would I be mad?" I bare my teeth in a rictus smile. "Best month ever."

Natalie frowns. "I'm *so* sorry. It appears you were collateral damage following my resignation. I had no idea, and I feel awful about it... Can we please just talk?" she asks like it's obvious, but is she kidding?

"What, because now you're ready? You know you don't just get to end things like that."

"What?"

Silence stretches between us, the sound of traffic and the outside world barely registering.

"Mia, I didn't end things," she says softly. "And last time we chatted, you didn't really want to have a conversation. In fact, you said you hated me."

I go to open my mouth, but nothing comes out.

Hate is such a strong word.

"I know I need to work on my communication skills, and I promise to do that. I also know that I owe you an explanation." Natalie steps closer, taking a seat on the couch beside me.

"Stay on your side," I warn and shuffle to the edge.

Natalie chuckles. "Okay. I remember from last time." Then she sighs. "The ranch trip. I sent you there on the spur of the moment because my father told me he was going to hit on you, and I freaked out. I didn't know how far he would've gone, and just the thought alone -"

"I don't need your protection."

"I know that. But if anything would've happened to you, I would've never forgiven myself. A sexual harassment suit was actually just filed against him two days ago. He's been stood down from the board pending the investigation." She rubs her brow. "I hope you can see that I didn't send you there to hurt you."

"Mmm."

"Look, you were right. Dalton Media was making me miserable. It's something I've known for a while. You know, I'm also acutely aware that I was becoming an ass."

I narrow my eyes. "Only a tiny bit."

A laugh bursts out of her. "Unlike you to keep me honest. Well, and what I couldn't tell you because of all the IPO nonsense is that I have been busy setting up my own business on the side. That's why I've been in San Francisco, working day and night, to secure funding, and I've finally got it. It's all set up and ready to go."

"Hang on." I pull back to study her. "You're not working in San Francisco for a second-rate marketing company with Lydia Longman lurking somewhere in the shadows?"

"What -" she pauses. "Margot?"

I nod, eyes tight.

"No. Mia, I'm not going anywhere. How could I leave? You're here."

I blink.

Oh, God. I want to kick myself. How could I actually let Margot get inside my head? Her voice fueling the flames of my insecurities.

"Last Friday, I wanted to chat with you in the office before my resignation became public knowledge. I didn't realize that you wouldn't be in. I tried to call, but... yeah, I understand now how things may have looked, and I'm sorry. I've come here for you, professionally. And more importantly... on a personal level," Natalie says with a look so earnest I want to bottle it, and my breath catches in my throat.

"I always had a bigger plan. Well, to get away from my father, and I'd started the groundwork a while ago, but I didn't have the confidence to follow through. Let's just say meeting you expedited things. You asked me if I was happy in Florida, and I wasn't. Not at work."

"I handed my father a letter of demand, and my hands were tied until he accepted. He wasn't really in a position to negotiate, but he finally accepted yesterday, and I was able to poach most of our team. Like ninety percent. You know, all the important people like Joan, Nancy, Theo, Kayley. I'll let you guess the people I'm leaving behind." Natalie lets out a long breath. "And I'm hoping to sign on one more as the Director of Digital Strategy. Superstar in her own right?"

Everything in my head comes to a standstill. Even my words are on hiatus. But Natalie is able to read my expression.

"Yes, you. Only you wouldn't be working for me. You'd be a partner. I can't run a business without someone of your caliber working by my side. And I wouldn't want to. What do you say?"

"I'd say you've got another virus. This one significantly more serious than the last."

Natalie just smiles. "Well?"

"Wait. You're not joking?" She shakes her head, and I look at her like she is insane – to be fair, she is. "You're nuts."

Natalie laughs. "So, *Media Guru* says. Sure, there's an element of risk, but we have all the ingredients to make it a success."

"But working together last time complicated everything."

"There would be clear boundaries." Natalie throws me a look. "Work boundaries. You would have your own team, and you wouldn't report to me."

Natalie gives a little grunt, then gets up and leans on her knees before me. She takes my hand, and my mind starts to panic. "Hang on, what are you -"

"Don't freak out. I'm not asking you to marry me. I strained my back, moving ten thousand boxes into the new office."

I narrow my eyes.

Natalie sighs. "Look, I didn't want to be in love with you. Actually, it was the furthest thing on my mind."

"You know, I'm not really sure about this speech."

I go to stand, and she pulls me down. "Mia. Please let me finish -"

"I don't want my heart smashed," I interrupt. "I also can't handle the trauma of one more Celine Dion ballad."

Natalie frowns. "You like Celine Dion?"

"At times. When it's called for," I say quietly.

She bows her head and looks contrite. "Look, I'm sorry. My head was all over the place the past few weeks with you, my job, this business, my idiot father, and all his threats. I got overwhelmed and wish I could go back and do some things differently." She looks up, all steely eyes on bended knee, and says softly, "You know, I also couldn't quite get over just how incredible you are... "

Velvety, butterfly wings tickle at my heart. "I'm incredible?"

Natalie nods.

I sit a little taller and bite back a smile. "Please continue."

She rolls her eyes. "You *are* incredible. No one is as funny as you. Or smart like you. You're passionate, caring, beautiful, naive. I could go on. You're also totally oblivious to all of the above. I knew the second you came barreling into work in my sweater, that yellow disc falling out from your skirt like a lucky penny... well, I knew you were special. I never thought I'd feel this way about someone. I'm lost when I'm not with you, Mia. And the truth is, I don't want to waste another second without you in my life."

I gulp down, acutely aware of my heart flapping in my ribcage. I also really need to explain that ridiculous lucky penny. I don't carry yellow discs around in my underwear, Natalie.

She continues. "Mia, can we see where this takes us? You and me? I mean, not in secret. Out in the open. You know, actively dating." All the time, her gaze is fixed on mine. "Because nothing makes sense without you in it, and I realize I'm even more cranky than I was before. Believe it or not. Joan called me unbearable," she winces. "And well, we all know how patient she is... What I really want to say is that I love you, Mia," she says, eyes burning darkly, her words liquefying my insides.

Finally.

Her fingers brush my cheek. "I love everything about you."

"The fact that I borrow your clothes and don't always return them in the same state?"

"We live in a sharing economy, so I feel like I'm making a positive contribution, and you know, I'm partial to a crop top every now and then."

"And how do you *really* feel about me being Fabio's numero uno?"

"Share the burden, I say. He's far too much cat for one person to handle."

"What about my knack for embellishing and throwing you under the bus?"

"Life is too vanilla without your little white lies and storytelling. I miss your smart mouth."

I lift an eyebrow.

"And your sparkling wit and big brain."

My brow furrows. "What about my boobs?"

Natalie looks affronted. "Of course, your boobs," she huffs. "Just wasn't going to lead with that."

I start laughing, and she rolls her eyes, then grins. And I know that look, I see it in the mirror often. She really *does* love me.

It's impossible to keep a smile from bursting across my face because she's exactly what I want in a partner. Natalie is not only brilliant and quietly funny, but she's also kind and surprisingly vulnerable.

"How did I do? It was mainly off the cuff, so... "

"A full five days, and you came up with this?"

"I know. I'm completely hopeless. No redeeming qualities at all. Honestly, what do you see in me?"

"Mostly the sex."

Natalie laughs. "Oh, right. I should've guessed it was only surface-level. You only wanted me for my body."

"I mean, you're not horrible to look at."

"Neither are you."

I jab her arm, leaning in closer, feeling the heat of her body. "But do you want to say it again? The important part?"

Natalie gives a short laugh. "You enjoy torturing me, don't you?" she sighs, then gazes straight into my eyes. "But I will say it again. A million times over if I have to. I love you, Mia Andrews, and -"

I put my finger to her lips and say softly, "That's all I wanted to hear. I love you too. Thank you."

Her face splits into the most genuinely happy smile I have ever seen, and before I can stop it, I feel my own smile explode.

"Oh, thank God for that." Natalie lets out a shaky exhale. She takes my hand, kissing it, and then moves it to her chest. "This is yours. Always... So, what now?"

"Well. Yes, to the job. As for us, I really want to kiss you, so how about we start with this?" My arms loop around her neck like it's the most natural thing in the world, and I kiss the heck out of her. I've waited long enough.

"We also need to get you changed out of these clothes," I add and feel her mouth smiling against mine, my body melting from the inside out, and the kiss quickly escalates. It's hard to keep my needy hands off her. One hand is up her shirt, and the other one wants to head south.

An earth-shattering scream pierces the room, and we jump apart, my hand dropping from Natalie's breast like a hot potato.

Amy throws her arms in the air. "Holy shit! They're getting married!" she yells at the top of her lungs.

Oh, God.

I can already see Amy mentally plotting our engagement party with dancing elephants and a string quartet.

"I knew the kneeling was a bad idea," Natalie mutters and staggers to her feet. I stand and giggle into her shoulder.

One by one, they file through the door with boisterous claps and whistles. Amy, Jules, a misty-eyed Joan, and Janet bringing up the rear. No comment.

"What's with the security detail? Should I be concerned?" I ask.

She smiles. "Not anymore. If you said no, it might've been a different story."

"Right. Lucky me then," I reply, still blissfully drugged.

Natalie's face turns into a frown. "Wait. Someone's missing."

There's an insistent scratching noise at the door, and it nudges open. A pair of whiskers appear first, then an unmistakable orange furry head.

It's Fabio, and I swear he's smiling. He prances across the room, happily whipping his tail back and forth.

I do a double-take, and my heart soars. "A bow tie, really?"

Natalie shrugs. "Totally his idea. Though he did say, he would've worn a clown suit as long as he got to see you again."

I pinch her waist. "You're ridiculous."

"Oh, and the real party is next door. There's a band, food trucks, and even trained parrots that sit on your shoulder." My mouth snaps open and then clamps shut when I see her smile. "I don't want you to ever go on another date unless it's with me. I promise I won't make the same mistake twice," she says softly, her eyes equally as shiny as mine.

I wrap my arms around my favorite human, pressing a kiss to her mouth. When her lips leave mine for a beat, I growl my protest, searching for them again.

Because suddenly, it's all mine for the taking.

Well, Natalie doesn't have to ask me twice.

This time I'm grabbing my dream woman, dream job, and dream cat with both hands and never letting go.

EPILOGUE

A FEW MONTHS LATER...

"So, no doubts about moving in together?" I reach across the console and take her hand.

"None. I should've moved out of that condo a long time ago." Natalie smiles, tapping her thumb on the steering wheel.

Obviously, this happened pretty quickly, but when you know, you know. Plus, I'm sick of always playing it safe. This time, I'm all in.

As fate would have it, Amy also decided to shack up with Priya not long after and followed us to a quaint neighborhood in La Jolla. We still see far too much of each other, but that will never change.

Our rental home sits on a larger-than-average block, perfect for our ever-expanding pet family. Fabio still rules the roost, but he's been joined by Daisy, a ten-month-old black Labrador, and a yellow canary named Heidi. Amy also drops by with Harriet, the hamster, for playdates.

All the females love to chase Fabio around the house, much to his hissing disapproval. He has already lost five pounds from the extra activity, and although they aren't friends yet, we have high hopes that they will be soon.

Right now, Natalie and I are driving to Scottsdale so she can finally meet my parents.

She squeezes my leg. "Thank God there's nothing to tie me to my father anymore. I'm a changed woman."

"You're certainly more relaxed," I reply, fiddling with the car stereo until I find a high-pitched pop song. Natalie doesn't even flinch these days. Like I said, more relaxed. Grinning, I settle back into my seat.

While Natalie's comprising photos of her father never made it to the press, it wasn't long until Ronald was papped in a hot tub with four topless women. Needless to say, the board pulled the plug on his planned IPO, and with all the employees jumping ship, Dalton Media is now running on skeleton staff.

Ronnie also served her hubby with divorce papers and intends to go after every last dime. It's not looking rosy for Ronald, but things are certainly looking up for us.

Work is great and such a cohesive space now that the axis of evil is no longer there. Last I heard, *Margot* was working at a second-tier marketing company. Sure, having our own business means there's an endless amount to do, but it's fun too.

Natalie throws me a love-soaked look. "You know, I'm also pretty happy with the woman I've moved in with."

"I bet she's amazing."

"Yeah."

"Also amazing in bed, knows exactly how to -"

Natalie lets out a groan and wriggles around in her seat. "Mia. This is a long drive. Four hours to Scottsdale if you don't remember?" she adds crossly.

I giggle and reach across to stroke her thigh.

She flings it off like it's a grenade. "Don't make me pull over to one of those gross rest stops."

"Okay, okay," I say but still smile.

How can I not?

Our couple-y vibes have continued even though we work together. Clearly, we're still in the honeymoon phase, but I hope we can stay here forever.

An hour later, Natalie almost veers off the road into a ditch when I tell her Mimi and dad are strict Catholics and we'll be in separate beds. She immediately takes an exit to the next rest stop, and half an hour later, we are a sweaty mess. Apparently, Natalie is full of good ideas.

Her smile is slow, mischievous, and only hers. "Wow."

"See." I peel the seatbelt off my back. "Rest stops aren't that bad."

"Yeah. You've opened my eyes to a whole new disgusting world."

I giggle. "I'm not the one with the handbrake jammed up their butt."

Natalie grumbles. "That was an accident."

"Why you want to pull acrobatic moves in such a confined space is beyond me," I say with a laugh.

"I've learned my lesson, Mia. Thank you very much." Natalie slides back into the driver's seat with a grunt while I button up my shirt.

But it's impossible not to smile because this woman... this beautiful woman. She is funny and smart and weird. All at the same time, and I want my days to start and end with her. Put simply, I'm head over heels. Even my eyes are heart-shaped.

Just over an hour later, we're in Scottsdale, and I feel a flicker of excitement when we turn into their street. Not much has changed. Same pale brick façade wavers in my vision in a heat mirage. The fence is still pitched on an angle and needs a paint, while the gardens remain littered with stones, prickly pear cacti, saguaro, and desert agave.

But it *is* July, so there is a life-sized Santa and sleigh in the yard with erratically flashing Christmas lights hanging across the front porch threatening to catch fire.

Dad must've been waiting by the window again because the instant we roll into their driveway, he comes hurtling out the front door, waving manically with his Santa hat bobbling in the sun.

He's wearing his red flip-flops, his beloved Rudolph Christmas T-shirt stretching over three-quarters of his pot belly, and a pair of beige golf shorts riding halfway up his chest while Mimi rushes past him, arms outstretched in her green crocs.

Her frizzy gray hair is tied back with a red scrunchie and her Ho! Ho! Ho! tank is tucked into a pair of elasticized linen pants. She's also sporting some fluffy reindeer antlers that look like they've been savaged by Alfie. Her shoulder pads so large she could double as a linebacker for the Cardinals.

My heart soars.

Christmas in July festivities are in full swing.

"Here they are, here they are!" booms dad, pausing by the hood of the car with his hand on his hips so Mimi can whip past for first hugs. He's a gentleman like that.

Natalie barely turns off the ignition when Mimi yanks me out of the passenger seat, and the desert heat smacks me in the face. My skin tingling under the merciless sun.

"Oh, I've missed you, sweetcheeks. I can't believe you're actually here!" Mimi squeals.

My laugh muffled by her monster padding. "Me too, Mimi. Your hugs are the best."

I pat her back, and after a prolonged hug, Mimi eventually peels off me, caressing my cheek. She scans my face, taking inventory. "Well, look at you. You're glowing like a diamond!" she beams, smoothing down my hair when her eyes catch on something. "Goodness. Appears I still need to dress you, though."

I glance down, and my buttons are askew.

Shit.

My eyes dart past Mimi to Natalie, who is standing there, completely unaware that her fly is undone. I gesture frantically to her shorts, and her face drops. As do her hands.

Mimi swings around a moment later, her heavy chest rising and falling to the rhythm of her breaths. "And hello, Natalie. Wow. Have we heard a lot about you!"

Natalie chuckles as Mimi gives her a monster hug. "All amazing, I hope." She gives me a wide-eyed glare over her shoulder.

"Appears you are nothing short of a demi-god!" Dad grins churlishly.

Of course, he takes this too far.

Natalie is positively beaming, and I roll my eyes. Great. I'll hear about this until the end of time.

Dad scoops us up in his arms. "So, *so* good to have you both here!" Pulling back, he tugs at his ill-fitting shirt. "And how was the drive? Relaxing? Do you need a rest before dinner?"

"No. We're fine. We stopped along the way," I say quietly, my cheeks flaming as red as his festive shirt, and when Natalie looks up, we share a conspiratorial smile.

"Fantastic," he says, pulling our suitcases from the trunk and almost topples under the weight. "Wow. I forgot how you like to pack bricks in your bags!" He winks at me and grins. "Now, let's get you inside, and I'll crack open a bottle of my vintage 2015 Italian Rioja!"

Not one to be left out, Alfie, their little Boston terrier, bursts out the screen door in his elf outfit, yapping and spinning in circles. It's hard not to be swept up in the excitement brought by our visit, and my heart squeezes.

Alfie immediately starts dry-humping Natalie's leg. "Oh, hi. You're awfully friendly… " she stammers, and I giggle at the look of alarm on her face.

"Alfie! Stop harassing our guest!" Mimi quickly scoops him up, shaking her head. "He has a girlfriend, you know. Mary, the poodle, from number twenty-seven. Three times his size. But still… "

Holding hands, Natalie and I share a grin and shuffle after Mimi. Natalie pauses by the entry. Wait. Is she nervous?

There's tension around her mouth, and I lean back, studying it. "You, okay?"

Her brow creases. "What if they don't like me?"

"What? Did you just see all that?" I laugh. "My family's mental. They love everyone."

She smacks my chest. "Not helping."

"Natalie." I look into my favorite set of eyes. "Are you kidding? They'll adore you."

"But you didn't like me initially."

"Huh?" I bite back a smile. "You tried to kill me in the coffee shop."

"You're infuriating. We will always have two different versions of that event. I had right of way," she frowns, and I giggle.

So easy to rile up, so easy.

I squeeze her hand, bringing it to my mouth and brushing my lips against the back of it. "You're impossible not to love, honey," I say softly.

"Really?"

I smile, going up on my toes, and push the hair back from her eye. "Yes."

And just like that, Natalie relaxes and grins, kissing the tip of my nose. Even with all her bluster, turns out the infallible Natalie Dalton also needs some gentle reassurance on occasion.

Honestly, I have so many hopes for this visit because, strange as they are, my parents are amazing. I want to show Natalie that people can love her without designs, and I know they will. Just like I do.

"This way, girls!" yells Mimi over a Mariah Carey jingle blaring from the speakers, and as Natalie turns to follow Mimi, I find myself smiling goofily after her.

We pass an empty fish tank, an alarming amount of green houseplants, and finally, a towering eight-foot Christmas tree with tasteful gold and silver-toned decorations in the living room. The dining table is covered in a soft red tablecloth, Mimi's favorite china, and freshly polished silverware while a mouthwatering aroma of succulent meat, gravy, and cinnamon wafts in the air.

"Sitting inside, so we don't melt." Mimi flits around the table, making last-minute adjustments, and then disappears. "It's hot as Hades out there! Home-made iced tea on the table."

I glance at the pitcher of her signature drink, peach slices floating lazily on top. "Can I help at all, Mimi?"

She pokes her flushed head out into the hallway and waves a flowery mitt. "Don't be silly. Take a seat and relax. I'll be out in a moment with food. You must be famished after such a long drive!" she replies in full mama bear mode, and I watch dad corner Natalie for a chat.

Grinning, I undo the top button of my shorts in preparation. Mimi always goes berserk in the kitchen. Her food honestly is like the eighth wonder of the world.

All of a sudden, two kids come tearing in, screeching like a pair of pterodactyls.

Leo and Marley.

They're knocking into walls and couches, candy-colored icing smeared around their lips. The hair on my neck prickles because it can mean only one thing. Janet is here.

"Oh, hi guys," I smile at them, and they give me toothy grins. Leo also kneecaps me with his little fist. "Ow. . . " Honestly, I shouldn't have such high hopes for Janet's kids. Just as I rub my knee, I notice them trying to mount an inflated reindeer by the window. Marley dangling precariously from the antlers. "Um. I wouldn't do that -"

"Greetings, little sister."

I swing around with a lump of dread in my throat, and there she is, swaying in the hall, clutching an open bottle of wine. She's barefooted, wearing denim cutoffs and a regular-looking UCLA t-shirt. Her eyes are ringed red and her hair is greasy and her skin is gray.

Holy shit, I think she's drunk too.

"Janet?" I blink in confusion. "Where's Harry?"

She wobbles over, waving her hands around. Her nails all bitten down. "Ask his secretary."

"Huh?"

"He's been fucking her. For two years."

I inhale sharply. "What? Not Mona?"

"Yes. Malnourished Mona."

"Wow. Sorry."

"Don't be. He's a shithead."

I want to smile, but that's odd. There's a strange pang in my chest. Hang on. Could it be a modicum of empathy for my sister? Reaching out, I hesitantly touch her shoulder.

"Don't be weird." Janet yanks me in for a tight, rigid hug, and naturally, the wine bottle smacks me in the back of the head. Being this close to Janet is the strangest feeling ever. Almost like an out-of-body experience. "I hate my life."

Her words ring around the room, seeping into the walls. I look over to Dad, who is slapping the table and laughing up a storm with Natalie. Hmm, slightly different vibe over there.

"But I thought you were happy," I say stiffly into her hair and pat her back, waiting for it to be over. "All those parties, holidays..."

Not to mention – irritating social media posts.

"Fake." Janet sculls wine over my shoulder. "So was the hoity toity lifestyle. We're mortgaged to the hilt, practically bankrupt. All those trips I told you about were straight out of a travel brochure."

Christ.

It's like she's sculled some truth serum. Is this really my sister?

Her bone-jarring grip on my body remains, and we are still locked in an uncomfortable embrace as I watch Alfie roll over on the couch with a worn hamburger toy and stuff his face between the cushions.

Trust me, Alfie, I feel the same way.

"I've been draining the joint account for the past six months in preparation, so I can get a new life. Sold a few of his hideous gargoyle sculptures too." Her mouth twisting in a bitter smile. "Quite the money spinners. Obviously, I'm divorcing the dirt-bag... Unfortunately, I get the kids."

"Janet," I gasp.

I've never heard her speak like this.

There's a massive bang, and thankfully, it's enough to prise us apart. The reindeer starts to deflate, and the twin blonde terrors make a guilty run for it, ripping open the screen door of the patio and launching into the kidney-shaped pool, fully clothed with cries of "Cannonball!"

"Ugh. Like I said, unfortunately," Janet sighs.

I laugh. I can't help it. "They're not that bad. Kind of reminds me of us. Well, you, more specifically. Remember the time you threw my cabbage patch doll in the bonfire, and it exploded? I think Amelia Dugan caught her shoe."

"How was I to know it had batteries?" Janet's hands settle on her hips with the odd sideways glance at her kids, now leisurely sprawled on the donut pool floats. "Come to think of it, I was a bit of a shit."

"Still are."

I probably shouldn't have said that. We were doing *so* well. But when I look at her, I'm surprised to see her smiling at me, her eyes starting to shimmer. Hang on. They never shimmer. They're made of rock-hard granite -

"God, I'm not hugging you again," I warn, our moment seemingly over. But I will absolutely be there if she needs me. Or to beat up Harry.

Janet scowls. "As if I'd want you to! Who knows where those hands have been?"

I'm leaving that hornet's nest well alone.

"Also, you should stop using organic deodorant. Doesn't work."

"Shut up, Janet," I hiss, and I don't need to look at her to register a snort.

And just like that, we're back to normal.

Janet disappears into the pool area, and I wander over to dad and Natalie. He's unscrewing a wine bottle. What are they talking about now?

"So, Natalie. Do you like Indy Car Racing?"

I cringe and almost turn around. "God. Dad -"

"Well, actually, I'm related to Mario Andretti. Distant but..."

Dad drops the corkscrew, and it clangs on the plate. "What?!" He booms. I'm sure the entire neighborhood heard that. "You've got to be kidding!" His eyes nearly popping out of his head, and just like that, a kinship is born.

My lips twitch with amusement, even though Natalie has told me this story more than nine thousand times. I pour myself a glass of wine and sink into a chair because this is one conversation I'm happy to sit out, but when I glance at their equally excited faces yammering about silly cars that go round and round in circles, my heart grows three sizes.

Janet strolls in with her wine bottle, picks up my glass, and sculls it. Seriously, this woman drives me mental. She refills the glass, and just when I think she is going to give it to me, she disappears.

I have to bite ten holes in my lip not to launch on top of her.

Luckily, Mimi appears in her holiday-themed apron, holding a tray full of festive food, which is enough to distract me. "You've got to try one of these pepper jelly pigs in a blanket!"

"This all looks amazing, Mimi," says Natalie. "You shouldn't have gone to so much trouble."

"Oh, nonsense," she beams and sits in a chair.

"Mimi got up with the sparrows to prepare all this-" Dad's top starts to sing 'Jingle Bells,' and he smacks at it to stop. A second later, it starts up again. "Goddammit. Apparently, I'm not allowed to breathe anymore."

We all start to giggle at his malfunctioning Christmas t-shirt, but the poor guy looks so disheartened.

"Perhaps just change the batteries, Rob," says Mimi gently. "Bottom drawer in the office."

"Now that's a great idea!" He leaps up with an energized smile. "Back in a minute!"

"So, tell me, Natalie and Mia. What have you two been up to? Heard your business is going gangbusters, and you've moved into a little love nest in La Jolla, complete with your own petting zoo?"

Natalie and I share a laugh.

"Certainly a lot of animals. And work is busier than ever, but we work well together. You know, really bounce off each other. Mia's *so* smart, *so* driven," Natalie says with an angelic smile, and the tiniest bit of suspicion creeps up on me. "She's taught me a lot. Haven't you, honey?"

"Oh, you two are so sweet," Mimi crows, and I nod cautiously, picking up a pig in a blanket, but my eyes remain fixed on my deviant girlfriend.

What is she up to?

Just as I take a bite, a foot starts moving up my shin, and I jump up, hitting the table. I almost choke on my peppery pastry.

"Oh, dear. You okay, Mia? Forget to chew again, did you?" Mimi tears at a savory Christmas muffin. "You know, it was a real issue when she was young, Natalie. Just throwing things whole down the hatch. I had to hand-feed her until she was four."

Janet gurgles somewhere behind me, and Natalie makes a pained sound. "Oh, poor little Mia. She's certainly come a long way since then," she says with mock seriousness, and I roll my eyes.

So, this is what payback feels like.

When Mimi looks away, Natalie flashes me a grin from across the table. Obviously, she's feeling far more relaxed now. Red and green fairy lights from the patio dance on her face, and you know what, who cares if I almost choked to death? Because I still feel a glow, that you-and-me feeling she gives me.

I've never felt more loved than I do under this woman's smile. Somehow, Natalie always makes me feel like I'm the one. Whether it is laughing with her eyes whenever I speak, wrapping me up in a hug in a crowd full of people, or finding a way to steal a moment with me under the table.

In all honesty, Natalie Dalton wasn't really that hard to crack. All it took was a collision, a cashmere sweater, Fabio the ginger cat, Joan's meddling, Lydia's third wheeling, sharing a bed, breaking a bed, a shit-talking parrot, a bottle of absinthe, a military extraction, and an epic amount of patience and understanding.

What can I say?

It's been an adventure.

Someone wise once told me (maybe Amy) that when you choose adventure, it becomes life, so that's what I'm doing, and I can't *wait* for what's around the corner.

Printed in Great Britain
by Amazon

21514754R00171